TRASH TALK

Cherie Bennett & Jeff Gottesfeld

BERKLEY JAM BOOKS, NEW YORK

THE BERKLEY PUBLISHING GROUP
Published by the Penguin Group
Penguin Group (USA) Inc.
375 Hudson Street, New York, New York 10014, USA
Penguin Group (Canada), 10 Alcorn Avenue, Toronto, Ontario M4V 3B2, Canada
(a division of Pearson Penguin Canada Inc.)
Penguin Books Ltd., 80 Strand, London WC2R 0RL, England
Penguin Group Ireland, 25 St. Stephen's Green, Dublin 2, Ireland (a division of Penguin Books Ltd.)
Penguin Group (Australia), 250 Camberwell Road, Camberwell, Victoria 3124, Australia
(a division of Pearson Australia Group Pty. Ltd.)
Penguin Books India Pvt. Ltd., 11 Community Centre, Panchsheel Park, New Delhi—110 017, India
Penguin Group (NZ), Cnr. Airborne and Rosedale Roads, Albany, Auckland 1310, New Zealand
(a division of Pearson New Zealand Ltd.)
Penguin Books (South Africa) (Pty.) Ltd., 24 Sturdee Avenue, Rosebank, Johannesburg 2196, South Africa

Penguin Books Ltd., Registered Offices: 80 Strand, London WC2R 0RL, England

TRASH TALK

A Berkley Jam Book / published by arrangement with the authors

PRINTING HISTORY
Berkley Jam edition / January 2005

Cover photography by Photodisc/Getty Images. Cover design by Rita Frangie.
Interior text design by Kristin del Rosario.

For information address: The Berkley Publishing Group,
a division of Penguin Group (USA) Inc.,
375 Hudson Street, New York, New York 10014.

ISBN: 0-425-20121-X

BERKLEY® JAM BOOKS
Berkley Jam Books are published by The Berkley Publishing Group,
a division of Penguin Group (USA) Inc.,
375 Hudson Street, New York, New York 10014.
BERKLEY is a registered trademark of Penguin Group (USA) Inc.
BERKLEY JAM and its logo are trademarks belonging to Penguin Group (USA) Inc.

PRINTED IN THE UNITED STATES OF AMERICA

10 9 8 7 6 5 4 3 2 1

Contents

GOOD GIRLS,
BAD BOYS

For the Wintons,
who know the true meaning
of friendship and family—
David, Suzanne, Sarah, Eric . . .
and Studly

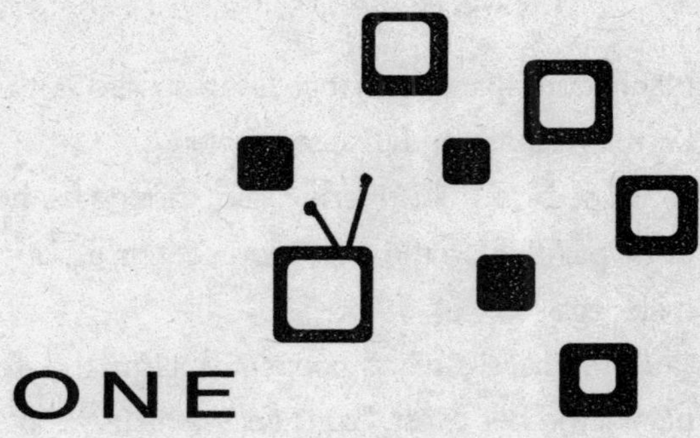

ONE

"I'm inviting you in, in the nicest way I know how," Harley said, pointing his gun at Lisha's head. He kicked the door to the apartment closed with the blunt heel of his motorcycle boot. "Long time no see, baby."

"You know him?" Demetrius asked Lisha incredulously.

"Yeah," Lisha said. "Demetrius, Karma . . . this is Harley."

Harley smiled, and shook the dark, shaggy hair out of his intense blue eyes. "Why don't we all sit down?" He kept his gun trained on Lisha, and she slowly sat in the nearest chair. Karma and Demetrius sat cautiously on the couch.

Harley sauntered around the living room of the Upper West Side

Manhattan apartment that Lisha shared with her two best friends, Karma Kushner and Chelsea Jennings.

"Nice digs, huh?" Harley said, turning his head sideways to check out a painting on the wall, representing a piano balanced on nude female legs.

I can't believe this is happening, Lisha thought, her heart thudding painfully in her chest. *I can't believe he broke into my apartment and he has a gun.*

And I know he's capable of using it.

Images flitted quickly through her mind—of Harley and her in London, of falling in love with him, of how it had all gone so very wrong....

"Harley, what do you want?" Lisha asked, careful to keep her voice low and neutral so she didn't betray the abject terror she was feeling.

Harley turned to her. "Hey, is that any way to greet me?"

"Look, whoever you are—"

"Harley," Harley spat.

"Harley," Demetrius repeated. "You really need to put that gun away."

Lisha snuck a look over at Demetrius. Even seated, at six feet four inches of golden, muscular perfection, he was an intimidating sight. Sitting next to him, tiny Karma looked like a lost child.

"Oh, I need to put the gun away?" Harley echoed innocently. "Now, lemme ask you a question, big man, whoever you are. I have the gun. And you have zip. So who gives the orders in this room?"

Silence.

Harley strolled over to Demetrius and jammed the revolver into his right temple. "I said," he began calmly, and then he screamed, *"Who gives the orders in this room?"*

"You do," Demetrius said quietly.

"Oh, much better," Harley replied cheerfully. He moved the gun from Demetrius's temple and went to lounge against the far wall, keeping the pistol trained on Demetrius. "I'm really hurt that you didn't tell him about me, Lish."

"Look, Harley, it's me you have the problem with," Lisha managed. She could hear her voice quavering. "Why don't you just let them leave—"

"No, no, I like a good party," Harley said. He marched over to Lisha and knelt in front of her. "Did you miss me?"

His gun shifted, so it was pointing straight up at her face.

"Wha-what we had was a long time ago, Harley . . ." Lisha began.

Harley's eyes glittered weirdly, staring up at her. "You look really beautiful, Lisha. Hot. And I know you still love me, Lish. Why won't you admit it?"

My God, he's crazy, Lisha realized. *And I think he's high on something, too.*

"You know I care about you," she lied carefully.

"I knew it," Harley said. "All that tough-girl talk over the phone was a big act. I told you I'd find you, Lisha. Remember?"

She closed her eyes, and her last conversation with Harley, in London, flew into her mind. *"It's all over,"* she had told him. *"I don't want any part of you, or your life. Just pretend you never even knew me."*

"But, Lisha," he had told her, *"don't you know it will never be over? You're mine, and it doesn't end unless I say it ends. I'll find you, wherever you go. Bet on it."*

Lisha opened her eyes, and found Harley's eyes glaring into her own. "I remember," she said.

"I went to a lot of trouble to find you, you know," Harley continued.

"The FBI is after me—ain't that a kick? I risked my life to come here. You need to thank me."

"Thank you," Lisha managed through tense lips.

"You're welcome," Harley said.

At that moment a siren began to wail on the street, and Harley ran to the window and looked out. "It isn't safe here," he mumbled.

Lisha looked over at Demetrius, who seemed ready to spring off the couch to tackle Harley. She shook her head no as frantically as she could. *He'll kill you,* she mouthed.

Harley turned away from the window and strode over to Lisha. He grabbed her left forearm and jerked her from her chair. His face was inches from hers. "It isn't safe here," he repeated. "I have to leave you now."

Thank God, Lisha thought.

"All right," she said.

"I'll be back," Harley promised. "You know I always keep my promises, right, Lish?"

"Right."

"Will you kiss me good-bye?" he asked, as innocent and hopeful as a starry-eyed suitor.

Hiding her disgust and fear, she leaned forward and kissed him.

"Ah, Lisha, we had it all, remember? I was the only one who saw how beautiful you really were, when no one else could see it, remember?"

She nodded at him all but imperceptibly.

"We can have it all again, Lish," he continued. "I'll be back for you, baby. We'll run away together and leave all this crap behind us, you know? Won't that be great?"

"Great," Lisha agreed, her entire body vibrating with fear.

"Hey, nice to meet you," Harley told Demetrius and Karma, as if they had just hung out together at a really fun party. He turned back to Lisha. "I know you won't go to the police about this. Right?"

"Right," she echoed.

"Because if the police knew what I know, you'd have to leave this nice apartment and these nice friends behind. And we couldn't be together, which really would be a crime, you know?"

Lisha tried to smile at him.

He kissed her again. "We're forever," he whispered to her. "Just remember, Lish, if I can't have you, no one can."

Then he strode across the living room, pulled open the door, and left.

"Oh, my gawd!" Karma exclaimed in her nasal, New York voice. "What just happened?"

Demetrius was already on his feet, reaching for the portable phone on the coffee table.

"What are you doing?" Lisha cried.

"Calling 9-1-1," Demetrius said, punching the numbers into the phone. "They can still catch him if they get here fast—"

"No!" Lisha cried, and grabbed the phone out of his hands.

"Are you insane?" Demetrius asked. "That guy is a crazed maniac with—"

"Please, you can't call," Lisha said. She held the phone behind her back.

"But, Lisha, he's really dangerous," Karma protested. "We have to do something—"

"You don't understand—" Lisha began.

"I understand that a pyscho-killer is on the loose!" Demetrius yelled. "Now give me the phone!"

"Please, I'm begging you," Lisha said, tears in her eyes.

The door to the apartment swung open, and Karma actually screamed out loud in fright.

But it wasn't Harley. It was Chelsea, their third roommate, returning from her boyfriend Nick's apartment, across the hall. "Hey, I came to tell you guys there's a great old movie on—"

Then she noticed their faces. "What happened?"

Karma rushed over to the door of the apartment and quickly locked all the locks. Not that those same locks had kept Harley out before, but it still made her feel safer. She turned back to Chelsea. "You know that psycho dude who keeps calling Lisha?" she asked.

"Harley," Chelsea said.

"Right," Karma said. "Well, we just met him, up close and personal. And he has a gun."

Chelsea went to Lisha. "Harley was here?"

Lisha nodded. "He broke in. He had a gun." She fell into the chair and buried her face in her hands. "Oh God, it was so awful. I was so scared."

"And now for some reason Lisha doesn't want us to call the police," Demetrius said with disgust.

"Something happened between Harley and Lisha in Europe," Chelsea said slowly, sitting on the armrest of the couch. "Something bad."

Demetrius threw his hands in the air. "What does that have to do with protecting a psychotic, drugged-out—"

"I'm not protecting him," Lisha said, lifting her tear-stained face from her hands. "I'm protecting myself."

Chelsea, Karma, and Demetrius just stared at her, waiting.

I have to tell them the truth, Lisha realized. *I owe them that now. Even if they hate me. Even if I hate myself.*

Lisha took a deep breath. "Here's what happened. I graduated from high school in Colorado a year early," she began, "and then my parents treated me to a trip to Europe. I was only supposed to stay for a month, but I stayed for seven. It completely changed my life." She smiled shakily. "You remember, Chels, what a little butterball I used to be—"

Chelsea, who had gone to grade school with her back in Nashville, before Lisha and her family moved to Colorado, nodded. "But you were still cute, Lisha—"

"No, I wasn't cute," Lisha said. "I was fat. And ugly. And that's how I looked when I arrived in London, too. Can you imagine—this fat, naive, little geek on her own in London? I was so pitiful! Well, fortunately, I had a friend who had a friend who kind of took me under her wing—maybe she thought I made her look good, I don't know. Anyway, she got me invited to this party for Crash—they were the hottest new band in London last year. I was scared to go—imagine fat little Alyssa Bishop at this hip rock party with these famous people?

"Anyway, I forced myself to go," she continued. "And I was standing there at that party, all by myself, feeling sorry for fat, little me, when Harley came up to me and started talking. Here was this gorgeous American guy who played the guitar in a band, he told me, and he knew all the guys in Crash, and he's paying attention to me! To *me!* I couldn't believe it.

"That first night, Harley introduced me to speed. He said I'd be able to lose weight without even trying, and I'd have all this energy. And I wanted to please him, and I did want to lose weight, so I took it, and—"

"Lisha—" Chelsea interrupted.

"No, let me finish, or I'll lose my nerve," Lisha said, shaking her bangs out of her eyes. "I did lose weight, more and more weight, and Harley became my boyfriend," she continued. "By this time I was addicted to his little pills. And I guess I was addicted to Harley, too.

"I knew it was bad, I knew I should stop, that I should just leave him and the drugs and get far away from the whole scene. But... but I couldn't. For a long time. I mean, I was finally thin. And cute. And... I thought I loved him.

"But one day I woke up and I said to myself, 'I can't do this anymore.' So I decided to go visit some friends I'd met who were in Paris. I told Harley we were through, that I wasn't coming back. You see, by that time I had found out that he didn't really make his living with his band, he made his living dealing drugs. I should have known, but I didn't. I was so stupid and blind."

Tears came to Lisha's eyes and she fisted them away quickly, gulping down the lump rising in her throat. "So Harley asked me to take a suitcase of clothes to a friend of his in Paris—American-made clothes, he said, that cost a mint in Paris. And... and I agreed. I don't know why—maybe I thought I still loved him or something sick like that. It was only later that I found out there were drugs under the clothes—"

"Oh, Lish—" Karma began.

"There's more," Lisha said. "Harley's drug-dealing partner got busted in Los Angeles. And to make the courts go easier on him, he went and turned state's evidence and told them all the dirt on Harley. So now Harley is wanted by the FBI. But if he's caught, he'll tell them that I transported drugs from one country to another. Don't you see? My entire life will be ruined!"

"But, Lisha," Chelsea said, "you can tell them that you didn't know there were any drugs in that suitcase—"

"They won't believe me," Lisha interrupted. "Everyone knew Harley and I were a couple. And I . . . I knew he was a drug dealer." Tears filled her eyes. "I know you all hate me now—"

"Lisha, we don't," Karma said firmly. "I mean, I could live without your psycho ex-boyfriend threatening my life, but I don't hate you."

"I'm sorry, Lisha," Demetrius said, "but I still think you need to go to the cops. Harley is still out there. He's clearly got some sicko thing for you. What are you going to do, be scared forever?"

"I won't let him ruin everything in my life!" Lisha cried. "I had to get myself off of speed. And I did it! I came home, and got my life together, and now I have this great job as an intern at *Trash*. I want to have a life, and I just want to put Harley and everything that happened in Europe far behind me! Can't you get that?"

Everyone in the living room was quiet as they all thought about what Lisha had just said.

"I do get that," Demetrius finally told her. "I don't think you came to the best conclusion, but I understand."

"Thank you," Lisha said gratefully.

"How about if we all agree not to do anything for tonight," Karma suggested. "But I think you should talk to a lawyer about this, actually."

"A criminal lawyer," Chelsea added.

"You're right," Lisha said. "I will."

"And you'll do whatever the lawyer tells you to do?" Demetrius asked.

"I will," Lisha agreed. "Listen, thanks. I . . . I never wanted to tell you all of this. And I sure didn't want you guys dragged into it."

Chelsea crossed the room and gave her a hug. "You were my best friend when I was a little girl. And you're my best friend now, Lish."

"Hey, what about me?" Karma asked, and she went over to them, too. "Excuse me for a moment of heartwarming girl-bonding," she told her boyfriend, Demetrius, over her shoulder.

"Bond away," Demetrius said. "I'm going to the bathroom. Excuse me." He left the room.

Karma hugged Lisha. "It's not like all three of us don't have problems and secrets, right?"

"Not like mine," Lisha said, laughing shakily.

"Well, I suppose being a Korean girl adopted by Jewish hippies isn't quite as scandalous," Karma conceded. "But then there's the fact that I just found out that I have an identical twin sister I never even knew existed. At least I think she's my sister. That's pretty out there!"

"And then there's my life," Chelsea added. "You have to admit, it's not exactly normal."

That's true, Lisha thought. *Even though Chelsea looks and acts like the most normal girl in the world, her father was actually a mass murderer. He shot and killed a restaurant full of people, then came home to kill his wife and child, meaning Chelsea—but his wife killed him first. And no one knows that terrible secret except Chelsea's mom, me, and Karma.*

"I guess the three of us really *are* in this together, huh?" Lisha said.

"Huh is right," Karma replied. "And I have only one thing to add."

"What?" Lisha asked.

"If ever there were three girls perfect to be interns for the world's trashiest teen TV talk show," Karma said, "it sure is us!"

Lisha lay in bed, staring up at the ceiling, which was, as it always is at night in New York, illuminated by the lights from the street.

No window blinds can keep it all out, Lisha thought idly. *Not in New York City.*

She could hear someone outside singing drunkenly, the sound of distant car horns, and the traffic on West End Avenue. She couldn't sleep.

I can't believe what happened tonight, she thought with a shudder. *Harley really was here. With a gun. And I finally told Chelsea and Karma the truth about what happened to me in Europe. I trust them to keep my secret, but what about Demetrius? He seems really nice, but I hardly know him! He's Karma's boyfriend, and I never would have bared my soul to him like that if he hadn't been held at gunpoint by my ex-boyfriend.*

My ex-boyfriend. Who is stalking me. Who told me he'd be back.

She turned over and tried to get comfortable. The luminous numbers of the digital clock on her nightstand read 4:01 A.M.

And I have to wake up at seven-thirty to get to work on time, Lisha thought, beating her pillow into a better position.

Trash. *I really and truly work at* Trash, she thought. *It's only the most popular talk show on TV, hosted by none other than nineteen-year-old-ultrahot-gorgeous Jazz, who claims to be the daughter of Rod Stewart.*

Thousands of eighteen-year-olds from all over the country entered the contest to pick six summer interns for Trash, *and I actually got picked. Of course, it probably helped that Madonna wrote me that letter of recommendation. She was so nice to me when I met her in London. After I got thin, we both modeled in that Rockers for AIDS Research fashion show. I was afraid she wouldn't even answer my letter when I wrote and asked for a recommendation, but she did it right away. And I'd only met her once before.*

And now here I am, living with Karma and Chelsea. We couldn't possibly be any more different from each other. Karma is tiny, with delicate Asian features, and long, gorgeous hair, and she's the world's greatest expert at mixing designer fashions with thrift-store chic. She's also a whiz at the stock market, and she sounds just like Fran Drescher on The Nanny*—strange combination!*

And then there's Chelsea, who has the biggest, darkest secret of all. You'd never know to look at her. With her cute, blond, Hilary Duff looks and preppie outfits, you'd never dream about her bizarre past. She was even valedictorian of her high school! How normal can a girl with such a totally abnormal past get?

And me. Karma insists I look and sound like a young Angelina Jolie. I sure didn't look like Angelina Jolie when I was fat. I can't get fat again. I just can't. I bet Sky wouldn't be so crazy about me if I still looked like the old me.

Sky. He was one of the three eighteen-year-old guy interns who lived right across the hall from them. Another was Alan Van Kleef, from Texas. A romantic, sweet, sensitive guy who wanted to be a writer, he looked kind of like Johnny Depp. Their other roommate was Nick Shaw, who was hot and heavy with Chelsea, a Canadian guy with a slacker kind of attitude, who looked a lot like Brad Pitt.

And Sky, Lisha thought, *looks just like Keanu Reeves. Only better. And I want him so much.*

Only no one knows it.

And no one is going to find out how much I want Sky, either. Not Chelsea, not Karma, and certainly not Sky. Because I wanted Harley that much once. And look what happened.

No, I'm never going to let Sky know how I feel.

And right now I have to concentrate on finding a way of getting Harley out of my life forever. There has to be another way, other than going to a lawyer. A lawyer will probably just tell me I should turn myself in, throw myself on the mercy of the court, or something. My entire life will be ruined.

No, there's got to be another way.

Because I know Harley isn't through with me. And I know he'll be back.

And the next time he shows up with a gun, he might really use it.

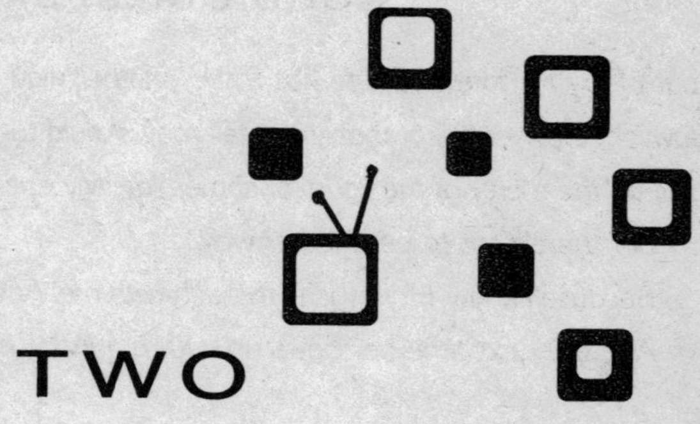

TWO

"Hey, Jazz, wow, I can't believe I'm talking to you!" the recorded, young, male-sounding voice exclaimed into Lisha's earphones. "So, listen, I have this idea for a show on bisexuality, right? Like, you'd be blindfolded, see, and a bunch of different people would kiss you, and you'd have to say if each one was a guy or a girl. Pretty cool, huh? And I volunteer to be one of the people who kiss you, for sure! Oh, my name is Linda Carson, and I'm a girl, even though everyone says I sound like a guy. So, call me, okay?"

Lisha moved the earphones off her ears and rubbed them. She had already spent an hour that morning listening to and recording the messages left on the 1-900-I'M-TRASH phone line, where people paid two dollars a minute for the privilege of leaving a message for Jazz with their best show idea.

Every day, there were thousands of such calls.

The interns had dubbed Room 401, the message-recording room, Sicko Central, in honor of how truly bizarre some of the phone messages were. They all spent many hours there, transcribing the outrageous messages from the tapes.

"Well, Linda Carson-who-sounds-like-a-guy," Lisha said out loud, "your idea is just trashy enough to appeal to Jazz, but you didn't leave your phone number, so you're outta luck."

"How's it going?" Sky called, sticking his head into the room. He took a sip from the cup of coffee in his hands.

God, he's so gorgeous, she thought, in spite of all her resolve. *I love the way his hair sort of brushes his eyes, and I love the way his arms look with the sleeves of his denim shirt rolled up like that, and—*

Stop it, Lisha, she told herself. *A guy like Sky is big trouble for you, so just forget it.*

"The usual sickos," Lisha said, her voice casual, betraying nothing of how she really felt. "How come I'm the only one in here this morning?"

"Guess you just got lucky," Sky said. He came in and sat at the desk next to her, straddling the chair backward. "They've got me following one of the camera guys out to Brooklyn in an hour. We're filming a convention of teen girls who have all had plastic surgery to look more like Barbie."

"As in the *doll?*" Lisha asked, making a face.

"The same." He took another sip of his coffee. "So, I heard you had company Friday night."

"Gee, word travels fast," Lisha said, her voice low.

"You want to talk about it?"

"Frankly, no," she said. "And I have to get back to transcribing these delightful tapes, so—"

"Lish . . ." Sky put his hand on her arm. "I really want to help—"

She shook off his arm. "I don't need your help, okay?"

He gave her a sweet, crooked smile. "Look, I know you aren't into me—it's a killer, but I got the message. But that doesn't mean we can't be friends, does it?"

If he only knew the truth, Lisha thought. *If he only knew.*

"We can be friends," she told him, her tone cool.

"So, friends help out friends," Sky said. "And I heard the guy who showed up at your apartment was some serious bad news, that he broke in and had a gun and—"

"Look, Sky, I know you mean well," Lisha said stiffly. "But I need to work this out myself."

He stood up. "Okay. Well, if you change your mind—"

"I know where to find you," she finished for him.

"Right," Sky agreed. "See you." He walked out the door.

Lisha looked down at her arm, at the exact spot where Sky had touched her. It still felt warm.

"My dawgs are totally killing me in these shoes," Karma whined, hurrying into the room. She had on one of her only-Karma-would-put-that-together outfits—very expensive zebra-striped cigarette pants by her favorite designer, Todd Oldham, a short, black plastic jacket over a hot-pink-and-tangerine Lycra T-shirt she had found at Target for ten bucks. Per usual, she wore high heels so she'd seem taller—today's version were hot pink with black polka dots.

Lisha half smiled, thinking of her own clothing choice—today she'd pulled on a pair of hip-slung jeans and a black suede vest with nothing underneath. The tattoo of a broken heart with a dagger was clearly visible on her shoulder.

I don't remember what Chelsea had on when we left this morning, Lisha thought, *but it was undoubtedly some good-girl preppie little outfit. One thing about me and my roommates, we definitely never swap clothes!*

"Slip 'em off and pick up a set of headphones," Lisha suggested.

Karma sat down next to her and eased her feet out of her shoes with a sigh of relief. "So, are we having a blast here at Sicko Central?"

"Oh, sure," Lisha said. "The usual laugh riot."

"Where's Chelsea?" Karma asked. "I thought she was on Sicko detail, too."

"I'm right behind you," Chelsea said, hurrying into the room.

Lisha grinned when she saw Chelsea—she had called it right, since Chelsea had on one of her usual preppie outfits. Today's was beige chinos with a denim shirt and loafers.

"I had to go walk Jazz's monsters." Chelsea rolled her eyes. "Y'all know I am an animal lover, but I truly detest those two creatures."

Jazz, the nineteen-year-old superstar who was the host of *Trash* had two snarling, nasty-tempered dalmatians that the interns had to walk twice daily. Jazz doted on her dogs as if they were children. They often had intestinal problems, which made walking them and cleaning up after them a particularly daunting enterprise. More than once Lisha had been tempted to disobey New York City's pooperscooper law.

"Hey, I almost forgot," Karma said, reaching into the pocket of her pants, "I asked my broker for the name of a good criminal lawyer, and she recommended this guy." She handed Lisha the piece of paper with the name and number of the lawyer scribbled on it.

"Thanks," Lisha said, sticking it into the pocket of her jeans.

"You will call, won't you?" Karma asked, sitting at the desk next to Lisha. "My broker says he's good—that he's even been on Geraldo's show at night on CNBC."

"I'll take care of it," Lisha promised, shaking her bangs out of her face. "I never wanted to drag you guys into all of this, I told you. It's bad enough that I have to take Harley's abuse."

"Hey, we're your friends," Karma reminded her. "If you can't abuse us, I ask you, who *can* you abuse?"

"Mail call, mail call," a guy said, wheeling a large mail cart into the room. He was medium height, his brown hair cut into a buzz, with a little mustache and beard around his thin lips. He was nice looking, basically, but he was so shy that he wouldn't ever look any of the girls in the eye.

"Hi, Brian," Chelsea said. "Why don't you just put our mail in our offices, like you usually do?"

"Well, I thought I'd do a special delivery and give you all your mail personally," the guy said. "Hi, Lisha," he added, his voice low. His eyes slid over to her, then looked away again.

"Hi, Brian," Lisha said.

"So, uh . . . what's happening?" Brian asked nervously.

"Oh, we're just working," Chelsea replied.

"Uh-huh," Brian said. "You guys are really lucky you got picked to be interns, you know?" He bit at one of his cuticles. "I bet you have fun, you know, hanging out together and everything."

"Sure," Karma said politely.

"Yeah," Brian agreed. His eyes looked everywhere except at them. "I bet you go to the movies together a lot, stuff like that. You know, like on *Friends* on TV."

"Well, we're pretty busy here at work," Chelsea said.

"Oh, yeah," Brian replied. "But you guys like movies and stuff, I bet."

"Sure," Karma said again, trading looks with Lisha.

"Listen, Brian, we really have to get back to work," Lisha told him. "And this really isn't a good place to leave our mail."

"Oh, yeah, okay, cool," Brian said quickly. "Okay, so I'll see ya." He wheeled his mail cart out ahead of him.

"What was that all about?" Karma asked.

"I think he's got a thing for Lisha," Chelsea explained.

They all knew that Brian Bassinger, nephew of executive producer Barry Bassinger, had been hired the week before for a summer job at *Trash,* thanks to his uncle. Brian was seventeen and about to go into his senior year at some private school in upstate New York. He was the only *Trash* employee who seemed to have a lower status than the interns—although his connections were better.

"You know, I just thought of something," Lisha said slowly. "You know how we've been trying to figure out who took the film out of the Trash-cam. What if it was Brian?"

The Trash-cam was the video camera the interns were secretly using to create an underground film about the dirty dealings and behind-the-scenes trash that really *was Trash*. They had decided to do it when they all realized they couldn't deal with the underhanded sleaziness of the place without doing *something* to keep themselves sane. Sky, whose father was an official in the TV technicians' union, had borrowed a tiny video camera from a friend of his father's, and the interns had been hiding it in the offices of various executives . . . and just letting the camera run. But the week before, when they retrieved the hidden camera from Jazz's office, they had discovered that someone had removed their film.

Which meant that someone had found their camera.

Which meant that they all expected "someone" to go to Jazz and get them all busted any minute.

"Why would Brian take our film?" Chelsea asked.

Lisha shrugged. "How should I know? But didn't you notice how he kept asking us about movies? What if that was his sly way of telling us he found our Trash-cam?"

"I don't know. . . ." Chelsea said doubtfully. "How would he even know it was our camera?"

"Oh yeah, like it would be hard to figure that one out," Karma snorted. "Lisha could be right."

"Well, even if she *is* right," Chelsea said, "what can we do about it? We can't very well ask him."

"How many?" Sumtimes asked, sticking her head in the door.

The girls were used to this question. Sumtimes, known only by her last name, as she changed her first name weekly, was one of their many bosses. They generally thought of her as the most hardworking *Trash* executive. She often barked out her infamous shorthand query of "how many?"—which basically meant how many or how much of whatever they were supposed to be doing had actually been done.

"I've transcribed a half hour of tape so far," Lisha said.

"Gotta get it done, guys," she told them, scratching a mosquito bite on her completely shaved pate. She was so beautiful that her baldness actually enhanced her beauty.

"We'll get on it," Chelsea assured her, reaching for her headphones.

"Cool," Sumtimes said. "Because this afternoon you guys—"

"Emily, have you seen Jazz this morning?" Winston Manroot, Jazz's to-die-for gorgeous, dreadlocked Jamaican secretary, asked in his sexy, mellifluous voice.

He looks like a movie star, has that sexy accent, and I heard he went to Harvard, Lisha thought as she studied him. *Now, there's another guy any thinking woman should stay far away from.*

"I just saw her in Barry's office," Sumtimes answered. "Why?"

"I paged her and she didn't answer," Winston said. "That obnoxious reporter from Channel I-forget is on her way over to ask Jazz about some kid in Oregon who is on a hunger strike unless he can marry Jazz. She's called three times this morning already."

"I'll go find her," Sumtimes told him. "Tell the guards not to let the reporter in, okay?"

"Yeah-mon," Winston agreed, his voice a sexy, musical singsong. "I got it covered."

Winston and Sumtimes disappeared.

"I guess Sumtimes is Emily Sumtimes this week, huh?" Chelsea asked idly.

"How cute is that Winston dude, I ask you?" Karma put in.

"Hey, I thought you were crazy about Demetrius," Chelsea reminded her.

"I am," Karma agreed happily. "But that doesn't keep me from appreciating beauty in other life-forms, ya know."

"All of which are male," Lisha added.

"Well, yeah," Karma conceded. "What's your point?"

"My point," Lisha said, "is that fine guys are not worth the trouble."

"Come on, Lish," Chelsea said. "They aren't all like Harley."

"Maybe not," Lisha admitted. "But how do you know ahead of time? I mean, I didn't think Harley was . . . well, like he is, until it was too late, and I was already in love with him."

"He's a really bad guy, Lish," Chelsea said.

"In the words of Jazz, big duh, Chels," Lisha said with disgust. *Big duh* was Jazz's favorite expression.

"Every great-looking guy isn't a bad guy, is what I mean," Chelsea explained.

"You never know," Lisha insisted. "They steal your heart, and then you're at their mercy."

"Yeah, but what's the alternative?" Karma asked.

Lisha reached for her headphones. "It's simple, really. All you have to do is become heartless." She put on her headphones. "And then you have no heart for them to steal."

"This could be it," Alan told Lisha as all the interns met outside Sumtimes's office late that afternoon. A memo had gone around to all of them a couple of hours earlier, telling them to meet Sumtimes at her office at four o'clock. Now they sat on the couches and chairs outside Sumtimes's office while her secretary—a gorgeous girl named Shyanne who was half-black and half-Tahitian, kept a watchful eye on them as she typed into her computer.

"Could be what?" Lisha asked.

"The ax," Alan whispered, eyeing Shyanne to make sure she couldn't overhear them. "Why else would all of us interns be called to a meeting?"

"He's right," Chelsea said anxiously. "We aren't important enough to have meetings—all we do is take notes for other people's meetings."

"No way is Sumtimes firing us," Karma insisted. "If we were busted, we'd get called to Jazz's office."

"Maybe we're not important enough for Jazz to even bother with," Alan said.

"Just chill, you guys," Nick said easily. "If Jazz had found out about the Trash-cam, it wouldn't come down like this."

"Don't you ever worry about anything?" Chelsea asked him.

"Not often," he admitted.

"You could be wrong about how Jazz would handle this, you know," Chelsea pointed out.

"I'm not," Nick said. "I know her."

"Yeah, we all know that you *know* her." Chelsea's voice was cold. "You *know* her really, really well."

I guess Chelsea is still ticked off at Nick for agreeing to be Jazz's date for the Rock of Ages Awards later in the summer, Lisha thought. *And I guess she feels insecure because Nick used to date Jazz. He told Chelsea he never slept with Jazz, though. Not that you can trust a fine guy to tell you the truth. Nick and Chelsea are supposed to be in love with each other, but who knows what he does behind her back?*

Which only proves my point: love stinks.

The intercom on Shyanne's desk buzzed, and she picked up the phone. "Fine," she said, and hung up. She turned to the interns. "You can go in now."

"We might be about to kiss our butts good-bye," Sky whispered as the six of them got up and filed into Sumtimes's office.

"No negative thinking," Karma admonished him, pushing the tiny braid at the front of her hair off her face.

Alan gave her a cynical look. "We who are about to die salute you."

"Sit anywhere," Sumtimes said from behind her desk. She waved them toward her kidney-shaped pink velvet couch and her bright orange chairs. Everyone sat down.

"Okay, interns, listen up." Fiddling with one of the multiple earrings dangling from her left ear, Sumtimes got down to business. "We need to have quite the serious little chitchat. Karma, shut the door."

As Karma complied, she and Lisha traded looks.

A serious chat with the door closed, Lisha thought. *That could be really bad news.*

"I guess you all know why you're here." Sumtimes folded her arms.

Lisha got a sinking feeling. The group eyed each other. *Should we just confess?* Lisha wondered. *Would it make any difference?*

"Well? Doesn't anyone have anything to say?" Sumtimes asked.

The silence in the room was deafening.

"Look," Sky finally said. "I'm really the one you should be talking to. They really didn't do anything."

"So it was *you!*" Sumtimes exclaimed.

"Sky, just forget it, man," Nick began. "You can't take all the blame when we all—"

"*All* of you?" Sumtimes interrupted, her voice incredulous. "The reporter told me it was only *one* of you!"

"What reporter?" Sky asked, obviously confused.

"You're supposed to be telling me that, don't you think?" Sumtimes responded.

"Uh . . . just exactly what are you talking about?" Sky asked carefully.

"The cover story for *Rave* magazine," Sumtimes said. "What did you think I was talking about?"

The interns just stared at her.

"Wait, hold up here." Sumtimes came around her desk. "Didn't one of you give a secret interview to a reporter named Lydia Love from *Rave* magazine?"

The interns all looked at each other blankly, then shook their heads no.

"You guys aren't just saying that because of that clause in your contract that says you can't give interviews about *Trash* without permission, are you?" Sumtimes asked.

"I didn't even know that clause was there," Chelsea admitted.

"I did," Karma said. "I always read the fine print."

"None of us gave an interview," Alan told Sumtimes. "Honest."

"For real?" Sumtimes asked. "Because she said . . ." She let the rest of her statement trail off. Then she laughed. "I can't believe it! That girl out-TRASHed me!"

"Uh, Sumtimes, we aren't exactly following you, here," Karma explained.

"Yeah, yeah, I know," Sumtimes said. "Okay, it's like this. You guys know *Rave*, right? The new one, that is supposed to be the hippest thing happening? Controversy is, like, their middle name. Well, they wanted to do this big cover story on the *Trash* interns—you know—what happened to the six of you since you got picked and all that. Jazz was not too psyched about that—*Rave* hasn't done a story on her yet—and she turned them down. So this reporter from *Rave*, Lydia Love, claimed she got an interview from one of you and that you blew the lid on Jazz and all the secrets of *Trash*. And if we didn't agree to the full story, they would just print what this unnamed intern had told them."

Sumtimes eyed all of them. "And none of you talked to her, for real?"

"This is the first any of us has heard about this at all," Alan assured her.

"So, what were you talking about, then?" Sumtimes asked Sky. "What was it I was supposed to blame you for and not them?"

"Uh, well, uh . . ." Sky stammered.

"The . . . coffee room!" Karma exclaimed. "Sky trashed the coffee room! Yeah, that's it! The guy is a total slob!"

Sumtimes looked dubious. "You thought I was gonna yell at you guys for trashing the coffee room? But the coffee room is always trashed. It's a permanent condition."

"Yeah, and Sky's responsible for it," Karma said firmly.

Sumtimes gave them a jaded look. "When I shaved my head, my brains did not fly off with my hair. Meaning something is up with you guys that I don't know about."

The interns just smiled at her.

Sumtimes sighed. "Okay, we'll drop it For the moment, anyway. So, back to this thing with *Rave*. None of you spoke to this reporter? Honest?"

"Honest," Chelsea assured her.

"Absolutely," Alan added.

"For some crazy reason, I believe you guys," Sumtimes said. "Well, anyway, Jazz says *Rave* can go ahead with the story now, providing it's her picture that appears on the cover."

"Figures," Nick said with a chuckle.

"Hey, she got where she is because she's really smart, you know," Sumtimes told him.

"And here I thought it was because she's Rod Stewart's love child," Nick said. "She says."

"Whatever," Sumtimes said breezily. "She's a marketing genius. The point is, she gets the cover, you guys do the story. Just don't say anything Jazz wouldn't want you to say, or your collective ass is grass."

She turned around and picked up an embossed card from her desk. "*Rave* is giving a private party tomorrow night at Tunnel of Love. They want all of you interns there. A photographer will be there to take some shots of you."

"What's Tunnel of Love?" Chelsea asked.

"It's that new club in the East Village, right?" Karma said. "Avenue C?"

"Right," Sumtimes confirmed. "It looks just like an abandoned subway station. They hire actors to pose as bums and junkies and stuff. It's supposed to be really out there."

"Gee, *quel* atmosphere," Karma quipped.

"So, how are we supposed to get in?" Lisha asked. "We're underage."

"Like I said, it's a private party," Sumtimes said. "So there won't be any problem." She handed the embossed card to Chelsea. "Here's the invite. I'll be there, too, to kind of make sure everything goes okay." She stuffed her hands deep into the pockets of her lime-green-and-acid-yellow plaid jumpsuit. "Okay, guys, that's it. Scram."

The interns hustled out of the office.

"Well, we just dodged a major bullet," Alan said as they walked by Shyanne's desk.

"I can't believe I almost opened my mouth and spilled everything," Sky said, shaking his head. "Guilt can do a major number on you."

"You would be one sucky double agent, you know," Karma told him.

"I'll be sure to cross that off my list of career choices," Sky replied as they headed for the bank of elevators.

"It's a good thing I've got the night off from Jimi's tomorrow," Karma said. "I wonder what we should wear to this *Rave* thing." She pushed the down button.

"Oh, one more thing, you guys," Sumtimes called to them, sticking her head out of her office. "For tomorrow night? Dress hot."

"Hot?" Chelsea echoed.

"Hot," Sumtimes repeated. She eyed Chelsea's preppie outfit. "Borrow something from one of your roomies, Chelsea."

"But I'd really rather dress like . . . well, like me," Chelsea said.

"This is an order from Jazz," Sumtimes said. "And you know what we say—"

"When Jazz says, 'jump,' we say 'how high?' " Chelsea recited dutifully.

"Good girl," Sumtimes approved, and disappeared back into her office.

"I don't do 'hot,' " Chelsea said, making a face.

"There's a first time for everything, Chels." Lisha put her arm around Chelsea's shoulders.

"Right," Karma agreed. "Tomorrow night, Lisha and I will turn you into a goddess of the night."

"Oh, you guys, one last thing," Sumtimes called, sticking her head out her door again. "Hot, but not too hot," she qualified. "Jazz will be at the party, too, if you know what I mean." She disappeared again.

"I know exactly what that means," Lisha said. "It means whatever we wear, we have to be sure not to outshine Jazz."

"Ha," Chelsea snorted. "*People* named Jazz one of the fifty most beautiful people in the world. I don't exactly think I'm comp for her."

Lisha looked over at Nick, waiting for him to say something, like that he preferred the way Chelsea looked to the way Jazz looked. But Nick didn't say a word.

Well, we'll just see who outshines who tomorrow night, Lisha thought. *I have a feeling that between Karma and me, we can make Chelsea into a vision so hot that it'll scorch Nick Shaw's eyeballs.*

"So, this could be fun tomorrow night, huh?" Sky asked Lisha.

She shrugged.

He cocked his head at her. "What is that, Lish?"

"What's what?"

"That shrug. You do it all the time. What does it mean?"

"Whatever," Lisha said breezily.

"Huh. An enigmatic woman." Sky smiled at her, and moved closer, gazing down into her eyes. "So, if I ask you to dance tomorrow night, will I get more than a shrug as an answer? I mean, if the music was slow, and I held you close, would you move away?"

Lisha pretended to consider for a moment. "Sounds confining," she decided.

"Confining," Sky echoed. He shook his head. "You sure do know how to hurt a guy, Lish."

She smiled and patted him on the back as if he were her brother.

But inside, her heart was talking.

If you only knew, Sky. If you only knew.

THREE

"White spandex hot pants and a cropped rayon shirt that shows your navel," Karma mused, considering Chelsea, who stood there in her bra and panties. She handed her a tiny tropical-print shirt. "It's totally you."

It was the next evening, and Lisha and Karma were planning an outfit for Chelsea to wear to the *Rave* party. They were all in Karma's room, which featured a king-size mahogany canopy bed and more bad art on the walls, compliments of the art-student son of the owners of the apartment. Half of Karma's wardrobe was spread out on the oversized Pakistani-print scarf she used as a bedspread.

"It is definitely not me," Chelsea insisted. "Besides, you wear a size two or something. I wear a size eight."

"I have a lot of stretchy clothes," Karma assured her, grabbing a neon-striped tube dress off of the bed. "How about this?"

"How about not," Chelsea said, pushing the dress away. "I would feel like I was at a costume party."

"Chelsea's idea of dress-up involves something virginal and flowing, with little flowers on it," Lisha teased.

"So what's wrong with that?" Chelsea asked.

"Nothing," Lisha said. "Except that Jazz will be at this party. And so will Nick. And Jazz will have on something outrageous. Compared to that, one of your little floral Miss Nashville numbers just isn't gonna make it."

"I didn't compete in pageants," Chelsea protested. "And I'm not in competition with her."

"Oh, yes, you are," Karma said. "Nick used to date her, right? Nick is going to the Rock of Ages Awards with her, right?"

"I could just kill him for that," Chelsea said. She sat on the bed, her eyes blazing with anger.

"It doesn't mean anything," Karma assured her. "She just needed an escort, and she asked him, and—"

"And he could have said no!" Chelsea exclaimed.

"She's his boss," Karma pointed out. "You don't get to say no to your boss and still keep your job." She tapped one green-polished fingernail against her lips contemplatively. "I have this Betsy Johnson black leather number that will make you look kind of Pamela Anderson-ish in the bosom department—"

"Her breasts are plastic!" Chelsea said, shuddering with disgust. "Why would I want to look like that?"

"Ask millions of men who drool over her for an answer to that question," Lisha said.

"No black leather," Chelsea said firmly. "No cleavage."

"Okay, okay, wait, I've got it," Lisha said. "I'll be right back."

She ran to her room and pushed through the clothes hanging in her closet. "Ah, perfect," she said triumphantly as she plucked a hanger from the back. She hurried back to Karma's room.

"Okay, Chels, this is definitely you," Lisha declared. She handed the hanger to Chelsea.

On the hanger was a pale peach bias-cut satin nightgown, sleeveless and long, fitted around the bust and dipping dangerously low in the back.

"Uh, Lish, this is a nightgown," Chelsea pointed out.

"Only if you wear it at night," Lisha deadpanned.

"Actually, it's very fabulous," Karma said, feeling the material. "Where did you get this?"

"My aunt Margaret," Lisha said. "She was the only cool relative I ever had, and she died from breast cancer last year. She left me all her clothes."

"So why aren't you wearing it?" Chelsea asked Lisha.

"I'm more into my downtown trash-rock phase these days," Lisha said. "Try it on."

Chelsea slipped the gown over her head. "Well?"

"Oh, my gawd," Karma gasped, "you are totally to-die-for, Chels."

"Really?" Chelsea surveyed her image in the mirror on the dresser.

"Really," Lisha confirmed. "You look like Gwyneth Paltrow at the Academy Awards."

"Yeah, I wish," Chelsea said, but she was smiling at her reflection. "Y'all really think I should wear this?"

"We-all do," Karma insisted. She looked at her watch. "We have to meet the guys in a half hour and I didn't even shower yet!"

"Are y'all really sure—" Chelsea began.

"We're sure, we're sure." Lisha pushed Chelsea toward the door. "Nick is going to totally die when he sees you, and—"

The phone by Karma's bed rang. Lisha was closest, so she picked it up. "Hello?"

"Miss me?" the voice said.

Harley.

Lisha's stomach dropped to her toes.

"What do you want?" she asked carefully.

"That's no way to greet me, Lish," Harley said, his voice low and sexy.

"I was just . . . just on my way out," Lisha said.

"Yeah, I know," Harley said. "You're going to a party at Tunnel of Love. Are you gonna wear something hot, Lish?"

"How did you know that?" Lisha gasped.

"Oh, I have my ways," he said. "Too bad I can't go with you. You're not going there with a guy, are you?"

She didn't answer.

"'Cuz you know I'd be really, really angry if you were going with some guy. And you don't want me to get really angry, know what I mean?"

"I . . . I think you should stop calling here," Lisha began, her voice tremulous.

"Hey, are you gonna wear that sexy underwear I love so much?" Harley asked, his voice low and insinuating. "That flimsy little black bra, and the G-string with the—"

Lisha slammed down the phone.

Chelsea and Karma stared at her.

"It was him, wasn't it?" Chelsea guessed.

Lisha nodded yes, too upset to speak.

"You have to call that lawyer, Lisha," Karma said.

Lisha nodded again.

"Don't just nod, do it!" Chelsea cried. "Lish, this guy is dangerous! You can't ignore this, because it doesn't look like he's going to go away!"

"I know," Lisha agreed, her stomach turning with fear.

You're going to a party at Tunnel of Love. Are you gonna wear something hot, Lish?

How did you know where I was going, Harley? How did you know? I'd better not tell Karma and Chelsea. They'll just freak out.

Lisha put her hands on her stomach, suddenly nauseous.

"In the meantime we'll stick really close to you," Karma promised. "We'll get the guys to watch out for you, too."

"Sky won't leave your side," Chelsea added.

You aren't going there with a guy, are you? Because you know I'd be really, really angry if you were going there with some guy. And you don't want to get me really angry, know what I mean?

He's watching me, Lisha thought. *I don't know how he's doing it, but he's watching me.*

Which means that no one around me is safe.

No one.

"Well, the six of you are looking really terrif," Sumtimes said, greeting them in front of Tunnel of Love. Normally a line of people would be waiting to get in, but tonight a big sign that read PRIVATE PARTY had been posted. The bouncer, a handsome bodybuilder type with a tattoo on his biceps that read DANGEROUS, stood vigil at the front door, which looked like the turnstile of a subway station.

The always fashionable Sumtimes had on black crepe hip-hugger harem pants with a matching bra top, and multiple chains wrapped around her tiny waist. Her bald pate shone with gold glitter, which matched the gold glitter on her cleavage and pierced navel.

Chelsea had on the pale peach gown, and Lisha and Karma looked just as fabulous. Lisha wore a tiny black miniskirt with a sleeveless baby-blue satin shirt that ended just below her bust, and black lace-up thigh-high boots. Karma had on silver lamé bell-bottoms and a tiny red-and-silver shirt covered with huge flowers, which matched the red-and-silver flowers on her purse and high heels.

The guys looked great, too. Nick wore his usual jeans, sneakers, and T-shirt, but over that he had actually managed to scrounge up a black jacket. Sky had on black jeans and a black shirt, and a black tie covered with Looney Tunes cartoon characters, and Alan wore a gorgeous dark green Italian suit and a collarless shirt.

"Glad we meet with your approval," Alan said. "Our mamas always said we clean up nice."

"So, listen," Sumtimes told them, "remember to follow the ground rules at this thing. Meaning, you only say nice things about Jazz and about *Trash*. Got it?"

"Be nice, got it," Karma agreed.

Sumtimes checked her watch. "Jazz should be here any minute. I want all of us to go in together."

Lisha looked nervously up and down the street. *I half expect Harley to pop out from behind some building,* she thought. *Is he watching me right now?*

"You okay?" Karma asked Lisha, her voice low.

"Yeah, sure," Lisha said halfheartedly.

"You should have let us tell the guys that you-know-who called you tonight," Chelsea whispered.

"I don't want to make a big thing out of it," Lisha insisted, still looking up and down the block.

"But it *is* a big thing!" Karma exclaimed. "Look at you! You're a nervous wreck!"

"What are you a nervous wreck about?" Sky asked, overhearing Karma's remark.

"Nothing," Lisha said quickly. "Forget it."

At that moment a limo with dalmatian-print doors pulled up to the curb. They all knew the unique limo belonged to Jazz.

The chauffeur, a hunky African-American guy whose muscles bulged in his well-fitted uniform, quickly got out of the car and hurried around it to open the door for Jazz.

She stepped out of the car and shook her famous mane of silver-blond hair back off her face. She wore faded jeans with holes in the knees, a man's white T-shirt, under which it was perfectly obvious she wore no bra, and a motorcycle jacket, which fell artfully off her shoulders.

"Trumped," Karma whispered.

"What do you mean?" Chelsea whispered back. "She didn't dress up at all!"

"Exactly," Lisha said. "Now we look like we're trying too hard, and she looks like she's so cool she doesn't have to try at all."

"Jazz!" Sumtimes said, hurrying over to her.

"Hi," Jazz said, cool as always. Her eyes flitted to the interns. "Hi, Nick."

"Hi."

Jazz sauntered over to him. "I came alone, you notice."

"Uh-huh," Nick said, clearly ill at ease.

Jazz took Nick's arm, then she turned to Chelsea. "You don't mind, do you?"

Chelsea's jaw set hard. She didn't say a word.

"Good, I knew you wouldn't," Jazz said. "Let's go in."

Nick shrugged helplessly at Chelsea as the bouncer held open the heavy door that looked just like the door to a subway train.

"I wish I was just about anyplace on the planet except here," Chelsea whispered to Lisha.

"Don't let 'em see you sweat," Lisha advised as they went through the subway-style turnstile. She took one last quick look around before she entered the club.

I'll feel safe inside the club, Lisha thought. *There's no way he could get into this private party.*

Of course, I thought there was no way he could break into my apartment, and he managed to do that.

The group entered the dimly lit club, which had graffiti spray-painted on the walls. A narrow subway car led to a cavernous room, featuring a giant dance floor surrounded by a circular set of subway tracks. The tunnel surrounding it all was lined with subway-type seats, above which were more graffiti-covered walls. Cans of spray paint were available so patrons could add their own graffiti. Various bums and junkie types were staggering around the room, bumping into people.

"Come with me," Jazz told Nick. "I feel like dancing."

As if she was Moses crossing the Red Sea, bodies parted as Jazz led Nick to the dance floor.

"I hate Jazz with every fiber of my being," Chelsea seethed, watching them walk away.

"Can you spare a buck, honey? I'm hungry," a drunken fetid-breathed bum said, sticking his hand in Chelsea's face.

"Are...are you an actor or is this for real?" Chelsea asked nervously.

"Chels, they don't let real bums in here," Lisha said patiently.

"Hey, watch who you're calling a bum, honey," the bum slurred.

"He seems so authentic," Chelsea said.

"Why, thank you," the bum said, his face lighting up, all traces of his drunkenness disappearing. "I study at the American Academy of Dramatic Arts!"

"Gang, follow me," Sumtimes ordered. "We're meeting Lydia Love in the private room upstairs."

Sumtimes led them across the dance floor, where bodies moved in slow motion to a steamy ballad by Alanis Morissette. They went down a dark hallway, hearing a tinny recorded voice announce that the subway had lost all power, then up some stairs and into a dimly lit room, decorated with giant pillows, low-slung couches, and tiny ultraviolet lights.

A young woman with long, straight brown hair, a pierced cheek, and a nose ring sat on a huge red velvet pillow, looking bored. With her was a tall, thin bald guy with three cameras slung around his neck.

"Lydia?" Sumtimes said. "I'm Diana Sumtimes."

Lydia got up gracefully. They shook hands. "And this is my photographer, Chase Gaines."

The photographer nodded at Sumtimes. "Love the hair," he declared.

Sumtimes ran her hand over her smooth pate. "Thanks."

"So, you're the lucky guys who got picked to be the *Trash* interns." Lydia looked them over as she spoke.

"Five out of six," Sumtimes said. "The sixth is downstairs dancing with Jazz at the moment."

Lydia raised her eyebrows. "Jazz dances with interns?"

"Sure," Sumtimes said. "*Trash* is a very laid-back place. Everyone parties with everyone."

"Yeah, right," Lisha muttered. Karma kicked her, meaning shut up, keeping a bright smile on her face at the same time.

Lydia reached for a small tape recorder that sat on the table next to her. She turned it on and held a microphone up to Lisha's face.

"What do you hate most about *Trash?*" she asked.

From behind her, Lisha could see Sumtimes's face go white.

"Getting up in the morning," Lisha said smoothly. "I'm kind of a night person."

"Oh, yeah, that's *real* interesting," Lydia said sarcastically. She turned to Sky. "What kind of drugs go down at *Trash?*"

"I'm a clean-living kind of guy," Sky replied.

"Uh-huh," Lydia said, making it clear that she didn't believe him. She turned to Karma. "So, who do you have to do to get a promotion at *Trash?*"

"Everyone," Karma said, deadpan. "Yeah, they force us to have sex with each and every employee if we want to have any hope of ever being anything besides a lowly intern."

Lydia smirked. "Can I quote you?"

"She was kidding," Sumtimes said, rushing forward.

"The name is Karma Kushner, and I was kidding," Karma said, leaning into Lydia's microphone.

"I got a more exciting interview from Donna Hanover," Lydia said with disgust.

"We're a drug-free, sex-free, hardworking group of crazy kids," Lisha said cheerfully.

"Okay, great interview!" Sumtimes announced eagerly. "How about we move on to the photo session?"

"I'll have lots more questions for all of you later," Lydia promised, turning off her tape recorder.

"Super-goody," Karma whined. "Can't wait."

"They're all yours for the moment, Chase," Lydia told the photographer.

"Cool," he said. "Okay, for the first shot, I want you three girls all hanging off of Stone Pony."

"Who is that?" Chelsea asked.

"And you guys will be wrapped around Torrid Zone," Chase continued, checking something on one of his cameras.

"Is that an area or a person?" Alan asked dubiously.

"It's me," a young woman said, walking over to them. "Hi, I'm Torrid," she said huskily.

Torrid had long, bright red hair, massive fake breasts, and equally massive muscles. She wore a teenie, tiny leopard-print bikini.

"And I'm Stone," a guy said, coming up next to her. He had long black hair and was also a massive wall of muscles, clad only in a tiny leopard-print thong.

"They're bodybuilding strippers," Chase said casually. "We thought they'd be great for our shots."

"What do they have to do with our interns?" Sumtimes asked nervously.

"Nothing," Chase said. "Does that matter?"

"Uh, did you clear this with Jazz?" Sumtimes asked, sweat breaking out on her bald head.

"She doesn't have photo approval for any photos except her own," Chase said. "Okay, girls, go wrap yourself around Stone. Let's have the blonde wrapped around his waist, the Asian wrapped around his legs, and the brunette in his arms."

"No," Lisha said. "And by the way, we have names. Mine's Lisha."

"No?" Chase repeated, incredulous. "What do you mean, no?"

"I mean, I don't want to," Lisha said. "And I'm not going to."

"Me, either," Chelsea agreed. "I would feel like an idiot."

"Yeah, and 'the Asian' agrees," Karma said. "Why don't you just take normal shots of us?"

"Because normal is boring," Chase replied impatiently. "And *Rave* is never boring."

He shook his head with annoyance. "Okay, we'll start with the guys and Torrid. Torrid, can you bench-press one of these guys?"

"Sure," Torrid said.

"Good, here's what we'll do—" Chase began.

"No, *here's* what we'll do," Sky broke in. "We'll go downstairs and dance. You can take pictures of us, or not. Your choice." He turned to his friends. "You guys with me?"

"Absolutely," Lisha said.

"They dance great!" Sumtimes said quickly. "I mean, dancing shots of them would be great—"

"Would be boring," Chase corrected. "If we don't get some cooperation here, I don't know if this article is going to be a go or not."

"Well, that's just a chance we're willing to take," Lisha said. "Let's go, you guys."

The interns headed out of the room.

"Don't worry," Lisha heard Sumtimes say as the group headed for the stairs. "I'll arrange for any kind of shots you want. I just need a chance to talk to them and to Jazz."

"Well, that was stupid in a major way," Sky said with disgust.

"I don't know," Alan said. "Having Torrid bench-press me would have been a unique erotic experience."

Lisha hit him in the shoulder. "You guys are all alike."

"Not true," Alan protested. "We're all different, and you know it. For example, I'm this sensitive poet who hates football and all those manly-man sports, remember?"

"How could we forget, when you keep reminding us?" Sky said good-naturedly. He gently pushed a strand of hair off of Lisha's face. "You did a really cool thing up there, you know."

"So did you."

"So . . . want to dance?" Sky held out his hand to her. A slow, sexy tune was playing through the sound system.

I would love to be in your arms, Lisha thought. *But I can't. I don't trust myself to resist you. And I don't want Harley coming after you. I'm not worth it.*

"I don't think so," she said.

"Aw, come on," Sky wheedled, holding out his hand. "Would it really be so awful to slow-dance with me?"

"Hey, hey you! Lisha!" a male voice called to Lisha.

For a moment she was rooted to the spot. *The voice sounds like Harley's,* she thought frantically. *But it can't be. I have to run, but where can I—*

"Lisha!"

She gritted her teeth and turned to face him.

But it wasn't Harley. It was Stone Pony. He had put on a pair of jeans over his thong, and thrown on a denim shirt, which was unbuttoned, revealing his perfect, golden, washboard stomach.

"It *is* Lisha, isn't it?" Stone asked.

"Right," she said.

"Sorry about that up there," Stone said. "I mean, that photographer who hired us was kind of rude, I thought."

"Yeah, me, too," Lisha agreed.

"So, let's start over," he suggested. He held out his hand. "I'm Stone Pony. And you are—?"

"Lisha Bishop," Lisha said, shaking his hand. She quickly introduced her friends.

"No one is really named Stone Pony," Karma told him.

"You're right," Stone said, smiling to reveal his perfect, white teeth. "It used to be Stan Poninski. But that didn't exactly cut it in my line of work."

"I see your point," Karma agreed.

"So, you guys are really interns at *Trash,* huh?" Stone said. "I love that show!"

"Thanks," Alan said. "I think."

"Well, it was nice meeting you," Lisha said politely, turning away.

Stone reached for her arm. "Wait a second."

Lisha turned back to him.

Stone grinned at her. "Look, I know this is going to sound like a big line, but it really isn't. The moment I saw you upstairs, I wanted to know you. You're really gorgeous. Would you like to dance?"

"Take a hike, muscle-brain," Sky said. "She doesn't want to dance with you."

"Sky!" Lisha hissed. "Kindly shut up!"

"What?" Sky asked. "You're not going to fall for that I'm-so-honest-and-disarming routine, are you? The guy just wants to get in your pants, Lish!"

"All he did was ask me to dance!" she exclaimed.

"Well, so did I!" Sky fumed. "And you turned me down!"

Lisha narrowed her eyes at Sky, then she whirled around to Stone. "I'd love to dance with you," she declared.

"Great," Stone said. He reached for her hand and led her to the dance floor.

Sky watched as Stone took Lisha into his arms. "I don't believe it," he muttered, his hands clenched into fists.

Lisha looked over at Sky, who just stood there, staring daggers at her. She moved closer to Stone, reached up, and wrapped her arms around his neck.

Then she closed her eyes, and wrapped in Stone's muscular arms, she swayed to the music.

I won't think about Harley, or Sky, or anything at all, she decided. *Sky has a helluva nerve getting all possessive about me. Forget him. Forget complications.*

All I want to feel is the heat of this moment.

And then she moved even closer into Stone's arms.

FOUR

Honk. Honk. *Honk!*

Honk honk honk honk honk!

All around the Kushners' health-food-store van, a cacophony of auto, truck, and bus horns started blaring. At first there were just a couple, and then other drivers chimed in, and then more and more, until it seemed like all the drivers backed up inside the Queens Midtown Tunnel, waiting to pay their tolls, were leaning on their horns.

"Why do they do that?" Lisha asked from her spot in the backseat of the van. She put her hands over her ears. "It doesn't accomplish anything!"

"New Yorkers love to make a racket," Karma said, throwing her head back against the headrest. "This is endless. We've been sitting in this exact spot for almost two hours!"

Lisha rubbed her temples, where a headache was starting to form. It was the next evening. And somehow Karma had talked Lisha into going with her to talk to her parents about how she, Karma, had actually met a person she strongly suspected was her identical twin sister. Karma had pleaded the need for moral support, and Lisha had said yes.

So Karma had called her parents from work and told them that she wanted to see them—could they pick up her and Lisha and bring them out to the house for dinner? Marty and Wendy were only too happy to oblige.

I guess I was flattered that she asked me instead of asking Chelsea, Lisha thought. *Or maybe I was her second choice, since Chelsea is off doing something or other with Nick. After Jazz made Nick dance with her all night last night, it's going to take some work for him to get back in Chelsea's good graces.*

Lisha looked at her watch and sighed.

"What can I tell you?" Karma said. "When you're stuck, you're stuck."

"Try meditating, girls," Mrs. Kushner suggested good-naturedly from the front seat. "It can do wonders for you."

"Oh, thanks, Mom," Karma whined, rolling her eyes. "That's very helpful."

The plan they had arranged was that they'd drive out to the Kushners' house in Hewlett, Long Island, and then, over dinner, Karma would talk to them about the girl she had met who she was now certain was an identical twin sister that she had not known existed. After that, the Kushners would drop them at the subway near JFK

Airport, and they'd ride the A train on its return trip to Manhattan.

The only problem, Lisha thought, looking at her watch again, *was that we were supposed to be at the Kushners' house an hour ago. And an hour from now, we're supposed to be on the subway back to Manhattan.*

"Must be an accident at the other end," Karma's former-hippie father, Marty, replied. "I'll put in another tape, honey." He reached into a box of cassettes that was sitting between him and Karma's mother, Wendy, on the front seat of the car.

Karma looked at Lisha and made a face. "Prepare your virgin ears for a Grateful Dead assault," she warned her friend.

"It's John Tesh," Wendy advised them with a smile as she reached behind her neck to free her waist-length straight gray hair from her seat belt. "Not the Grateful Dead."

"Oh great," Karma quipped. "New Age music to have your blood boil by. A concerto for synthesizers and automobile horns?"

Lisha laughed, even though she was as frustrated as Karma was by the unmoving traffic.

"You'll love it, honey," Marty said to her. He seemed unfazed by the intense traffic backup.

"Yeah, right," Karma groused. "Can't you play something by Good Charlotte or Tori Amos instead?"

Lisha tapped her watch as she looked at Karma, who made a face in return.

She doesn't want to have this conversation with them, Lisha realized. *It's making her really nervous.*

"Just do it," Lisha advised out loud, her voice muffled by the honking car horns.

"I don't want to just do it here," Karma said.

"Putting it off isn't going to change anything," Lisha pointed out.

"Oh, yeah?" was Karma's retort. "If you're so good at doing stuff you dread, why haven't you called that lawyer yet about you-know-what?"

"I'll get to it," Lisha said defensively, "and don't change the subject." She checked her watch again. "Look, your father is going to have to turn around at the tollbooth and take us home anyway, or you'll be late for your shift at Jimi's, and you won't have—"

"What are you two talking about?" Wendy asked conversationally.

"Oh, nothing," Karma said quickly. She smiled at her mother. "Just, you know . . . talking."

Wendy turned around in her seat. "Karma Kushner," she admonished her daughter gently, "I'm your mother. Don't you think I know when you're hiding something?"

"Yeah, and overhearing your conversation didn't hurt, either," Marty added with a grin.

Wendy made a face at her husband, then turned back to Karma. "Spill it, please."

The traffic wasn't moving at all, so Marty Kushner took his eyes off the road and turned around to face his daughter, too.

Lisha couldn't help it. She stared at her friend, too.

What's she going to say? she thought. *And how is she going to say it?*

Karma seemed to shrink in her car seat and appeared even tinier than she really was.

"And so?" Wendy prompted her. "You're about to tell us that you're giving up black coffee and hot dogs forever and becoming a macrobiotic vegetarian?"

"Worse," Karma said meekly.

"Honey," Marty said, his voice full of kindness, "if you haven't been arrested and don't have a fatal disease, there's nothing you can say to us which will throw us. I guarantee it."

"You sure?" Karma said.

"Sure," Marty and Wendy said at the same time.

These two are amazing, Lisha thought. *How come my parents couldn't be more like them?*

"I think... well, that is I'm pretty sure that... I have a sister," Karma said. "A twin sister. An identical twin sister."

"We know," Marty said.

They what? Lisha asked herself, shocked.

"You *know?*" Karma asked incredulously. "Do you want to run that by me again?"

"We know you think you may have a twin sister," Wendy said.

"But how?" Karma asked. "I never—"

"Look, honey," Marty said. "Ever since you started working at *Trash,* we tape it every day and watch it before we go to bed."

Lisha could see that this statement took a second for Karma to digest.

"You watch *Trash*?" Karma asked.

"I just said that," Marty said. The car behind him gave a couple of quick beeps on the horn, and Marty pulled forward three or four feet in the traffic. Then the wall of cars and trucks stopped again.

"We saw that advertisement that had your picture on it," Wendy said.

"You did?" Karma said dully. "I can't believe you guys watch *Trash.* You are the last two people on the face of the earth that I ever thought would—"

"We watch it because you work there," Wendy said, "and we're your parents. When we saw that ad, we guessed that you thought you had a sister. Why else would you advertise on TV for someone who looks like you?"

"So why don't you explain to us what's going on, exactly?" Marty said. He reached for the volume knob on the van's tape deck, and turned the John Tesh music way down, until it was no more than a hum.

Karma sighed. "I guess I should start at the beginning."

"That would be a good place," Wendy agreed.

Lisha listened, fascinated, as Karma let the story unravel for her parents, beginning with how Demetrius mistook someone for her on the street, going through how she had seen someone who looked just like her on a city bus, and concluding at Jimi's when a girl who looked just like her, whose name Karma found out later was Janelle Cho, came into the club and ordered a drink from Karma.

As she talked, Lisha recalled how Karma, after she'd been convinced that there was another girl in New York City who looked just like her, had convinced the powers that be at *Trash* to run a short advertisement on the show featuring Karma's picture, and asking anyone who thought they looked like her to contact *Trash* immediately.

We got thousands of photos, Lisha thought. *And most of them didn't look like Karma at all. In fact, that had nothing, finally, to do with how Karma found Janelle!*

When Karma finished, fifteen minutes had passed, and the traffic had moved forward a bare two hundred yards.

"So, that's it," Karma concluded. "Except for the fact that when Janelle and I had coffee together, she told me she doesn't want anything to do with me. She says her life is fine the way it is, and doesn't want any complications. I've called her four times, and left her messages on her machine, but she never calls me back."

"Wow," Wendy said.

"I'll second that," Marty added.

"So if you saw me on *Trash*, with the ad," Karma asked, "how come you didn't say anything to me?"

"We were waiting for you to come to us," Marty explained. "We thought that was the right thing to do."

Cool, Lisha thought. *Very cool. That's the kind of parent I want to be. That is, if I'm ever a parent. Which I never will be. Since I plan never to fall in love and get married.*

"But if you didn't bring it up by the end of July, we were going to bring it up with you," Wendy added, reaching for a small bottle of mineral water that was perched in the center console, and taking a sip.

Even cooler, Lisha thought.

"So what do you know?" Karma asked them.

"Not much," Marty said. "We adopted you when you were two days old. The adoption agency told us that you didn't have any brothers or sisters, and certainly didn't say anything about a twin."

"That's for sure," Wendy added.

"And I have to admit, it really troubles me. I don't like the idea that they lied to us, or that they separated twin sisters like that."

"Would you . . . would you have adopted both of us, if you'd known I was a twin?" Karma asked hesitantly.

Marty and Wendy traded looks. "I honestly don't know," Wendy finally said.

"Unreal," Karma said. "I mean, if you had known about my twin, you might not have adopted me. And I might never have been your daughter."

"I know this sounds terribly fatalistic," Wendy said, "but I believe you were destined to be our daughter."

"And we can't imagine life without you," Marty added.

"The two of you ought to give lessons in how to be terrific parents," Lisha told them.

"Oh, we've made plenty of mistakes, believe me," Marty said. "But thanks for the compliment."

"So, Karma, do you want us to contact the agency again?" Wendy asked.

Karma nodded.

"Don't be disappointed," Marty warned her. "They may not be able to tell us anything."

"Well, they don't have to tell me she's my twin," Karma said, "because I already know that. I sat across the table from her and it was like looking at myself, minus the great fashion sense, of course."

Wendy reached for her daughter's hand. "So, how do you feel about all this?"

"Weird," Karma said.

"Bad," Lisha corrected.

"Okay, weird *and* bad," Karma admitted. "How would you like to find out you had a twin sister who didn't want to have anything to do with you?"

"Give her time, honey," Marty said gently, looking at his daughter through his rearview mirror. "This has to be a shock for her, too. Maybe she'll come around."

"I doubt it," Karma said unhappily. "See, the people who adopted her are Korean, too. And no one knows she's adopted. That's how their whole family wants it."

Wendy patted Karma's hand again. "Well, we'll do everything we can to get you information, sweetie."

"I know," Karma said with a sigh.

Lisha smiled at her friend, and hugged her shoulders. "Hang in there."

Karma gave her a small smile. "Well, Lish, I guess now you know all the family secrets."

"If my family was more like the Kushner family," Lisha said, "there'd be a lot fewer secrets in my parents' house."

Like what happened to me in Europe. My parents don't know a thing. And I could never, ever tell them, she thought.

"We'll be happy to take you as one of our kids," Marty said.

"Yeah, we could be fraternal twins," Karma cracked.

Everyone laughed as the car horns started up again, and within seconds the decibel level in the tunnel was once again completely excruciating.

I can't believe I'm out of shampoo, Lisha thought, as she turned her bottle of Aussie Miracle upside down and watched as nothing dripped out.

It was very late that evening. Marty and Wendy Kushner, had, in fact, turned around and driven Lisha and Karma back to their apartment, when they'd finally gotten out of the Queens Midtown Tunnel, at 9:30 P.M. that night. The holdup had been caused by an actual *holdup* at the toll takers' booth, and the police were conducting a thorough investigation. Karma had hurried off to work, worried that her boss, Arnold, was going to kill her for her tardiness.

Shampoo, shampoo, who uses my brand of shampoo? Lisha thought as she stepped out of the shower. *Not Chelsea and not Karma, and I hate the stuff they use.*

"Alan uses Aussie Miracle," she recalled out loud as she wrapped herself in an oversized terrycloth bathrobe and wrapped a towel around her wet hair.

That's right, she thought. *We laughed together one night over how particular we both are about using that shampoo. I'll go across the hall and borrow some from Alan.*

Lisha stuck her head into the hallway and looked around carefully. *No sign of Harley,* she thought. *I've got to do something about him. I just don't know what.*

She looked down under the door of the guys' apartment and saw some light, so she knew that someone was awake inside. She gave the quadruple code knock they'd all worked out. Then she knocked again.

The door opened.

Alan stood there, clad only in a small towel wrapped around his hips, his hair wet and tousled.

"Hey, Lisha," he said, his voice betraying a slight south-Texas drawl. "What's going on?"

"You look like you just stepped out of the shower," Lisha commented.

"Looks like you did, too." Alan smiled. "Come on in."

Both the girls' and the guys' apartments had been rented fully furnished by *Trash,* and while they were about the same size and layout, they couldn't have looked any more different. The girls' apartment featured overstuffed furniture and bad erotic art, but the guys' apartment was done in industrial chic. Everything in the apartment was made of metal, from the hard-edged frame on the uncomfortable black sofa, to the coffee table made from gray pipes. Sky, who was from Brooklyn, had a buddy of his bring the comfortable BarcaLounger from his family's living room over in his van. The brown easy chair sat incongruously amid the black-and-gray metal furnishings.

"I came to beg some shampoo, actually," Lisha said, stepping into their living room. For a moment she felt keenly aware that Alan had on nothing but a towel, and she had nothing on under her robe. "You use—"

"Aussie Miracle," Alan filled in. "Yeah, I remember you do, too."

"And I'm out," Lisha said.

"No problem," Alan said easily. "I'll get it—"

The phone rang.

"Just a sec," Alan said, snatching up the phone on the metal coffee table. "Hello?"

As he talked into the phone Lisha couldn't help but notice how cute he looked, clad only in a towel, with his hair all wet and tousled. *For someone who doesn't like sports, he sure is in great shape,* she thought, checking out his lean and muscular torso. *In fact, he's incredibly cute. Huh. I never think of Alan that way. Maybe it's because he used to have such an intense crush on Chelsea. Or maybe it's because he doesn't come on like a macho man, like Sky. I always just think of him as my bud.*

"Listen, I'm telling you the truth," Alan was saying into the phone. "Yeah, I promise I'll give Nick your message. Yes, word for word. Okay, bye." He hung up the phone.

"One of Nick's admirers?" Lisha asked.

"An ex, I guess," Alan said. "There are many."

"And they still call him here?"

Alan nodded. "His old roommates give them this number. They call all the time."

"Does Chelsea know that?"

"No," Alan said. "I tried to warn her once, that Nick isn't ready for the kind of serious relationship she wants, but—"

"She wouldn't listen," Lisha filled in.

"Something like that," Alan agreed. "Listen, I'm not busting Nick. He's a great guy and I know he really cares about Chelsea. In fact, they're out somewhere together right now. They even took Belch with them."

Belch was Nick's dog, who was famous for his ability to belch on command.

"Is Sky home?" Lisha asked casually.

"He went out for a burger," Alan said. "You know we never have any food in this apartment. So, I'll get my shampoo for you."

"Thanks," Lisha said. She sat on the couch and tried to get comfortable, failed, and got up to plop herself down in the easy chair.

There's some button here that makes this thing vibrate, she recalled, and she fumbled around with the knobs at the bottom of the chair.

She pushed the wrong one. The chair slid backward until the back was practically parallel with the floor, the footrest came up, and Lisha found herself facing the ceiling, her bathrobe all the way up her thighs.

"Hey, man, I brought you back a burger—" Sky said as he came into the apartment.

Lisha fumbled wildly, caught in the chair, trying to adjust her bathrobe and reach for the knob to set her upright at the same time.

"Great outfit," Sky said with a grin.

"Shut up," Lisha snapped, her face blazing with embarrassment. She pulled down her bathrobe.

"You know, I've fantasized about you dressed just about like that, in that chair—" Sky began.

Lisha managed to right the chair, and she stood up. "I don't want to hear about your fantasies, okay?"

"Lish, I'm only kidding," Sky said. "I just meant that I'm glad to see you."

"I just came to borrow some shampoo from Alan," Lisha said stiffly.

"Oh," Sky replied. He set Alan's burger down on the table. "I shouldn't have gotten my hopes up, huh?"

"Right," Lisha agreed.

Sky moved closer to her. "I just . . . I feel this heat between us, you know? You keep denying it, but I keep feeling like it's there."

It is, Lisha thought, barely breathing. *Do you know how much I want to touch you? But it's too dangerous. That kind of passion got me into big trouble before. And I'll never, ever let it happen again.*

"There's nothing there from my point of view," she said coolly.

Sky stood so close to her that she could feel his warm breath on her face, his lips were so close to hers.

"Nothing?" he asked, his voice low.

Now his lips were almost on hers. *It would be so easy to give in. So easy.*

"Sorry I took so long," Alan said as he came back into the room. "I was trying to find a new bottle and it was all the way in the back of my—" He stopped, taking in the sight of Sky and Lisha. "Oops. Guess I'm interrupting."

Lisha jumped away from Sky. "Not at all," she said, her voice a little too loud.

"Lish—" Sky began.

"Forget it," she said quickly.

"Lish, come on—"

Lisha ignored Sky, went over to Alan, and took the shampoo. "Thanks. You're a lifesaver."

"Lisha, come on, stay and we'll talk," Sky said.

"There's nothing to talk about," she said firmly.

And then, before she had a chance to think about it, to prove her point that there was absolutely nothing going on between her and Sky, Lisha leaned over and—to the shock of all three of them—kissed Alan softly on the lips.

Then she turned on her heel and walked out of their apartment, leaving two speechless guys behind her.

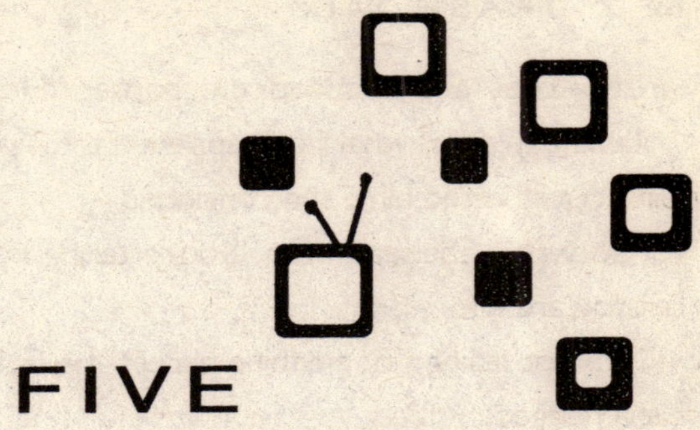

FIVE

"You did *what*?" Chelsea asked Lisha.

"I kissed Alan," Lisha said.

It was the next morning, and Chelsea and Lisha were walking to work together. Karma, even though she'd gotten hardly any sleep the night before because of her late shift at the hip teen downtown club, Jimi's, had gone in early to *Trash* to prepare for a meeting. Later that day she was scheduled to see their most hated boss of all, Roxanne Renault—also known as Bigfoot, because of the gigantic size of her feet.

"You and Alan?" Chelsea asked. "I never thought of the two of you together." They sidestepped a street vendor selling knockoff wristwatches and rounded the corner. "How did this happen?"

Lisha explained what had happened the night before. "And then I just . . . I just kissed him," she concluded.

"So wait," Chelsea began, "you're telling me you're not into Sky but you are into Alan?"

"I'm not telling you anything except the facts of what happened," Lisha hedged.

Chelsea looked at her sideways. "Is it possible that you really are into Sky, but you're only pretending not to be?"

"Why would I do that?" Lisha asked nonchalantly.

"I don't know," Chelsea confessed. "I just get this feeling sometimes."

"It makes much more sense for me to be with Alan," Lisha said firmly.

"Why?" Chelsea asked.

"Because chemistry is highly overrated," Lisha declared as they approached the glass doors of the building where *Trash* was taped daily in front of a live audience.

"Oh, so you *do* want Sky—"

"Just forget it," Lisha said quickly. "I'm not looking for any kind of big relationship with anyone."

They walked into the cool, air-conditioned lobby and stood with all the other people waiting for an elevator.

"Did you call that lawyer yet?" Chelsea asked Lisha.

"I've been busy," Lisha said, blowing the bangs out of her eyes.

"You have not," Chelsea accused. "You're just scared to do it."

"I'm not scared," Lisha denied.

"Lish, you can't just blow this off, I mean it!" Chelsea exclaimed. "Harley could show up anywhere, at any time, and he's really sick!

How about if Karma and I go to see the lawyer with you, would that help?"

"Don't push me, okay?" Lisha said. "I said I'll get to it, and—"

"Hi, how are you, how's it going?" Brian Bassinger said eagerly, sidling over to them. He was holding a pile of manila envelopes, which Lisha recognized as interoffice memos.

"Hi, Brian," Chelsea greeted.

"I got here an hour ago," Brian said. "The early bird gets the worm, Uncle Barry says."

"Great," Lisha managed.

He gazed at her with adoration. "Wow, Lisha, you look really, really nice today."

Lisha looked down at herself. She had on a plain black slip dress, very short, and combat boots. "Thanks, Brian."

"And I love your perfume," he added.

"I'm not wearing perfume, Brian," Lisha said.

"Wow," he repeated, unable to take his eyes from her.

The elevator arrived, and the girls piled in with the rest of the crowd. Brian was wedged right up against Lisha. He stared at her all the way up to the fourth floor.

"Bye, Brian," Lisha said, since he seemed rooted to the spot and unable to move, and blocked her exit from the elevator.

"Oh, yeah, bye," Brian said, and he edged out of the way, letting Lisha and Chelsea pass by.

"That guy has it really bad for you," Chelsea commented as they headed down the hallway toward the tiny cubicles that masqueraded as their offices.

"He's kind of creepy," Lisha said, making a face.

"Oh, he is not," Chelsea replied with a laugh. "He's just crazy about you, that's all."

"Speaking of people who are crazy about people, how was your date with Nick last night?" Lisha asked.

"Great," Chelsea said with a sigh. "And you're right. I *am* crazy about him."

They had reached their offices. Lisha leaned against the wall. "Did he talk about what's going on with Jazz?" she asked.

"No," Chelsea said. "He steered clear of that subject."

"Bummer," Lisha commented.

"Hey, interns!" a female voice barked at them. They turned around. It was Roxanne Renault, a.k.a. Bigfoot. A Gwyneth Paltrow look-alike, except with red hair, she limped toward them on crutches, one of her massive feet encased in a cast covered by orange-and-pink silk, which matched the orange-and-pink silk of her minidress.

Bigfoot had recently been shot in the foot by a crazed guest on *Trash*. She was still recovering from her injury, and the interns were bearing the brunt of the wrath her pain induced.

Not that she was a pleasant personality before she was wounded, Lisha thought. *Hardly.*

"Good morning, Roxanne," Chelsea said cheerfully.

"I'm not interested in morning chitchat, okay?" Roxanne snapped. "My foot is killing me and a pipe burst in my office this morning and soaked a bunch of my files. Which means I'm in a bad mood. Get it?"

"Got it," Lisha confirmed.

"Good," Roxanne said. "I expect the two of you at the one o'clock meeting about the Kids of Serial Killers show we're planning."

"I'm not working on that," Lisha reminded her.

"Look, if I say I want you at the meeting, then your butt will be at the meeting, right?"

"Right," Lisha agreed.

"Good answer," Bigfoot said. "And Chutney, go clean up the mess in my office. Bring a squeegee." She hobbled away.

Roxanne called Chelsea Chutney because Chutney was the name by which Jazz had mistakenly referred to her, on the air, after Chelsea had saved Jazz from the crazed gun-toting teenager, Sela Flynn. All Sela had done was taken the entire *Trash* set hostage, Jazz included.

Just another day at the Trash-bin, Lisha thought to herself.

"What a charmer," Chelsea muttered.

"I'd like to shoot her in her other foot," Lisha said.

"Can you imagine if she ever found out the truth about me?" Chelsea asked, shuddering.

She means that mass murderer Charles Kettering is her father, Lisha thought, *and that Bigfoot would love nothing more in this world than to uncover her secret, and expose her in front of the entire world.*

"Bigfoot is not going to find out," Lisha said firmly. "Karma scammed her into believing that Chelsea Kettering lives in Australia and turned down the chance to be on *Trash,* remember?"

"I remember," Chelsea said. "But I always feel like I'm *this* close to getting busted."

"Don't worry," Lisha told her. "Roxanne isn't nearly as smart as she thinks she is. If she wasn't doing the nasty with Barry Bassinger, Executive Producer, I bet she wouldn't even have a job here."

"Maybe," Chelsea said dubiously. "I just get so nervous around her."

Lisha hugged Chelsea. "Karma and I told you we'd keep your secret, and we will, Chels. Not to worry."

"Thanks," Chelsea said gratefully. "So, why is it that you'll help me with my problems but you won't let me help you with yours?"

"I don't need any help!"

"You need to go to see that lawyer—"

"I will—"

"Just call him," Chelsea insisted. "Promise me you'll call him today."

"Boy, you can be a real pit bull when you want to be," Lisha groused.

"A pit bull who cares about you," Chelsea said. "I guess I'd better go clean up Roxanne's mess." She sighed. "I'll see you later. Oh, and don't forget what I said about the lawyer, okay?"

"Yeah, yeah." Lisha waved her off, then went into her tiny cubicle and sat behind her desk. On top of a pile of papers sat an envelope, with *Lisha* written on the front.

"What's this," she murmured to herself as she opened the sealed envelope. A typed note fell out. She read it quickly.

Dear Lisha,

I can't stop thinking about you. Meet me on the third floor, in the film storage room, today at one-thirty. Or else.

The note wasn't signed.

Lisha's hands began to shake.

Harley, she thought. *He got past the guards downstairs, and he got into my office. He's watching me. He's right here at* Trash.

Oh God . . .

"What should I do?" she whispered out loud to herself. "Please, I don't know what to do—"

"Hey, you okay? You look like someone died."

It was Alan, sticking his head into the doorway of her cubicle.

"Oh, sure," she said, her voice shaky. "Fine."

"You don't look fine," Alan said, his voice concerned. He came into the office. "Can I help?"

Lisha stood up and went to him. "If it wouldn't sound too crazy, you could put your arms around me and hold me," she whispered.

Alan opened his arms, and she moved into the comfort of his embrace. For a long time she just stood there, her eyes closed, feeling momentarily safe.

Safer, anyway.

"Lish, what is it?" he finally asked, his mouth in her hair. "You're shaking—"

"I can't talk about it," she said quickly. She took a step away from him. "But, thanks. You helped."

He gave her a small smile. "I know you can take care of yourself, Lish. But I just want you to know that I'm your friend. And I care about you."

"I know you do, Alan." She walked over to the window and looked down at the street. "Did you ever wish you could just erase your past?"

"I'm afraid my past isn't exciting enough to harbor a wish like that," Alan admitted. "If it was, I'd probably be a lot better writer than I am—you know, you can't write it unless you've lived it, and all that."

"Well, I've lived it," Lisha said, still staring out at the street. "And now I have to pay for it." Her eyes filled with tears until the street scene below was just a blur.

She heard Alan cross the room, and then she felt his hands ever so gently on her shoulders. He turned her around. Then, without saying a word, he took her in his arms again.

This is what I need, Lisha thought. *To feel safe. I'll never feel this way with Sky. He's too dangerous. And I never, ever want to feel that out of control again.*

And then she lifted her lips to Alan, and she kissed him. For just a moment he hesitated, and then . . . then, he more than answered the warmth of her kiss with his own.

"Okay, let's review," Bigfoot said, her cast-clad foot, as usual, propped up on her desk. Lisha, Chelsea, and Karma had to lean to one side or the other in order to see Roxanne's face from the other side of her humongous foot.

"Karma, update, Teen Kids of Serial Killers," Bigfoot barked.

Lisha snuck a quick look at her watch. *One o'clock. I'm supposed to meet Harley in the film storage room in a half hour. What should I do? Should I go? By myself? But what if he has a gun? No, he couldn't possibly have snuck a gun past the metal detectors downstairs. But what if I don't meet him? And he goes to the police? My whole life would be ruined and I—*

"Lisha, are you with us?" Roxanne asked.

"Oh, yes, of course," Lisha said, her attention snapping back to the meeting.

"So, what did Karma just say, then?" Bigfoot demanded.

"I, uh . . ." Lisha stammered.

"What is this, junior high?" Roxanne asked. "What is your problem?"

"No problem," Lisha said, trying to sound like her usual cool self. "Continue."

"Oh, I have your permission?" Roxanne sneered. "Karma just gave us short sketches of the three teen kids of serial killers who have already agreed to be on our show. You daydreamed through the whole thing."

"Sorry," Lisha said.

"I brought you into this because I thought you had it together enough to contribute to this show. Jazz expects us to pull incredible ratings with this. I expect your full attention. Got it?"

"Got it," Lisha assured her.

"Yeah, I bet." Roxanne turned to Karma. "Okay, continue. Move on to the Chelsea Kettering recap."

"Okay," Karma said, scanning her notes. "Well, let's see, we wanted to get Chelsea Kettering, but when we spoke to her in Australia, where she's attending college, she absolutely refused to be on the show."

Actually, Bigfoot only thinks she spoke to Chelsea Kettering, Lisha recalled. *The person she really spoke to was some actress in Australia who was pretending to be Chelsea. Karma somehow arranged the whole thing to throw Bigfoot off of the real Chelsea's trail. Because if she knew that the real Chelsea Kettering was her intern, Chelsea—or should I say Chutney?—Jennings, it would be all over the front page of the* New York Post *tomorrow morning.*

"I've tried to call Chelsea in Australia three more times to see if I could get her to change her mind," Roxanne said, adjusting her foot on her desk. "All I ever get is an answering machine."

"She was pretty adamant about not wanting to have anything to do with *Trash,*" Karma said innocently.

"I didn't get where I am by taking no for an answer," Bigfoot snapped.

Yeah, we know exactly how you got where you are, Lisha thought. *You sure didn't say no to sex with Barry Bassinger.*

"The three guests we have lined up are excellent," Chelsea said.

"Right," Karma agreed. "So we won't really miss Chelsea Kettering at all."

"We won't have to miss her," Roxanne said smugly.

The interns looked at her blankly.

"We won't have to, because I have a plan to get her to say yes."

Chelsea's face grew pale. "Wha-what would that be?"

Bigfoot leaned forward as far as her cast would allow. "Jazz wants us to offer ten thousand dollars to anyone who can convince Chelsea Kettering to come on *Trash*."

"Bad idea, won't work," Karma said quickly.

"Right," Chelsea agreed. "Because . . . she can't be bought!"

"Clearly you don't get the *Trash* motto—it's all *Trash*. You see, everyone can be bought, it's just that some people have a higher price than others," Roxanne replied. "Here's the deal. We do this publicity blitz, with the story of what happened with her dad, and then photos of her then and now. We say we know she's in Australia, her address, and all that. And anyone who can convince her to come on *Trash* gets this money. And if it doesn't work, we up the sum."

Lisha snuck another peek at her watch. *One-fifteen. Fifteen minutes until I'm supposed to meet Harley,* she thought. Sweat began to break out on her forehead.

"But . . . but isn't that an invasion of her privacy, or something?" Chelsea asked nervously.

"Why would I care?" Roxanne asked.

"Because of legal implications," Karma said. "Yeah. I'm sure it's illegal. You could get sued."

"I doubt it," Roxanne said dismissively. "Jazz loves this idea. And freelance photographers are going to go nuts down in Australia, trying to catch this chick and get a current photo of her. It's kind of brilliant, if I do say so myself."

"I don't really see why you're so obsessed with this one particular girl," Chelsea said, trying to sound nonchalant.

"I'm not obsessed," Bigfoot corrected her. "But I always win, and I always get what I want." She turned to Lisha. "What do you think?"

"I think you're obsessed, too," Lisha said.

"Oh, really," Roxanne said sweetly. "Well, in case it escapes the combined and extremely limited wisdom of you three mental giants, you were not hired to *think*."

"But you just asked me what I—" Lisha began.

"It was a trick question," Bigfoot replied. "You were hired to follow orders and I have a whole bunch of them. Get ready to take scrupulous notes."

Roxanne went on and on, giving them a million assignments, everything from publicity for the Ten Thousand Dollars for Chelsea Kettering Campaign, to cleaning the employees' lounge.

Lisha furtively looked at her watch again. *It's one-thirty. But I can't just leave—I'll lose my job. And Bigfoot is on a roll. Who knows when she'll be done? But what if I don't show up to meet Harley? What will he do?*

". . . and another thing," Roxanne continued. "About walking Jazz's dogs. Sumtimes hasn't been hard enough on you. The dogs aren't getting enough exercise. I expect you to trot with them for at least three blocks. . . ."

One-forty. Will she ever stop talking?

". . . when you seat the audience for the shows, you need to look a lot better than you guys look today," Roxanne said. "I mean, Chelsea, what is that pathetic little outfit? You don't even look like someone we'd let into the studio, much less like someone who is hip enough to work here. . . ."

One forty-five. I can feel the sweat pouring off of me. I feel like I'm going to faint. Or throw up. Or—

"Lisha, are you okay?" Chelsea asked, breaking into Lisha's thoughts.

Lisha could feel Bigfoot, Karma, and Chelsea all staring at her.

Here's my chance, she thought.

"No, I . . . I think I'm sick," she said, rising quickly. "Excuse me—"

"You want me to come with—" Chelsea began.

"Sit!" Bigfoot barked. "She can go hurl by herself."

Lisha rushed out of the office, ran down the hall, and quickly took the stairs to the third floor. No one was around. She ducked into the film storage room, breathing hard.

At first the room seemed completely black. Then, as her eyes adjusted to the lack of light, she could make out shadows, bins of stored film stacked high.

"Harley?" she whispered.

No answer.

She wiped the sweat from her brow and took a few tentative steps toward the stacked film. "Harley?" she asked again.

Something crawled over her hand, and she screamed in fright.

A spider. She shook it off.

"Harley?" she called one more time.

But the only answer was the fearful pounding of her own heart.

He must have thought I stood him up, and he left, Lisha thought. *Which means he's mad. Really mad.*

I don't have any idea what he'll do next. But I know there's one thing I can be sure of.

He'll be back.

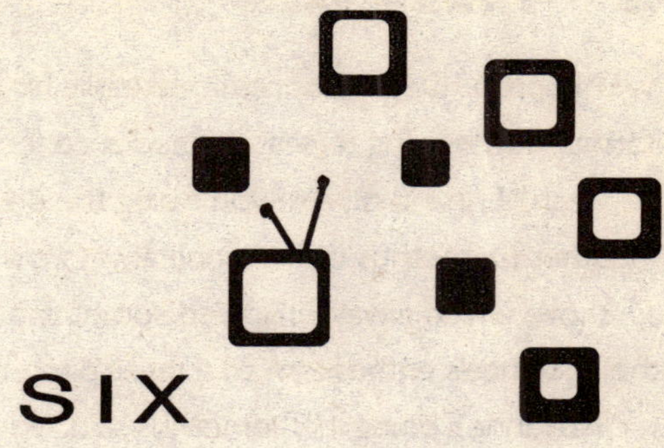

SIX

Lisha rounded the corner on her way to the studio where *Trash* was actually taped, lost in thought.

I know I should have called the lawyer last night, but I didn't, she thought guiltily. *I keep thinking that if I can just talk to Harley, I can reason with him. Which is crazy. But a lawyer is going to tell me to talk to the FBI before they come to talk to me, or something. For all I know they'll extradite me to France, and I'll end up in a French prison, and—*

Ooof.

Lisha bumped into something tall and hard. It was huge Demetrius, standing in the hallway outside the studio, his arms around tiny Karma.

"Sorry," Lisha said.

"No prob," Demetrius returned easily, his arms still wrapped around Karma. "You helping to seat the audience for today's show?"

"Yeah," Lisha said. "Are you doing the preshow?"

Either Demetrius or Roxanne always did the show before the on-air show, which always involved something wild, guaranteed to raise the audience's enthusiasm to a fever pitch.

"Roxanne's doing it," Demetrius said. "I'm on audience patrol, too."

"Me, too," Karma added, leaning her head against Demetrius's chest, which she barely reached, even in high heels.

"The two of you look disgustingly happy together," Lisha said.

"I know, we're nauseating," Karma agreed happily. "Hey, did you get the memo about the *Rave* interviews tomorrow?"

"No," Lisha said. "But my desk is a mess, so I could have missed it."

"Well, that Lydia Love is coming here tomorrow at three," Karma said. "We're all supposed to be available. I think the idea is that Sumtimes can exert more control over the interviews if they get done here at the Trash-bin."

Lisha shrugged. "I wasn't exactly planning to bare my soul to *Rave*, anyway."

"Have you called the lawyer about your boyfriend?" Demetrius asked.

"He's my ex-boyfriend," Lisha corrected. "And I'm—"

"Lisha!" Brian Bassinger called to her as he came barreling down the hallway, carrying a stack of Xeroxed papers. "Hi!"

"Hi, Brian," Lisha replied. "What is it?"

"Oh, nothing," Brian said. "I'm just in a good mood!"

"Oh, well, that's nice," Lisha said.

"Yeah, well, see ya." Brian stared at her dreamily, then he walked away.

"Strange guy," Karma commented.

"We were talking about Harley," Demetrius reminded them.

"As I was saying," Lisha said, "I'm on top of the situation."

Demetrius gave her a jaded look. "I take it that means you haven't called."

"Don't pressure me—"

"I'm sorry, Lisha, but I *am* going to pressure you," Demetrius said. "You need to—"

"I can't talk about this right now," Lisha interrupted, and she hurried into the *Trash* studio.

"Lish—" Karma called after her, but Lisha ignored her.

I know they're right, Lisha thought. *Okay. Right after the show, I'll go call the lawyer. I'll see if I can get information without giving him my name or anything. That's a good plan.*

"Hi," Chelsea said as Lisha joined her in the back of Studio A.

"What are you waiting for, an invitation to the prom?" Bigfoot hissed as she hobbled by them. "Get to work!"

Work meant that when Demetrius gave the signal, the rear doors would open, and the long line of young people waiting to be seated in the audience would stampede into the studio.

"Bigfoot is such a lovely person," Chelsea said.

"The loveliest," Lisha agreed. "Okay, I take it it's the usual—pretty people down front where the camera will pick them up, unattractive people in the back—"

"Sumtimes says she has to talk to us before we seat anyone today," Karma said, hurrying toward them.

Sumtimes finished a conversation with one of the cameramen then hurried over to the girls. A portable walkie-talkie headset was wrapped around her head, the mouthpiece near her mouth. "Okay, you guys, today don't seat any pretty people down front. Today's different. Gorgeous people go in the back row. Pleasant-looking people go in the middle. Unattractive people go in the front row. Got it?"

"How come?" Karma asked.

"Because that's how Jazz wants it," Sumtimes said patiently.

"But you always tell us to put the hip, good-looking people in the front—"

"Not today," Sumtimes said. She turned on her walkie-talkie. "D? You about ready?"

"Ready," came Demetrius's voice through the headset. "You want me to let 'em in?"

"It's a go," Sumtimes told him. "Let's open the pearly gates." She turned her head back to the interns. "Remember what I told you about the seating. And remember the *Trash* motto: You're too cool to care."

Chelsea made a face. "I hate being rude to people just because—"

"Don't think of it as rude," Sumtimes said. "Think of it as performance art."

As the rear doors opened, hordes of people streamed into the studio.

"You take the rear," Lisha told Karma, "you take the middle," she told Chelsea, "and I guess I'll take the front," she finished, hurrying down the aisle.

Two gorgeous girls in tiny miniskirts were heading for the front row.

"Sorry, these seats are reserved," Lisha told them.

"They are not," the blonder of the two girls stated. "And the front row gets on camera."

"I know, and you won't be sitting there," Lisha said coolly.

"We don't have to put up with that," the other girl said, outraged.

"True," Lisha said. "You could leave. I don't care."

The two girls made huffy sounds, but they turned and marched to the back of the studio. Meanwhile Karma and Chelsea were sending unattractive people down to Lisha.

"Great, just fill in these seats," Lisha told them, waving them down the aisle.

"This is way rad, Tracey," a skinny girl with braces and a bad perm told her friend as she settled into the front row.

"Way," her friend agreed. She had a huge nose, a bad complexion, and massive thighs. "I never thought we'd score front-row seats!"

"Hi, I got sent to help," Nick said, strolling over to her. "What's the deal with the unattractive people down front today?"

"Ours is not to reason why," Lisha said. "We are but lowly interns, who live to serve." A couple came in with matching beer bellies, as well as matching denim jackets, and sauntered down the aisle.

"Yeah, here is cool," Nick told them.

"Wow!" the girl said, staring at Nick. "Did anyone ever tell you you look just like Brad Pitt?"

"He *is* Brad Pitt," Lisha said.

"He ain't really Brad Pitt," the boyfriend said as they found their seats. But the girlfriend kept looking back at Nick, as if she wasn't sure.

"This is so bogus," Nick told Lisha. "Separating people on the basis of their looks—pure *Trash*."

"Well, Jazz would say life is *Trash*," Lisha said. "I mean, people judge people on the basis of their looks all the time."

Like me, Lisha thought as she waved more people into the first few rows. *When I was fat and ugly, I had no life. If I hadn't been so insecure about my looks, I never would have fallen for Harley. Harley. How did he get past the* Trash *guards?*

What does he want from me?

"Okay, here we go," Karma said as she stood up in the *Trash* control room, looking down at the set.

Lisha, Chelsea, and Nick were there, too, having been given permission for the first time to watch the show from the booth. Sky was in there, too, but he was sitting with a set of acoustic headphones on, in front of one of the soundboard panels. Down below them, Roxanne was just finishing her warm-up with the audience, something having to do with finding money hidden inside the clothing of people who were total strangers to each other.

"It's great watching from in here," Nick said.

"Hey, Nick, mon, Jazz is wanting you," Winston Manroot, Jazz's secretary, said in his lilting accent as he stuck his head in the door.

"For what?" Nick asked, scowling.

"If you think she tells me, you are on some serious drugs, mon," Winston said. He shook his head and his dreadlocks went flying. "She says jump—you know the drill."

"Unfortunately," Nick said.

Winston flashed his fabulous grin. "It could be worse, mon," he said cheerfully. "Bigfoot could be callin' on you."

Lisha's jaw dropped open. "How did you know we call her—" She stopped herself. The director and his assistant could hear every word they said.

Winston winked at Lisha. "No secrets around here, mon," he said, and disappeared out the door.

"I'll catch you guys later," Nick said, and left.

Chelsea's jaw set hard.

"Don't get weird about Jazz and Nick," Karma told her. "It's probably nothing."

"Yeah, but what if it's—"

"Okay, guys, cut the talking," Sky said. "We're on in ten."

"Count it down," the director said, focusing in on the main monitor.

"Ten, nine, eight . . ." Sky began.

"We're live," the director said into his headset, when Sky finished the countdown. "Camera one, stage right to Jazz."

As a rule, Jazz made a creative entrance. The audience—both in the studio and at home—never knew what to expect. Roxanne had driven the audience into a frenzy, and now they all stood up, chanting "Jazz! Jazz! Jazz!"

Today, two cute guys dressed in medical scrubs entered from stage right, wheeling a hospital gurney, on which there lay a body.

The gurney was upended, and the body practically flew off into the air, and then landed deftly on its feet.

It was Jazz, her body completely swathed in bandages, like a mummy. Only her face, and her perfect, long white-blond hair were free.

"She's trussed up like a mummy?" Karma asked, bewildered.

"Now, this is out there, even for Jazz," Lisha said.

"Shhh!" Sky instructed them.

The audience had no idea what Jazz was up to, but they went wild, anyway, as the "applause" signs flashed on and off.

Jazz held up one finger to quiet them, and they obeyed, sat, and leaned forward to hear what Jazz's latest stunt would be.

"Well, well, well," Jazz said, standing in the middle of the *Trash* set, surveying the audience, "what have we here? In the front two rows?"

Lisha looked, through the control-room glass, at the people in the front rows. They were looking at each other uncomfortably, wondering what Jazz had in store for them.

"So, you guys have read all the tabloid crap they write about me, I'm sure," Jazz said conversationally. "Last week I read that I had sex with the entire cast of *CSI: Miami,* including the dog!"

The audience laughed and applauded.

"How utterly *Trashy,*" Jazz continued. "This same article said I have had plastic surgery on every part of my face and body. Well, that's not true."

"Close-up on camera two," the director called into his headset. A camera moved in on a close-up of Jazz's face.

"For example, I was born with this forehead," Jazz said with a wicked smile. At that moment two incredibly fine guys came out from the wings, and cut Jazz out of her bandages, as the audience roared their approval. Underneath she was wearing a simple white bikini.

"I was not, however," Jazz said, "born with this body." Her eyes scanned the people sitting in the front rows.

"Who put these people here?" she demanded.

No answer.

"You people in the first two rows, stand up!" Jazz commanded.

They all stood up.

She walked up to one of the people in the front row—Lisha saw it was one of the first two girls she had seated.

"Hi," Jazz said, draping her arm around the girl.

"Hi," the girl squeaked, staring up, awestruck, at Jazz. "It's really you!"

Everyone laughed.

"What's your name?" Jazz asked conversationally.

"Tracey Angier," the girl said.

"Tracey," Jazz said, "I wasn't born gorgeous, you know."

"Really?" Tracey asked, wide-eyed.

"Anyone can look good," Jazz said. "Have you ever thought about plastic surgery?"

"Well, yeah," Tracey said. "I guess. I mean, it's really expensive and stuff—"

"What if it wasn't expensive?" Jazz asked her. "What would you have done?"

"You need everything done, baby!" some guy yelled from the back of the house.

Some of the audience laughed. Tracey blushed.

"Too bad we can't do plastic surgery on his mind, isn't it?" Jazz said coolly.

Tracey hugged Jazz. "You're my idol."

"Thanks," Jazz said. "Now, back to the subject at hand. If cost was no object, what would you have done?"

"A nose job," Tracey said. "Something on my skin to get rid of the marks—I used to have all this gross acne. And, um, that liposuction stuff on my thighs."

"Cool," Jazz said. "And how many others in these front two rows have thought about plastic surgery?"

Most of the people raised their hands.

That's why she wanted not-so-good-looking people down in front, Lisha realized. *But where is she going with this whole thing?*

The answer came soon enough.

"Fantastic!" Jazz said, taking Tracey's arm, and then pointing with her handheld mike at two other girls and three guys in the front rows. "You, you, you, you, and you," she ordered. "Up on the set. In the director chairs. And Tracey here, too."

Lisha watched, amazed.

When the six teens were all seated, Jazz sat down on the famous *Trash* couch, with her arm around the male half of the ever-present plastic blowup doll couple that graced the set of *Trash*. Today both dolls were also swathed in white bandages.

Jazz reached for a handful of M&M's from the jar she kept on the coffee table. "So, who's under the age of eighteen?" She threw a handful of candy into her mouth.

Nobody said anything.

"Cool," Jazz said. "And if you're lying, we'll find out, and you're outta this. Okay, we're going to play a little game now. I call it the Obnoxious Game. I'm going to ask you guys a question, and we'll see who can come up with the most obnoxious answer."

"What do we win?" a guy with no chin and less hair asked from his place in the center chair on stage.

"Not telling," Jazz said coolly. "But it's something fantastic, I promise. Wanna play, anyway?"

They all nodded yes. "Okay," Jazz said, "here goes. What's the most obnoxious thing that you can say to someone at a funeral, about the dearly departed?"

"Uh . . . this girl I know got treated by the same doctor. She's dead now, too," the girl on the end offered.

"Oooooo," the audience reacted.

"You know, he owed me ten bucks!" the balding guy shouted out.

The audience laughed.

"I wish she could know that she looks a lot better now with short hair!" Tracey called out.

This time the oohs and ahhs and whistles were loud enough to be heard in the control room.

"He's allergic to dirt, you know," another guy cried.

The audience cracked up.

"Damn, I can't believe I'm missing *Oprah* for this!" the last guy said.

The audience cracked up even louder.

"You would have thought there'd be more people here, huh?" the last girl said.

This time even the people in the control room had to laugh.

"Okay, it's sick," Karma said, "but it is funny."

Lisha nodded, her eyes glued to the stage below.

Jazz turned and faced one of the cameras, which came in tight as the director issued orders into his headset. Lisha shifted her gaze to the monitors in the control room, all of which showed Jazz in extreme close-up.

"Beauty is skin-deep, right, gang?" Jazz asked. "And it's what's inside that counts, isn't that what adults love to tell you? We'll see. Because on today's *Trash,* we're going to have a contest to pick which of these six plastic-surgery candidates is the most obnoxious of them all. And then *Trash* is going to give that person, all expenses paid, all the plastic surgery they ever wanted! And then we'll see how it changes their life! Or not! Back in a moment with more *Trash.*"

The audience whooped and hollered and cheered and stood and applauded as the studio lights went out for a commercial break.

"Genius," Karma repeated. "Demented, sick, disturbed, perverted, and thoroughly ill. But genius, all the same."

Lisha was lost in thought as she got off the elevator on her floor. Right before she'd left the office, she had tried the number of the criminal lawyer that Karma had given her. He had not been available, but Lisha left a message for him to return her call.

At least I did something, Lisha thought, secretly glad that the lawyer hadn't been available. *At least it's a step.*

"Hi," Sky said as Lisha rounded the corner to the hall of her apartment. Sky had his key in the lock of his own apartment, about to enter.

"Hi," Lisha responded. "Just get home?"

"I went out for sushi with Alan."

"Raw fish?" Lisha said, making a face.

"Yeah, I agree. Alan could live on it. I pushed it around on my plate hoping it wasn't going to flop on its own. Did you eat?"

"I stayed late at the office to finish some filing Bigfoot wanted done."

"We could go and get a burger on the corner," Sky offered.

"No, thanks," Lisha said. "I'm beat."

"Or maybe you're just avoiding me," Sky said.

"I'm not, I'm just tired," Lisha insisted.

Sky scratched his chin. "Would you say yes if Alan asked you?"

"This isn't about you or Alan, okay?" Lisha said.

Sky came over to her and looked into her eyes. "Are you and Alan in a thing with each other?"

"I don't even know what that means," Lisha said crossly.

"Yeah, you do," Sky said. "Alan is my friend. But you don't belong with him."

Lisha gazed back up at Sky. She tried to keep her voice cool—much cooler than she really felt, every time he was near her. *You'll hurt me, Sky,* she wanted to blurt out. *And I'll hurt you. I know it.*

"Look, Sky, you don't know me at all, really—"

"That's not true—"

"There's just . . . it's complicated," Lisha said, her voice low.

"I can handle complicated," Sky said.

"Not this complicated," Lisha replied.

"Give me a chance—"

"I don't want to get involved—"

"With me?" Sky interrupted. "Or at all?"

"Just . . . you just have to back off," Lisha said. She took a step away from him. "Just . . . back off."

"You don't really want Alan," Sky said earnestly. "I just don't believe—" He stopped himself. Then he took Lisha in his arms, and kissed her passionately.

For a moment she was lost in the best, hottest kiss she had ever had in her life.

But then she pulled herself away from him. "You jerk!" she yelled.

"Yeah, I'm a jerk!" Sky said, his eyes blazing. "So tell me you didn't really want me to kiss you, that you didn't feel that, and I'll leave you alone—"

"I don't have to tell you anything," Lisha said furiously as she quickly began to unlock the many locks on the door to her apartment.

"Lisha—"

"Leave me alone," she said as she slammed into her apartment, leaving Sky in the hallway, still staring after her.

"Sky," she whispered to herself, leaning her back against the door to the apartment. "Sky."

The apartment was dark and deserted. Karma had plans with Demetrius before her shift at Jimi's. Chelsea was with Nick.

Peace, that's what I want, Lisha thought. *Everything is so peaceful with Alan. I don't want to feel a passion that sweeps me away. I don't. I just want to get rid of Harley, and not think about Sky, and simplify my life.*

She pushed out of her sandals and padded over to the answering machine.

The on-light was blinking.

Lisha shuddered. She had a very bad feeling. She pressed the button.

It wasn't Harley. It was Lydia Love, asking for an off-the-record interview for *Rave*.

"Yeah, I'll bet it's off-the-record," Lisha muttered.

The phone rang. Lisha picked it up.

"Yeah," she answered.

"Lisha," a voice whispered to her.

Male. Low. Disguised.

Lisha froze. Unable to say anything, unable to put the phone down.

"Listen, Lisha," the eerie, whispered voice repeated. "You missed our meeting. That wasn't smart. But I'm a nice guy and I'm offering a second chance. Your last chance. Tomorrow, eight-thirty in the morning. Same place. You—"

Lisha slammed the phone down.

"Damn you, Harley!" she cried as tears ran down her face. "I'm not running scared anymore! Do you hear me? I'm going to find a way to get rid of you. Once and for all!"

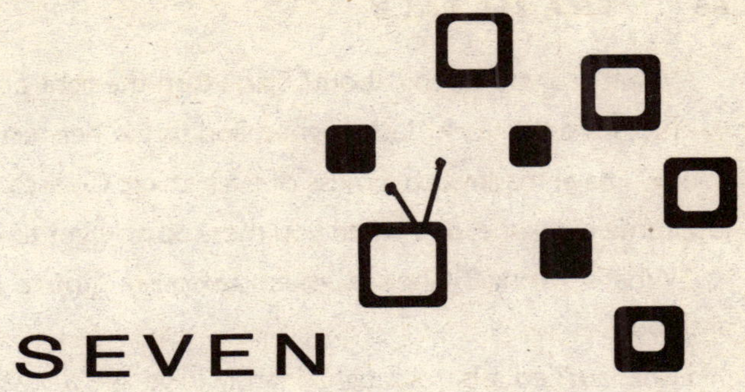

SEVEN

Sometime after midnight, Chelsea unlocked the front door of the dark apartment and tiptoed in so that she wouldn't wake up her roommates.

"Hi," Lisha said, from where she sat on the couch.

Chelsea yelped and jumped into the air. "Lish? You scared me to death! What are you doing sitting in the dark?"

"Contemplating the sewer that is currently called my life," Lisha said.

"What happened?" Chelsea asked, coming over to sit next to her on the couch. "Oh, God, was Harley here?"

"Who knows?" Lisha shrugged. "Sometimes he leaves calling cards, and sometimes he doesn't."

"What are you talking about? Can I turn the light on?"

"No, I like the dark." Lisha sighed and threw her head back on the couch. "I have made such a mess of everything, Chelsea. I wish life was just some big game, and when you mess up you get to call 'do over.' "

"What's wrong?" Chelsea asked anxiously. "You're not pregnant, are you?"

Lisha laughed a bitter laugh. "Hardly. I live like a vestal virgin these days."

"I thought maybe you and Sky finally admitted that you're crazy for each other and then something went wrong," Chelsea admitted.

"I told you, there's nothing going on between me and Sky," Lisha said firmly.

"You and Alan, then—"

"My problem is not a current-guy problem, it's a past-guy problem," Lisha said. "Namely—you guessed it—Harley." She turned toward Chelsea. She could barely make out her friend's features in the darkened living room. "Here's what happened."

Lisha told Chelsea about the note on her desk, about how she had gotten to the meeting late, and how Harley had called and threatened her if she didn't meet him at the same place tomorrow morning at eight-thirty.

"He sounded so creepy on the phone," Lisha recalled with a shudder. "He whispered, like something out of one of those bad psycho murder movies."

"Wait, you're telling me that after you got that note from him, you went to meet him alone yesterday?" Chelsea asked incredulously. "Are you out of your mind?"

"Probably," Lisha replied. "What was I supposed to do, bring the welcome wagon?"

"You have to go to the police!" Chelsea exclaimed.

"And get extradited to France? And thrown in prison for transporting drugs?" Lisha asked, her voice rising hysterically. "Are you out of your mind?"

Chelsea was silent for a moment. She reached for Lisha's hand in the dark. "Let's try to look at this logically. Do you have the note he left where he threatened you? In case the police need it?"

"I have it," Lisha said. "But he didn't sign his name."

"Then how do you know Harley left the note?" Chelsea asked. "It could have been anybody!"

"I'm so sure," Lisha snorted. "I don't know any other psychotics who are stalking me."

"But how could Harley have gotten into the *Trash* offices?" Chelsea asked. "There are guards downstairs, and they check ID, and Harley doesn't have clearance—"

"I don't know how, but he managed," Lisha said. "I wish I could just—"

They heard their front door being unlocked, and both girls froze. Then, as if by unspoken agreement, they both jumped up and ran into the kitchen, ducking behind the counter. Chelsea grabbed the portable phone, ready to dial 911.

Someone came into the apartment. Slowly, Lisha raised her head so that her eyes peeked over the top of the counter. "It's Karma," she said with relief. She and Chelsea both stood up.

Karma whirled around. "Have you two lost it?" she asked. "What are you doing in the dark on the kitchen floor?"

"It's the best way to find the cockroaches," Lisha joked, her voice flat.

"We were afraid you were Harley," Chelsea said, turning on the kitchen light. She looked at her watch. "It's too early for you to be here."

"It was a slow night at Jimi's, so Arnold let me leave early," Karma explained. "What's going on?"

"You tell her," Lisha told Chelsea. "I can't go through the whole thing again."

Chelsea brought Karma up to date. "Did I leave anything out?" she asked Lisha, when she'd finished.

"Only that I called the lawyer today," Lisha said. "I didn't get a chance to tell you that. He wasn't available—some flunky told me he'd return my call."

"So, you're saying that the note wasn't signed, and that Harley whispered over the phone?" Karma asked, massaging her tired feet. "What if it wasn't Harley?"

"I asked her the same thing," Chelsea pointed out.

"Wishful thinking," Lisha said.

"Not necessarily," Karma pointed out. "It really is hard to get past those guards downstairs at *Trash*, you know. What if it's . . . Brian!"

"Brian *Bassinger*?" Lisha asked incredulously. "Brian Weenie *Bassinger*?"

"Well, you have to admit, he seems to have this huge crush on you," Chelsea said.

"And he'd have access to every place at *Trash*," Karma pointed out. "He'd know about the film storage room. How would Harley?"

"He's psychotic, not stupid," Lisha said. "He followed me. He skulked around or something—"

"Sounds dubious," Karma decided.

"Who cares if it's dubious?" Lisha asked. "I'm just telling you, it's Harley! And if I don't meet him tomorrow morning, my butt is fried!"

"But if you do meet him, he could do something terrible to you!" Chelsea cried. "He has a gun, remember?"

"So what am I supposed to do, then?" Lisha asked. "And don't tell me to go to the police, because—"

"I have an idea," Karma interrupted. "You go meet this mystery guy—"

"Karma, it isn't safe—" Chelsea began.

"Hold your horses, I'm not through," Karma said, chewing on a piece of her hair contemplatively. "Lisha meets the guy, but we go with her. We call Demetrius tonight and bring him in on this. Then tomorrow we have Demetrius stand guard for us outside the door, but the mystery guy inside won't know Demetrius is outside. That way if it's Harley, and he has a gun, Demetrius can go for help before anything can happen."

"Are you on drugs?" Lisha asked. "I'm not letting all of you risk your lives because my ex is crazy!"

"It's either that, or we call the cops tonight," Karma said. "Because no way are we letting you go to this meeting alone."

"It's a stupid plan," Lisha said. "But okay."

"I feel like throwing up," Lisha said, her hands on her stomach.

"Hang in there." Demetrius patted her back.

It was the following morning, about eight-fifteen, and Lisha, Chelsea, Karma, and Demetrius were all in the lobby of the *Trash* building.

"I'm kind of nervous, too," Chelsea admitted.

"Look, this is crazy," Lisha said. "I'll go by myself—"

"Forget it," Karma said. "This is going to work."

"But this is it, Lisha," Demetrius said sternly. "You speak to the attorney today or we're going to call and speak to him for you."

"I will, I promise," Lisha told him. "I can't live my life like this anymore."

"Okay," Karma said. "One for all and all for one, right?" She put her arm straight out, and one by one they each laid their hands on top of hers.

"Let's go do it," Demetrius said.

The guard knew them, and he nodded as they passed. Silently, they took the elevator up to the third floor.

"Now remember," Demetrius said, "you have to talk loud enough in there so that I can hear you outside in the hallway. There's no other way out of that room except by me."

Lisha nodded, and the three girls walked down to the door of the film storage room and opened it.

Lisha went in first.

It was pitch-black, even darker, it seemed, than the afternoon before. Lisha could feel Karma and Chelsea right behind her.

"Harley?" Lisha whispered. "I'm here, just like you told me."

No answer.

Now Lisha could make out the tall piles of film canisters that surrounded her. But she couldn't see Harley.

"Harley?" she called again. "We have to talk. I... I want to help you...."

They heard the sounds of something rustling between two of the stacks of film. Lisha jumped, and grabbed Karma with one hand and Chelsea with the other.

"I'm going to turn on the light," Lisha said, reaching toward the light switch on the wall.

"No!" a male voice whispered frantically from behind a tall stack of film.

Lisha's grip tightened on her friends' hands.

She gulped hard. "Wha-what do you want?"

"You," the voice whispered.

"Harley, is that you?" Lisha asked.

No answer.

"I'm not alone, Harley," she said, trying to sound confident. "My friends are here, too."

"What friends?" the voice whispered.

"The ones you met at my apartment the other night," Lisha said, her voice loud enough to carry to Demetrius in the hall.

"Who's Harley?" the voice said.

Lisha's jaw dropped open. "Are you playing mind games with me, Harley?"

No answer.

"Brian?" Karma called tentatively. "Is that you?"

"Brian Bassinger?" Chelsea called.

"Forget it," the male voice whispered. "Just go away and forget it."

"It *is* Brian," Chelsea said. "I'm turning on the light."

"No—!"

It was too late. The light was flipped on. The girls peered behind the stack of film.

Crouched down, looking up at them, was Jazz's gorgeous Jamaican secretary, Winston Manroot.

"Winston?" Lisha cried in disbelief. "Are you out of your mind?"

Winston stood up and brushed some dust out of his dreadlocks. "Surprise," he said weakly.

"What is all this?" Chelsea asked. "Are you crazy?"

"Well, now that you mention it, I do feel like somethin' of an idiot," Winston admitted. "This was just supposed to be a goof, mon. Who is Harley?"

"A goof?" Lisha echoed. "That note and that phone call, a *goof?"*

"And what were you threatening Lisha about, anyway?" Chelsea added.

"The film," Winston said. "The hidden camera in Jazz's office. What did you think I was referrin' to, girl?"

The girls' jaws dropped open.

"Well, you interns planted that hidden camera, didn't you?" Winston asked, brushing one of his dreadlocks out of his face.

"Wait, I'd better go call off Demetrius," Karma said. "He'll come running in here with the guards in about thirty seconds. Don't say a word till I get back, because I have to hear all of this."

Karma went out to Demetrius, quickly explained that they weren't in any danger, then returned into the storage room. "Okay, spill it," she demanded.

"Well, I feel like quite the fool now," Winston said. "See, I found your camera—it *was* your camera, right?"

"Maybe," Lisha hedged.

"Yeah-mon, it's yours," Winston said. "I saw one of your buds, Sky, goin' into Jazz's office one morning, carryin' something small. He didn't see me. When I was sortin' through Jazz's bookcase, I found the camera, and then I put two and two together. I took the film home."

"So you were threatening Lisha about the hidden camera?" Karma asked. "Why didn't you threaten Sky?"

"Sky doesn't have anything I want," Winston said, flashing his killer smile. "My guess was that all of you interns are in on something together, something with that camera. Am I right?"

The girls traded looks. "What is it that you want?" Lisha asked.

"Well, now I'm feelin' kind of like the hind side of a donkey," Winston singsonged. "This was supposed to be a cute way to get to know you."

"You're kidding," Lisha said flatly.

"No," Winston said. "I'm not."

"Didn't you ever hear of asking a girl out for coffee?" Karma asked, exasperated.

"I was trying to be creative," Winston admitted. "By the way, who is Harley?"

"Never mind," Lisha said quickly. "What are you planning to do with the film you found?"

"Nothing," Winston said with a shrug.

"Nothing?" Karma repeated.

"What, you thought I was goin' to turn you in to the teen-queen she-devil, Jazz?" Winston asked. "Not on your life."

"But... but why?" Chelsea asked him.

"Just because I work for her doesn't mean I like her," Winston said. "What are you plannin' to do with that film, anyway?"

"Never mind," Lisha said quickly.

"Hey, is that any way to treat a nice guy who is going to keep your secret?" Winston asked.

"He's right," Chelsea said. "He could have busted us, and he didn't."

"He could still bust us," Lisha pointed out.

"Yeah, and we can bust him for his anonymous threatening notes and phone calls to a fellow employee," Karma pointed out.

"Okay, we're even," Winston said. "You'll tell me sometime, though, won't you?"

"Maybe," Lisha said.

"How about if I ask you out for coffee," Winston said, with a grin. "Will you tell me then?"

"Look, Winston, no offense, but I am just not looking for a relationship right now," Lisha said. "Besides, this whole thing has me really wigged out. That stupid note, and the phone call . . . say—how did you manage to disguise your voice and hide your Jamaican accent, anyway?"

"Oh, it's not difficult," Winston said, and there wasn't a trace of his singsong accent as he spoke. "I'm actually an actor. I have an audition for *Days of Our Lives* next week." He reached for Lisha's hand. "I'm really sorry if I scared you."

"You did," Lisha said, taking her hand back.

"Does this mean no coffee date?" Winston asked.

"What are you planning to do with our film?" Lisha asked.

Winston went back behind the film stack, reached for something, and handed it to Lisha. "Your film. I'm an honorable guy."

"Thank you," Lisha said.

"Now, about the coffee date—"

"How about if I think about it," Lisha said. "I have some important business to take care of before I think about anything else." She nodded at Chelsea and Karma. "I have to call a certain lawyer, and straighten out my life."

Lisha outlined her problem to the criminal lawyer, whose name was Sandy Dweck, in the broadest possible terms—that she might have done something illegal, even though she hadn't known she was doing it, that now someone was blackmailing her and stalking her about it. As she spoke she doodled nervously on the notepad on top of her desk. Then she looked around her tiny cubicle, worried that she'd be overheard, anxious about what Dweck would tell her.

Dweck had refused to talk to her unless she told him her name. And gave him an address where he could send his bill. Lisha did both.

Because I just can't live like this anymore, she realized. *Anything would be better than this.*

"Well, Miss Bishop, I will really need to hear your story in detail, in my office, so that I can take notes. And then I can give you some advice. When would be convenient for you?"

"How about tonight?" Lisha said quickly.

"I'm sorry," Mr. Dweck said, "I don't have evening office hours. And I'm booked up for the next couple of weeks. If you speak to my secretary—"

"No, you don't understand," Lisha said, gripping the phone. "The person who is stalking me—he broke into my apartment. He has a gun. He's dangerous. I . . . I have to do something right away!"

"You could go to the police—"

"No, I can't!" Lisha exclaimed. "Please! Couldn't you just help me? I'll only take a few minutes of your time, and then if you tell me I have to go to the police, I'll do it."

Mr. Dweck sighed into the phone. "If you could get over here right away, I could give you some time—"

"I will!" Lisha cried. "I'll get a taxi and I'll be right over. What's the address?"

Lisha quickly scribbled the lawyer's address in the notebook, thanked him again, and hung up. Then she grabbed her purse and hurried down to Sumtimes's office.

"Sumtimes?" Lisha said, trying to make her voice sound weak and pathetic.

Sumtimes looked up from the memo she was reading.

"I'm really feeling sick," Lisha said. "I think I need to go home."

"What are your symptoms?" Sumtimes asked.

"Headache, stomachache, chills—I think I have a fever."

"Okay, go home and go to bed," Sumtimes said. "Chicken soup works miracles."

"Thanks," Lisha said.

She dashed to the elevator, but couldn't stand the wait, and finally ran down the stairs to the lobby, where she almost collided with Winston, carrying some take-out food in a cardboard container.

"Hey, watch yourself, girl," he said, feinting to avoid her.

"Sorry," she said, hurrying past him.

"Wait up a second," Winston said.

Lisha sighed impatiently, but she stopped and turned to him. *He knows all about the Trash-cam,* she thought. *I don't want to tick him off or he could change his mind about turning us in to Jazz.*

"I'm sorry about this morning," Winston said sheepishly. "I'd like to do something to make it up to you."

"Just forget about it," Lisha said. "I have."

"Well, good." Winston smiled. "Then we can start all over again and I can impress you with my charming Jamaican ways."

"Look, I'm in a hurry, I've got an appointment," Lisha said. "We'll talk... later, okay?"

"Yeah-mon," Winston said. "I'll look forward to it"

Lisha hurried out to the street. "Taxi, taxi, where is a taxi when you need one?" she muttered, scanning the traffic down the block.

And then she realized something. She had forgotten to bring Mr. Dweck's address that she had scribbled in her notebook. *I can't go back up there and get it,* she realized. *What was it? Think, Lisha. Fifteen-forty Broadway. That's it!*

Lisha walked down the street and then turned uptown, desperately searching for a taxi. *That stupid cliché is true,* she thought. *There is never a taxi in this city when you need one.*

"Come on," she pleaded under her breath, "just one lousy empty cab is all I need—"

A hand reached out and grabbed her arm, pulling her in between two parked cars, and then across the sidewalk and into a building's entryway.

Lisha screamed, but another hand clamped over her mouth, muffling the sound.

Harley.

His eyes glittered at her. His grip was like a steel vise on her arm.

"Hi there, Lish," he said, smiling crazily. "I told you I'd be back."

EIGHT

"Now, if I take my hand off of your mouth, you have to be a good girl, and promise not to scream," Harley said, his voice low. Lisha was so scared her entire body was vibrating. She managed to nod her head yes.

"Good," Harley said. "And just in case you try to pull anything, feel this." Lisha felt something hard poking into her back. "I would hate to use it on you, Lish. I really would."

She nodded again, her eyes two huge pools of fear.

Slowly, he took his hand away from her mouth. The sharp object—a knife, a gun?—was still poking into her back.

"This is amazing, Lisha, really. I didn't think I'd get to see you until you went out to lunch. But maybe your mind kinda heard my mind calling to you, or something. What do you think?"

"I don't know," she managed to say.

"Did you miss me?"

What should I say? What should I do? Lisha thought desperately. She forced her voice to sound steady.

"Harley, if you really care about me as much as you say you do, why do you keep pulling a gun on me?"

"Because I know how fickle girls can be," he said. "Especially you. You left me once. In London. Remember? You said you didn't want to have anything to do with me. That wasn't very nice, Lisha. I mean, I was the only guy who would even look twice at you when you were fat, remember?"

"You got me hooked on diet pills," Lisha reminded him angrily.

"Hey, baby, I didn't get you hooked. You got yourself hooked," Harley said.

A couple walked by on the street, arm in arm, laughing. Harley pulled Lisha farther into the entryway.

Please, look this way! Lisha thought. But the couple walked right by without ever glancing her way.

"What do you want?" Lisha asked desperately.

"First of all, I want a little respect!" Harley said, his voice rising dangerously. "You are going to talk to me with respect, got it?" He pushed the sharp object into her spine for emphasis.

"I got it," Lisha replied.

"That's better," Harley said. "Now, I have my buddy's car parked a block from here. You and I are going for a ride."

"To where?" she asked fearfully.

"Someplace where we can be alone," he said.

"I was on my way to an appointment," Lisha said thinking frantically. "The person is expecting me, and then they're expecting me back at work. Everyone will be really suspicious if I don't show up. And my friends already know you broke into our apartment. They'll go to the police."

"Nice story, Lish," Harley said. "First of all, it takes twenty-four hours before the cops will bother to look for you. By that time you and I will be long gone."

"To where?" she asked again.

He didn't answer. Instead, he took his free hand and ran it from her cheek, down her throat, and over her right breast.

Lisha shuddered in revulsion.

"You used to love that," Harley said, his voice low. "Remember?"

Lisha tried to smile at Harley, but all she could manage was a slight grimace.

"Just walk in front of me, Lisha," he ordered. "If you do anything dumb, I *will* hurt you, baby. I mean, it would bum me out, but I'd do it. Okay, let's go."

Harley prodded her in her back, and she walked out of the doorway. Various people walked on the street, but they ignored her. No one seemed to find it odd that a white-faced young woman was walking down the street with a guy walking six inches behind her.

Please, God, Lisha prayed as she forced herself to put one foot in front of the other, *please let me figure out how to get out of this.*

Please. Let me get out of this alive.

"Lish?" Chelsea said, sticking her head in Lisha's cubicle late that morning.

The cubicle was empty. Chelsea had been so busy all morning that she hadn't had time to breathe. She hadn't even seen Lisha at all.

Sumtimes was walking by the area, recording a memo for herself into her tiny tape recorder. "If you're looking for Lisha, she went home sick a couple of hours ago," she said.

"She did?" Chelsea asked with surprise.

"Yeah, she said she thought she had the flu."

"Thanks for telling me." Chelsea went into Lisha's cubicle and sat behind her desk. Then she picked up the phone and called their apartment. The answering machine picked up. "Lisha, if you're there, pick up," she said into the phone. "I want to make sure you're okay."

"Hi, Chels," Alan said, stopping by the desk. "You heading up to Sicko Central? Because I am, and as you know, misery loves company."

"Yeah," Chelsea said, her voice troubled. "I stopped to get Lisha. She went home sick."

"No kidding?" Alan hesitated before continuing. "She's been really upset about something lately, hasn't she?"

"Yeah," Chelsea admitted, "she has."

"She wouldn't tell me what it was," Alan said. "You know how Lish is—Miss Mysterious."

"I know," Chelsea agreed, still staring at the phone.

"Do you know what's bothering her?" Alan asked.

Chelsea nodded yes.

Alan leaned against the wall of the tiny office. "And I have a feeling you're not going to tell me what it is."

"I can't," she said unhappily. "Lisha would have to tell you herself."

"So, did you call home to see how she's feeling?"

"I just did," Chelsea said. "The machine picked up."

"Maybe she's sleeping," Alan suggested.

"Maybe," she echoed, but her tone was doubtful. She looked down at Lisha's desk, and there, on the top of her notepad, was the name Mr. Dweck, and a Broadway address. Then, written in large letters and circled many times, were the words SEE ME NOW!!!

"Hello beloved *Trash*ophiles," Karma said in her nasal whine, coming up beside Alan. "I hear Sicko Central calling us. Where's Lish?"

Chelsea filled her in.

"But she didn't pick up the phone when I called home just now," Chelsea said anxiously. She lifted the notepad to Karma. "Do you know who Mr. Dweck is?"

"That's the lawyer I told her to call!" Karma said, taking the pad. "See me now," she read out loud. "You think that's where she went?"

"I think we should call him," Chelsea decided.

"Okay, now you're scaring me," Alan said. "Why does Lisha need to see a criminal lawyer?"

Chelsea and Karma exchanged looks.

"We can't tell you," Karma said reluctantly.

"Come on," Alan cajoled. "I care about Lisha. A lot."

"We know you do," Chelsea said.

"But we can't tell you," Karma added. "Call the lawyer, Chels."

Chelsea quickly called information and got the phone number for Dweck, Levine and Powell, Mr. Dweck's law firm, and dialed the number.

"Mr. Dweck, please," Chelsea said when a female voice answered the phone.

"Who is calling?" the woman asked.

"Chelsea Jennings—"

"No, no," Karma said, grabbing the phone from her. "Hello? Tell Mr. Dweck that Primrose Jensen is on the phone. Yes, I'll hold."

"Who is Primrose Jensen?" Chelsea asked.

"My broker," Karma said. "She's a friend of his. This way he'll take the call."

"Rose?" a male voice said into the phone.

"I'm sorry, Mr. Dweck, but this is actually a client of Ms. Jensen's," Karma said quickly. "I just needed to make sure you would actually get on the phone."

"Look, Miss—" Mr. Dweck began.

"I'm sorry I misrepresented myself," Karma continued, "but this is really important. Like life-and-death-type important. I'm a friend of Lisha Bishop's. I think maybe you had an appointment with her, and I'm concerned with whether or not she ever made it to the meeting."

"I'm sorry, Miss—whoever you are—but I don't give out information as to whom I meet with or who my clients are. It's privileged information. Now, if you'll excuse me—"

"No, you don't understand," Karma said. "I'm the person who recommended you to Lisha, through Primrose. You can call Primrose and check me out, if you don't believe me. The name is Karma Kushner. And I know all about attorney-client privilege. But see, Lisha was coming to see you because her ex-boyfriend was stalking her. And now we think she might be missing. So, that's why I need to know if she had an appointment with you, and if she showed up. I really need your help."

Mr. Dweck sighed into the phone. "All right. I did receive a call from Miss Bishop," he admitted. "She mentioned something about... well, she mentioned that she might be in some trouble. I told her that if she came over right away, I would try to offer some advice. She told me she'd be right over."

"What time did you speak with her?" Karma asked.

"Early this morning," Mr. Luger said. "And in answer to your next question, no, she did not show up."

"Thank you for your help," Karma said, and hung up. She quickly told Chelsea and Alan what the lawyer had told her.

"I'm getting a really terrible feeling about this," Chelsea said.

"About what?" Alan asked in frustration. "What am I supposed to do, just assume the worst? You guys have to tell me what's going on!"

Chelsea and Karma looked at each other again.

"Should we tell him?" Chelsea asked.

"Let's try our number again first," Karma said. She dialed their home phone quickly. And got the machine again. "Lisha, if you can hear me, or if you get my message, call us at work right away. We are really worried about you!"

She hung up.

"Okay, that's it," Alan declared. "We're not leaving until you tell me what's going on."

"I think we should," Chelsea decided.

Karma nodded in agreement.

Quickly Chelsea filled Alan in on the whole story. Alan grew more and more shocked as the story progressed.

"Wow, I couldn't have invented this plot if I tried to," Alan said, shaking his head, when Chelsea had concluded Lisha's story. "We've got to go to the police."

"That's exactly what Lisha didn't want us to do," Karma pointed out. "Her whole life could be wrecked."

"Yeah, well, she could also get killed by this Harley nut, which somehow seems worse, don't you think?" Alan said sharply.

"One of us should go back to the apartment to see if she's there," Chelsea suggested. "I'll make some excuse and go—"

"What is going on in here?" Roxanne demanded, storming into the cublicle and throwing a stack of files on Lisha's desk. "Where's Bishop?"

"She went home sick," Alan replied.

"Interns don't get sick," Roxanne said. "And what does that have to do with the three of you in here wasting time?" she asked suspiciously, balancing herself on her good foot.

"We were just on our way to Sicko—I mean, to work in the transcribing room," Karma told Roxanne.

"So, go!" Roxanne ordered.

"I, uh, think I'm not feeling very well, either," Chelsea improvised. "Would you mind very much if I went home—"

"Yes, I'd mind," Bigfoot snapped. "If I can put in more than a full day with my foot killing me, you can finish out your day with a little sniffle."

"It's more than a sniffle," Chelsea lied. "It's... my stomach. Food poisoning, maybe." She held her stomach and tried to look ill.

"So go barf and then get back to work," Roxanne said. "If you die, we'll call an ambulance." She hobbled out of the cubicle.

"So much for that idea," Karma said. She looked at her watch. "We can probably get out of here in an hour or so for lunch. We'll just have to go right back to the apartment, and see if Lisha is there."

"But what if she isn't?" Chelsea asked. "What do we do then?"

No one had an answer.

"I know it's not the finest of accommodations," Harley said as he prodded Lisha into the small basement apartment. "My friend is a little low on funds at the moment."

With one hand on the steering wheel and an eye glued on Lisha—he'd tied her hands with a bandanna so she wouldn't try to jump out of the moving car—he had driven them to Alphabet City, east of the East Village, and parked the car on a street with mostly abandoned, deserted buildings.

Then he had walked with Lisha, the hard object still embedded in her spine, to an ancient brown building in the center of the block, and forced her down a flight of steps to this apartment.

Lisha looked around. It was tiny, and filthy, with a threadbare couch, a small TV set, and a card table with a scale on it, and some lengths of rope. Cockroaches crawled over the top of some pizza remains on the floor.

"Make yourself comfortable, Lisha," Harley said, motioning her toward the couch. "I got us a bottle of wine." He opened the grimy refrigerator and took out a bottle of white wine.

"I don't want any." Lisha stood near the couch, her arms wrapped tightly around herself.

"Oh yeah, you do," Harley said. "I remember how much you like to party, baby."

Still watching Lisha intently, he got two cracked glasses out of a cupboard and poured them each a glass of wine. Then he handed one to Lisha.

"I can't drink it," she said.

"Drink it!" Harley thundered. *"I say you'll drink it and you'll drink it!"*

Lisha put the glass to her lips.

"That's better." Harley's voice returned to normal. "Let's sit on the couch together."

Lisha sat down, a spring from the ancient couch pushing into her thigh. Harley sat next to her, so close that their legs were touching. He put his arm around her.

"Remember when we used to sit like this?" he asked dreamily.

"Uh-huh," Lisha said cautiously.

"We really had a great time together, didn't we?" Harley asked. "You were so crazy about me. You couldn't get enough of me. Remember?"

She nodded her head yes.

"Do you still feel that way, Lish? I really need to know. I mean, I risked a lot to come find you. And I need to know that you appreciate it."

"I . . . do," Lisha managed to lie.

"But see, here's the thing," Harley said, taking a sip of his wine. "You don't act like you appreciate it."

"But I do," she said quickly.

"Yeah?" he asked hopefully. "Prove it to me, baby."

Please, God, please . . .

"Just sitting here like this proves it, doesn't it?" Lisha asked.

"I don't know," Harley said. "I'm afraid maybe you're only here because I forced you." He took another sip of his wine. "Is that true?"

"No," Lisha lied. "I . . . I want to be with you."

"Yeah?" he asked again. "Like how we used to be?"

"Ri-right," she said faintly.

"Well, you never used to sit around with me with so much clothes on," Harley said.

No, no, please.

"I think you should take them off," he said, his tone conversational.

Lisha's eyes flitted to the door, the window, any possible avenue of escape. But the window was tiny, below street level, and obscured by overflowing garbage cans. And Harley had locked the door.

"Take off your clothes, Lisha," he said, his tone dark and threatening.

"I... it's really filthy in here, Harley," Lisha said. "I don't want to sit around in here naked."

"Down to your underwear, then," Harley said. "I always did like the way you looked in them."

She hesitated, but the strange, hard, crazy look on his face convinced her.

Slowly, she reached down and pulled the oversized men's white T-shirt she was wearing over her head. And then she tugged the black Lycra biker shorts off.

She stood before him in a floral-print bra and matching panties.

It's not any skimpier than a bathing suit, she told herself so that she wouldn't fall over from fear. *I have to stay alert. I have to figure out a way to save myself.*

"Cute," Harley said. "Now, come and sit on my lap."

No. I won't do it, Lisha thought. *But I want to live. Would he really kill me? Please, God, I don't know what to do.*

"I have some really romantic plans for us, Lisha. But you know what? You can't have the romance without the finance. Isn't that a good one?"

She managed a smile.

"I heard some dude on a talk show say that," he said, laughing. He looked at his watch. "I need to go make a pickup."

He took her arm and led her to a wooden chair. "Have a seat." Lisha sat. "Put your arms behind you." She did.

Harley picked up one of the ropes from the card table and tied her hands behind her back, around the back of the chair.

"What are you doing?" she asked fearfully.

"What does it look like I'm doing?" he asked. He got another rope and tied her feet to the legs of the chair.

"But . . . but I thought we were going to be together," Lisha said desperately. "Why are you tying me up?"

"So I can go pick up my finance," Harley said. "I thought I just explained that. This dude owes me some money. And some happy pills. I'll only be gone a little while, baby. Will you miss me?"

Maybe if he leaves I can try to escape, she thought. *Maybe it's the only chance I have.*

"I'll miss you," Lisha assured him.

"I knew you would," Harley said. "And when I come back, I'll drop some of my special little happy pills on you. You won't believe how good they make you feel, Lish. I feel like I'm completely alive, for the first time, ever."

He knelt down in front of her and stared into her eyes. His glittered oddly, and a horrible, terrifying thought hit Lisha in the pit of her stomach:

He's completely insane.

"Bye, baby," Harley said. "When I come back, I'll have a big surprise for you." He softly kissed her lips. Then he left, locking the door behind him.

NINE

"It's twelve o'clock," Chelsea said, pulling off her headset. They had been in Sicko Central, transcribing tapes, with one eye on the clock. The minutes ticked by with agonizing slowness. Every ten minutes they called the apartment again. But Lisha never picked up.

"Let's get out of here," Karma said, grabbing her purse.

"I'm coming with you," Alan insisted.

"Hello, group," Winston said, sticking his head in the door of Sicko Central. "Did Lisha get back from her appointment? I thought I could redeem myself and take her to lunch."

"When did she tell you she had an appointment?" Chelsea demanded.

"This mornin'," Winston answered. "I ran into her in the lobby. Why?"

"Let's go," Karma said.

"Are you going to see Lisha?" Winston asked as the three of them hurried past him. "Tell her I owe her one, mon!"

"She isn't going to be at the apartment," Chelsea said as they practically ran down the hallway to the elevator. "Y'all know that."

"Well, if she's not there we have to go to—" Alan began.

"Interns!" Bigfoot yelled, hobbling toward them on her crutches. "Just where do you think you're going?"

"It's called lunch," Chelsea snapped, so concerned about Lisha that she forgot to use her usual measured tones with her boss.

"No, it's called *working* lunch," Roxanne contradicted. "I need the three of you in my office. Pronto."

"But... we have plans we can't get out of," Karma invented.

"Do they involve *Trash*?" Roxanne asked.

"No, but—"

"Then you don't have plans, do you," Roxanne pointed out dismissively. "You can order sandwiches in." She hobbled away from them.

"I truly loathe and despise her." Chelsea was fuming.

"Bigfoot can shove it," Alan said fiercely. "I'm going to the apartment to check on Lisha. If Roxanne wants to fire me, she can fire me."

"Hey, you guys heading out to lunch?" Sky said, walking toward them. "I've got my mind wrapped around a huge pastrami sandwich from Zabar's, how about it?"

"Bigfoot just ordered us to eat in her office," Chelsea explained.

"Tell Roxanne I'll be back as soon as I check on Lisha—" Alan began.

"Check on Lisha for what?" Sky asked.

"It's a long story," Karma said.

"Wait, I have an idea," Chelsea said quickly. "Let Sky go check on Lisha. That way you won't risk your job, Alan."

"I repeat, check on Lisha for what?" Sky said confused.

"See if she's back at our apartment," Chelsea said, fishing her apartment keys out of her backpack and handing them to Sky. "She told Sumtimes she went home sick, but she hasn't answered the phone, and we're worried about her."

"Look, I said I'll go," Alan began.

"No problem," Sky said. "I'm there."

"If she's not there, call us right away and let us know," Alan urged him.

Sky took in their worried faces. "Hey, why do I have the feeling there's more going on here than I know about?"

"Just go," Karma told him.

"Is Lish in some kind of trouble?" Sky asked, clearly concerned.

"If she was, she'd tell me, not you," Alan said brusquely.

"What makes you think so?" Sky asked coldly.

"You guys, this is not the time to pull your macho crap about Lisha, okay?" Karma said in exasperation. "Just go, Sky!"

"And call us," Chelsea called after him.

All they could do was go to Bigfoot's office.

And wait.

Sweat poured down Lisha's face, mixing with her tears. She didn't know how long it had been since Harley left, since there was no clock in the room. She had tried and tried to free her hands, or her feet, or to move the chair close enough to the window so that she could try to butt her head into it. But all that she had accomplished was to chafe her wrists and ankles so hard against the rope that they burned.

"Somebody! Anybody!" Lisha screamed as loudly as she could. Her throat felt as raw as her wrists and ankles, she had screamed in vain so many times.

"Somebody! Please! Help me!" she screamed again. The tears coursed down her cheeks as sobs were torn from her throat.

Why didn't I do something about Harley a long time ago? Lisha thought in despair. *Why was I so stupid? Oh, God, please, don't punish me because I was so stupid. I'll do anything....*

"Somebody!" she yelled again between her sobs. "Help!"

A key turned in the lock. Lisha held her breath.

Harley.

"Why did you do that?" he asked, his voice dangerously soft. "I heard you when I was opening the door."

"Be-because I'm scared," Lisha said.

"Why?" Harley asked.

"Because you kidnapped me and tied me to a chair!" Lisha screamed, crying again.

"If you treated me better, Lish, I wouldn't have to do these things. It's your own fault."

"Please, Harley, untie me," Lisha begged.

"Well, since you asked so nicely." Harley took out his pocketknife and cut through the ropes that held her hands, then her feet.

Lisha sprang to her feet, and stumbled, as the circulation had been cut off in her legs.

"Oopsie," Harley said, righting her. "Come on and sit with me on the couch, Lish. I've got great news."

He held her upper arm in a viselike grip and forced her over to the couch. They sat. "I got money and I got everything we need!"

"For what?" Lisha asked.

Harley looked at her as if she should know the answer to that question. "Our honeymoon, of course!"

He's totally insane. He could do anything. I see that now.

"It's kind of like that *Romeo and Juliet* story, you know?" Harley asked. "They were totally in love. And they were willing to die for it." He stared intensely at Lisha. "That's how much I love you, Lish. Don't you think you should be willing to die for love?"

Lisha hesitated. At that moment the lock turned in the door, and the door opened. Harley jumped up from the couch as a skinny, young guy with bad skin sauntered into the living room.

"What the hell are you doing here, man?" the skinny guy asked.

"Just hanging with my lady, bro," Harley said.

The skinny guy took in Harley's crazed face. "Get the hell outta here. I told you not to come here anymore. I didn't even know you still had a key."

"Hey, chill out," Harley said. "I'm just kickin' it, you know."

"You ain't kickin' it, fool," the skinny guy spat. "You got a chick in here in her underwear, and you're way high, man. Don't mess with me, Harley."

"You shouldn't be talking to me that way," Harley said, scowling.

"I told you, man, I don't want you around here anymore. You're friggin' crazy. A lunatic. You're stupid enough to take them pills and mess yourself up, it ain't my problem. Now get the hell outta here, I got business to do here."

Harley raised his right hand. The one with the weapon in it.

"Don't even think about it, man," the skinny guy said with disgust. "You waste me, the big guys will be all over you, and you'll wish you were dead way before your heart stops beating. Now get the hell outta here, Harley. I mean it."

"Please call the police—" Lisha cried, running over to the skinny guy.

"Yeah, right," the skinny guy snorted. "I don't know who the hell you are and I don't wanna know."

"I'm—" Lisha began.

"Hey, shut up!" the guy yelled. "I ain't gettin' involved! Now, both of you, get the hell outta here."

"Please!" Lisha yelled desperately. "He's going to kill me!"

"He's a wuss, he ain't gonna kill you." The skinny guy swiped his hand over his buzz-cut hair and sat at the table. "I mean, the dude is psycho, but he's still a wuss."

"Let's go, Lisha," Harley said, "This place isn't good enough for us, anyway."

Lisha reached for her clothes.

"Uh uh," Harley said. "Leave 'em."

"But—"

"Just the T-shirt. Move!" Harley repeated, his voice tight. Lisha quickly pulled the T-shirt over her head.

"Let's go."

He grabbed a length of the rope, and then pushed Lisha across the room and out the front door.

"You lied to me, Lisha," he said from behind her, his voice low in her hair.

"No, I—"

"You lied," Harley said dangerously. "You didn't really come with me because you love me. You came because I made you."

"Maybe if we could just go someplace and talk, we—"

"Yeah, right," Harley snorted. "Now that I see your true colors?

What do you think I am, stupid? We're going for another ride, Lisha."

She gulped hard. "Where to?"

"Someplace where no one will find us," Harley said.

He prodded her toward the car. Two young boys zoomed by on their bikes, but they didn't seem to take any notice of the fact that Lisha was wearing nothing but a long T-shirt.

Maybe I should try and make a run for it, she thought. *That guy in there said Harley would never shoot me. But what if he's wrong? I don't know what to do!*

They had reached the car. Lisha reached for the door.

"No," Harley said quickly, and he prodded her around to the back of the car.

"What?" she asked fearfully.

"I hate to do this to you, Lisha, but I can't trust you anymore." His eyes slid significantly to the trunk of the car. "You have to travel in the trunk."

"No!" Lisha yelled, and she looked desperately down the block to see if there was someone, anyone, who could help her.

It was deserted.

"In," Harley ordered, opening the trunk.

"No, please—"

Harley turned Lisha around and gave her a crazed smile, and nodded his head toward the trunk.

She climbed in. He slammed it shut.

And then, there was only darkness.

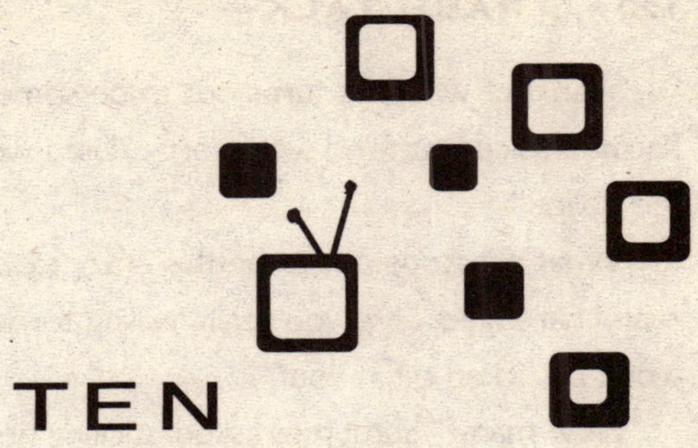

TEN

"Yeah, like this makes sense," Karma said, putting yet another credit-card carbon into the pile accumulating in front of her. "We had to stay in for lunch to file credit-card receipts."

Chelsea separated two copies of a Visa bill and put them into the appropriate piles. She kept looking over at Bigfoot's phone.

"I wish Sky would just call, already," she said anxiously.

"You know Lisha's not going to be home," Alan said flatly.

"We don't know anything yet," Chelsea disagreed halfheartedly.

"Your gut is speaking to you, big time, and so is mine," Alan insisted. "We can't mess around with this! We're going to have to go to the police!"

"Yeah, but what if it turns out to be some totally innocent thing?" Karma's voice was filled with worry. "Lisha would kill us if we went to the police."

"What if it turns out to be this crazy ex-boyfriend with the gun?" Alan challenged. "Are you really willing to risk Lisha's life just so she won't be ticked off at you?"

"How many?" Sumtimes asked, sticking her head in the door.

"We lost count," Alan replied, scowling as he pulled apart another set of receipts. "A lot."

"Good," Sumtimes said. "Hey, Roxanne told me you guys volunteered to stay in for lunch to do this. Thanks. You want to order lunch up?"

"We're not hungry," Chelsea said.

"Oh, well, if you get hungry, use Roxanne's phone to order out. Charge it to *Trash*." She smiled and left.

Chelsea stared at the phone again. "Ring!" she commanded it. "Ring right now!"

As if on cue, the phone rang, startling them all so much, they nearly jumped out of their seats.

Chelsea picked up the phone. "Roxanne Renault's office," she said. "Chelsea Jennings, intern, speaking."

"Yeah, it's me," Sky said. "I'm at your apartment, and she's not here."

"Is it Sky?" Karma asked hopefully.

Chelsea nodded. "Is there any sign that she's been there at all?" she asked Sky.

"None that I can see," he told her. "I checked your answering machine, and other than a whole lot of calls from you, and a message from Lydia Love from *Rave*, there was nothing at all."

"What's he saying?" Alan demanded.

"He says there's no sign of her," Chelsea told Alan.

"Chels," Sky said urgently into the phone, "what the hell is going on?"

"Come on back here," she said, "and . . . and I'll tell you," she decided. "You might as well get Nick and Demetrius, too. We can all try to figure out what to do together." Chelsea hung up.

"Are you sure that's the right thing to do?" Karma asked.

"No," Chelsea admitted. "The only thing I'm sure of is that I'm scared. Really scared. Like deep-in-the-pit-of-my-stomach scared."

She closed her eyes and an image of Lisha, with her bangs in her eyes, her hands on her hips, flashed into her mind.

And then she saw another image of Lisha, back when she was still little Alyssa Bishop, Chelsea's very best friend. Feisty. Strong-willed. Funny. And tougher than anyone that Chelsea knew.

I know you're in danger, Lisha. I feel it.

"You think Harley has her, don't you," Alan said, crossing the room to take Chelsea's hand.

Chelsea nodded, too scared to even speak.

She closed her eyes again. *Wherever you are, Lisha, you have to fight. Do you hear me? You have to fight back! You can't give up now. We love you.*

Now, fight back!

I have to stay alert, I have to keep breathing, Lisha thought as the car bumped along the road. It was totally dark in the trunk, and she could feel herself hyperventilating from fear. Right before she'd gotten into the trunk, Harley had tied her hands with the piece of rope he'd brought from the apartment, and slipped his red bandanna over her mouth, tying it behind her head. The bandanna made it difficult to breathe through her mouth at all, and the rope cut into her already tender and bleeding wrists.

Breathe deeply, she told herself. *Keep taking long, slow breaths.*

The air was so thin in the trunk, she felt as if she was suffocating. Sweat poured down her face, stinging her eyes. She was folded into a fetal position, her feet tucked under her.

"Ugh," she grunted as the car went over a huge pothole. Her head bounced against the top of the trunk.

Breathe. Keep breathing. Through your nose. That's it. Keep thinking. You have to save yourself. You have to live.

She felt the car speed up, and then the ride got smoother.

The FDR, she thought. *Or maybe the West Side Highway. Less potholes than the streets. Where is he taking me?*

Beep! Beep-beep-beep!

The car slowed down abruptly, and Lisha heard cars honking all around her.

A traffic jam. Wherever we are, there's a traffic jam.

Honk! Honk-honk-ho-o-o-o-nk!

Now more cars were sounding off.

A thought flashed through her head. Something she had seen on a talk show. Something about what to do if you were ever abducted and stuck in the trunk of a car.

And I thought it was such a stupid show at the time, Lisha recalled. *Just designed to scare people and get ratings. What did that expert say? He said to do anything to attract attention to the car. But what? What was it?*

I remember! He said if you kicked the taillight hard enough from inside the trunk, you could kick it out. A busted taillight might attract the police. And it would also let more air into the trunk so that I can breathe.

Honk-honk-ho-o-o-onk!

The car was still not moving, stuck somewhere.

The cars honking will muffle any noise I make, Lisha thought. *Harley won't know to get suspicious. If I can only turn over and try to kick out the taillight.*

Lisha tried to turn her body, but the space was so small that she was stuck in her position, on her side. She tried to kick backward, with her heel, toward the light, but her efforts were awkward and ineffectual.

Come on, Lisha, she told herself. *You have to find a way to do this. You have to try to save your own life.*

Slowly, grunting with the effort, little by little, she managed to edge her body onto her back.

Thank you, God, thank you, she prayed. Her breaths were rapid and shallow now. There was barely enough air in the trunk for her to breathe at all. Sweat dripped into her eyes, her mouth. She felt light-headed, faint, dizzy, and nauseous.

You can't pass out, she told herself. *You have to fight. Fight!*

But she could feel the lack of oxygen dragging her down, down to some place where all the fear went away, where she never had to see Harley again, or be afraid, or be ashamed about everything that had happened in Europe.

It would be so easy to just give up, give in, Lisha thought dreamily. She closed her eyes. *You'll never have to face any of the bad stuff ever again. You can just sleep.*

Chelsea.

Chelsea's face sprang into her mind. It was almost as if she could hear her old friend calling to her, willing her to stay awake, to try, to fight.

Lisha's eyes sprang open.

Fight! Fight, dammit!

Lisha forced her mind to concentrate. Everything felt so fuzzy, out of focus.

What was I trying to do? The taillight. Right. Kick out the taillight.

Just do it. This may be the only chance you have, she told herself. Lisha willed herself to stay awake and alert. She bit her own lips, hard, just to jar herself.

You still have your cowboy boots on, Lish, she told herself. *And just think, you hardly ever wear them anymore. Thank God Harley didn't make you take off those when he made you strip.*

She got angry all over again when she thought of how demeaning that had been. *Anger is good,* she told herself. *Get pissed off.*

And save your life.

She raised her knee as best she could in the cramped space, and aimed for where she thought the inside of the light would be.

She hit metal. Hard.

Try again, Lisha, she told herself, panting now from fear, exertion, heat, and lack of oxygen. *You have to find the strength to try again.*

She lifted her booted foot again, and aimed, farther to the right this time.

She hit something, not metal, something smoother, a different surface.

Glass.

The inside of the light. Maybe even the brake light. Or the turn signal.

Honk, honk, ho-o-o-o-nk!

She lifted her foot again, and jammed it as hard as she could at what she hoped was the same spot. Yes! She felt a splintering, and quickly she jammed her foot into it again, and again.

Daylight! She could see daylight coming in from where the light had been! Lisha took huge gulps of fresh air, drinking it in hungrily.

The car began to move, picking up speed quickly. Lisha was able to see through the hole where the taillight had been, but all she could make out was the edge of a car or the wheels of a truck.

They traveled for a long time, Lisha staying alert, trying to catch anything through the tiny spot into the outside world that might give her a clue, might help her save her life.

The car rolled to a stop. Where were they? She could feel that the motor was still running. She tried her best to see out of the busted taillight. There was another car just behind them. But even though neither car was moving, this time no one honked their horn.

Now the car moved forward a little, then stopped again.

A tollbooth! Lisha thought. *That could be it! We could be at a tollbooth. That means we're leaving Manhattan.*

The car rolled forward, then stopped yet again. Now the car moved again, not too fast, but it didn't stop again.

If only I could scream! Lisha thought desperately. She tried to make some sounds around the bandanna, but all that came out was a puny, muffled sound.

The car sped up, and she tried frantically to think of something, anything else she could do. When the car slowed down again, as if they were once again in some traffic, an idea flew into her mind.

Rock the car, she thought. *I've got to try to rock the car while it's standing still.*

Using all her strength, she threw her body forward, then backward, over and over. She moved as much as she could, grunting from the exertion.

The car started up again, and Lisha felt Harley switch lanes, and then put on a burst of speed. A good burst of speed.

No one saw, Lisha thought despairingly. *And no one is going to see the busted light, either. Probably the only thing I accomplished is that I made Harley mad for rocking the car that way. And I don't know what he'll do to me if he's mad. What if he—*

"Pull over into the right lane," came a loud authoritative voice through a megaphone.

The car sped up.

"Brown Ford Mustang, pull over to the right immediately. I repeat, pull over immediately!"

Oh, my God, that's this car! Lisha realized. *And that must be the police! Please, God, please, let me be saved. Please, don't let anyone shoot anyone.*

Lisha felt the car swerve to the right, then slow down, then stop. Harley turned off the motor.

She did her best to scream around the bandanna. She rocked the car as hard as she could, flinging herself around the trunk.

"New York Police Department," Lisha heard a deep, masculine voice say. "You're speeding, mister. And you've got a broken taillight. Please step out of the car, sir."

Lisha felt Harley's weight leave the car. "What's up, Officers?" she heard him yell as he closed his door.

"What is in your trunk, sir?"

"Nothing!" Harley said.

Lisha tried to scream again. She rocked the car.

"Step to the side of the car and put your hands on the hood," she heard the cop say over his loudspeaker.

"Hey!" the cop yelled. "Drop the—what do you think you're doing? Hey!"

And Lisha heard a shot. And then another.

Oh, no, she thought. *They're shooting at each other.*

And then there was no more shooting.

He's dead, Lisha thought. *Or the cops are dead. Or—*

A few moments later the trunk was being pried open. It was one of the policemen, an older black man with a kindly face.

"Sweet Lord," he said as he looked down at Lisha. He reached in and pulled her up, and then lifted her out of the trunk.

"Where's Harley?" she tried to ask, but her voice was still muffled by the bandanna.

The cop pulled the bandanna free.

"Where's Harley?" Lisha repeated.

The cop pointed to the railing of the bridge, which Lisha knew spanned the confluence of the Hudson River and the East River, just as more police cars were arriving.

"Miss, he jumped, miss," the cop said.

Gently, he untied her hands.

"He jumped?"

"Are you okay, miss?"

"Yes," Lisha said shakily, tears of relief falling down her face.

"Do you know this man?" the older cop asked.

"Yes," Lisha said, fisting the tears off her cheeks. Cars were going by at a snail's pace, everyone staring at her, gawking. She turned back to the older cop. "His name is Harley McCloud. He's been stalking me. He abducted me from work.

"He has a gun, somewhere," she added.

"He used it," the cop told her. "But he missed."

"Thank God," Lisha said.

"It's a long way to the river," the cop observed to Lisha. "I don't think you have to worry about this guy Harley stalking you ever again."

ELEVEN

Chelsea and Karma hurried up the walkway to the downtown headquarters of the New York Police Department.

Chelsea had received a call from Lisha about one o'clock, and the call had been transferred to Bigfoot's office. Sky was back, and the group was just on the verge of calling the police when Lisha called from the police station.

All she had told them was to please bring her some shorts, and to come and get her. Chelsea had begged Sumtimes—their only boss who ever revealed a trace of humanity—to let her and Karma go. Something in the desperation of her voice seemed to make Sumtimes say yes.

They had hopped into a taxi, and Karma waited in front of their apartment while Chelsea hurried upstairs and grabbed a pair of shorts for Lisha, then they sped downtown. For once, traffic was relatively light.

Lisha had told Chelsea almost nothing about what had happened. Or why she needed shorts. Or why she was at police headquarters.

The only thing she said was that it had to do with Harley, and then she started crying so hard she couldn't speak.

"Can I help you?" the female officer behind the front desk at reception area asked Chelsea and Karma.

"Yes, we're here for our friend Lisha Bishop," Chelsea said.

"Your names?" the officer asked.

They gave their names.

The officer scanned a printout on a clipboard, then she called someone, gave some information, and hung up again. "Miss Bishop is waiting for you in Room two," the officer said. "Down the corridor, second door on the right."

"Thank you," Chelsea said.

They hurried down the corridor, and opened the door marked "2."

Lisha was sitting in a wooden chair, her head in her hands.

She was wearing the jacket to a police officer's uniform over a T-shirt and her floral-print underwear.

"Lisha!" Chelsea cried.

She and Karma ran to their friend, and the three of them embraced. Lisha rested her head on Chelsea's shoulder. She didn't cry. When she looked up, Chelsea handed her the shorts.

"What happened?" Karma asked anxiously.

"We were so worried about you," Chelsea added.

Lisha finished dressing and sat down with her two friends. "You could say that today was the worst day of my entire life," she said shakily.

Chelsea and Karma waited.

And then slowly, painfully, Lisha told them everything that had happened, ending with Harley's high dive into the murky water.

"Do they—do they think he's dead?" Chelsea asked, wide-eyed.

Lisha nodded. "I guess they wait to see if a body ever floats up. But the police didn't seem to think he could live after falling that far. And no body surfaced that they could see. They've been checking."

"Oh, my God," Chelsea breathed, her hand to her mouth. "Oh, Lish..."

"I just... I feel like I'm having some terrible nightmare, you know?" Lisha said. "I keep thinking I'll wake up—"

"At least you know he can't hurt you anymore," Karma said gently.

"If he's dead, he can't," Lisha said. "But what if he isn't?" Tears came to her eyes. "And what if he is? Is it my fault?"

"No, no, of course not!" Chelsea exclaimed. "He was sick! And crazy! He did it himself!"

"He could have killed you, Lish," Karma added.

Lisha wiped the tears from her eyes. "I keep thinking about what that guy said in the apartment. That Harley would never really use his gun. He was right, sort of. He didn't use it on me."

"But you had no way of knowing if he really would or not," Chelsea reminded her.

Lisha's eyes filled with tears again. "I loved him once," she said. "Or at least I thought I did."

"Can we take you home?" Chelsea asked her.

Lisha nodded. "I just have to sign some papers. I gave the police a statement already. Some detective said he'd be calling me soon."

"They don't know anything about... the thing in Europe, do they?" Chelsea asked carefully.

"Only that Harley was my boyfriend back then," Lisha said. "And that he was a drug dealer. Nothing else."

"So, you really *are* free now," Karma said. "You know what I mean."

"Yeah," Lisha said. "I'm really free." Her eyes filled with tears again. "And all I feel is really, really sad."

"You want more, Lish?" Alan asked, holding the white carton of noodles with sesame paste over Lisha's dish.

"No, thanks," Lisha said.

"How about some rice?" Sky offered.

"No, I'm full, honest," Lisha replied.

It was later that evening, and the six interns were gathered at the girls' apartment, eating Chinese food they had ordered in. Demetrius was working late, but he was supposed to come over later. The girls had filled the guys in on everything that had happened to Lisha, and everyone was being very solicitous of her feelings.

"You hot or cold or anything?" Chelsea asked.

"Want Belch to do a trick for you?" Nick offered. Belch wagged his tail violently at the mention of his name, and Nick scratched the little dog behind his ears. "Belch can cheer up anyone."

"You guys, I'm not an invalid," Lisha said. "I'm okay."

"Well, I wouldn't be if what happened to you today happened to me," Chelsea said, shaking her head. "I'd be a wreck."

"What's the point?" Lisha asked.

"See, when most people are, like, losing it, they're too upset to ask 'what's the point?' " Karma explained.

"I'm not most people, then," Lisha replied, shaking her bangs out of her eyes.

"Supergirl, that's you, Lish," Sky said. "Nothing gets to you."

Lisha shrugged, but she couldn't look at him. *You get to me,* she wanted to say. *I wish I could just cry in your arms. But it's too scary. And I refuse to be that weak.*

"At least something good came out of all of this," Nick said. "Now we know who took the film from the Trash-cam."

"You really think Winston won't turn us in?" Sky asked Lisha dubiously.

"He said he wouldn't," Lisha said.

Nick fed Belch a piece of shrimp. "And Winston planned all the woo-woo stuff just to get you to go out with him?"

"He thought he was being clever," Karma said, getting up to pour herself a cup of coffee. "And I supposed if all this weirdness with Harley hadn't been going on, it might have been kinda funny."

"He seems like a nice guy," Alan offered.

"Too many guys want you, Lish," Sky said, his voice a little too hearty. "How are you ever gonna choose?"

"I'm not, okay?" Lisha snapped.

"Hey, don't bite my head off," Sky said. "It's not my fault if you're irresistible."

"Look, I don't need to hear that right now, okay?" Lisha said sharply. She got up and strode to her room. From behind her, she could hear Sky asking the others, "What did I say?" but she slammed her bedroom door shut before she heard anyone's answer.

Lisha threw herself on her water bed and stared up at the ceiling. *I want to cry, but I can't,* she realized. *It's like there's this huge lump of pain, and it's blocking my tears. And I can't let myself... I just can't let myself.*

There was a soft knock on her door.

"Who is it?" Lisha asked.

"Alan."

She got up and opened the door. Alan stepped into her room. Then he closed the door behind him. Lisha returned to the water bed. Alan sat on the edge. They didn't speak.

Then slowly, wordlessly, Alan lay down next to her. He opened his arms. And Lisha moved her head to the comfort of his shoulder. His arms circled her, and the water bed gently rippled underneath them.

Then the tears began to fall. Alan didn't make her talk, or say anything himself, he just held her, and let her cry.

"No, no, don't!" Lisha screamed, fighting Harley off. He was reaching for her, his hands wrapped around her neck. She managed to feint out of his grasp, and then she was falling backward, into the water, falling, and she couldn't breathe, couldn't breathe, couldn't—"

"Lish? Lish, honey?" Alan said softly. "Wake up. You're having a nightmare."

Lisha opened her eyes. Moonlight streamed in through the window, illuminating Alan's beautiful, kind, dark eyes.

"It was so horrible," Lisha whispered. "Harley was strangling me. And then I jumped, and I was drowning. . . ."

"He put his arms around her. "It's okay," he said. "You're safe. I'm right here."

She breathed in the comfort of him, burrowing into his embrace. When she could feel her heartbeat returning to normal, she kissed his cheek. "What time is it?" she whispered.

He looked at the hands of his luminous watch. "Three o'clock."

"In the morning?" Lisha asked, shocked.

"You slept," Alan said.

"I can't believe I slept for so long. Have you been awake all this time?" she asked.

"Watching you," Alan answered.

"Watching over me is more like it," Lisha said, touched by his caring. "You didn't have to."

"I know."

"I'm really okay," she insisted.

"I know."

Her lips trembled as tears sprang to her eyes again. "That's a big, fat lie," she said.

"I know that, too." He wrapped her in his arms again.

"How did you get so sweet?" Lisha asked, when she managed to stop crying again.

"Let's see, must have been all those protests against my macho dad," Alan said, a half smile on his lips.

"He's lucky to have you for a son," Lisha said fervently.

"I'll tell him you said so," Alan said wryly. "That is, if the two of us ever have an actual conversation."

Lisha rolled over and reached for some Kleenex on her nightstand. "Life is so crazy, Alan. I really don't get it at all." She blew her nose hard. "There was a time when I really, really thought I loved Harley. And now he's... he's..." She couldn't bring herself to say it.

"But the guy that died today isn't the guy you loved," Alan pointed out.

"Who was he, then? I mean, why did I think I loved him? What is love, anyway?"

"The greatest writers in the world have tackled that one," Alan said. "I'm out of my league. Hell, I can't even get past page fifty of my novel."

"Are you ever going to let me read what you're writing?" Lisha asked.

"Maybe someday. If I ever think it's any good." He stroked her hair softly.

"Well, I know one thing," Lisha said. "Love is stupid. It hurts. It makes your life crazy. And it's not worth the pain and trouble."

"That's how you feel now, Lish. But it's not forever," Alan said gently.

"Yes, it is," she insisted. "And another thing. Lust. I mean, just because you want to jump someone's bones doesn't make it love. It's just some stupid physical thing, and people make it something it isn't."

"Like you and Sky?" Alan asked softly.

"I don't love Sky!" Lisha denied sharply.

"It's okay if you do, Lish—"

"I don't," Lisha stated firmly.

"You want him, though," Alan said, his voice low.

"No."

Alan didn't say anything, he just held her.

Lisha got up on one elbow and looked into Alan's eyes. "No one makes me feel the way you do, Alan. Safe. Peaceful."

"But no fire," Alan said. He smiled a small, sad smile. "Someone else told me that once."

"I never said there was no fire," Lisha whispered.

Then she leaned down, and softly, slowly, she kissed his lips. Then she kissed him again, until his arms tightened around her, and he began to return her kisses passionately.

And finally, after they got lost in the sweetness and heat of each other, as dawn was coming up outside their window, Lisha fell asleep, safe in Alan's arms.

"Alan!" Karma said, when Alan padded into the kitchen later that morning. "Hi!"

"Hi," Alan responded. He found his sneakers under the couch and put them on.

Karma was dressed for work, in a black-and-white Betsy Johnson, geometric print, op-art shift, with chunky white high-heeled loafers. Her hair was in a fat braid that started high on her head and flowed down her back.

"So . . . you spent the night with Lisha," Karma said brightly, pouring coffee from the Mr. Coffee.

Alan didn't reply; he just tied his shoes.

"So, do you want coffee?"

"Nah, I'm gonna go catch a quick shower before work," he said. "Thanks, though." He slipped out the front door.

Lisha came into the living room, her hair tousled from sleep, clad in a T-shirt and panties. "Where's Alan?"

"He went across the hall to take a shower," Karma said, sipping her coffee. "He was here the whole night, huh?"

"Huh," Lisha agreed, pouring herself a cup of coffee.

"Oh," Karma said. "I'm dying of curiosity, of course, but I'm much too discreet to ask you anything."

Lisha got the milk out of the refrigerator and poured some into her coffee.

"The gossip of the morning, besides you and Alan, is that Chelsea spent the night across the hall with Nick. Demetrius never made it over here last night. Which means that I'm the only one who slept alone."

"What time is it?" Lisha asked, stirring her coffee.

"Eight," Karma answered. "How are you feeling?"

"Better," Lisha said. "I mean, I still have a ways to go. And the whole thing was just so horrible, but... better." She sipped her coffee.

"Alan helped, huh?" Karma asked.

"Yeah," Lisha replied.

"Like, how did he help?" Karma reached into the brown bag on the counter for a bagel.

"Just by being Alan," Lisha said.

"Uh-huh," Karma murmured. "Is that as in friend-Alan, or as in lover-Alan?"

"Lover," Lisha mused. "What an old-fashioned word. You don't hear that word much anymore, huh?"

"Because it's, like, out of some romance novel," Karma said. "You know, the ones with the cover where some hunky guy is holding some girl with her clothes falling off. And speaking of clothes falling off—"

Lisha plopped down in the chair in the living room. "What?"

"You're not wearing much," Karma noted.

"That's because I didn't get dressed yet," Lisha said.

"Yeah," Karma agreed. "I was wondering if you had ever gotten *un*dressed." She got the cream cheese out of the refrigerator and spread it on her bagel.

"You're trying to find out if I made love with Alan, aren't you?" Lisha said calmly, sipping her coffee.

"Would I do that?" Karma whined. She brought her bagel into the living room and sat on the couch. "Now, tell me every steamy detail."

"Well, it was nice," Lisha said.

"There are many kinds of nice," Karma pointed out.

"Alan is... well, he's really special," Lisha said dreamily.

"I know that," Karma said. "I love him like a brother. The question is, do you love him like a brother?"

"No," Lisha said.

"No?"

"No," Lisha confirmed.

"You mean you... but I thought you and Sky..."

"Okay, okay, I'm attracted to Sky," Lisha admitted. "But that's just my body. My heart says... Alan."

"Are you sure?" Karma asked.

No, Lisha thought. *That's the truth. I'm not sure. I don't think I've ever been as attracted to anyone as I am to Sky. But I can't handle that now, not after what happened yesterday.*

"Physical attraction isn't everything," she told Karma, sipping her coffee.

"Okay, it's not everything," Karma agreed. "But it's a lot. So, do your knees get weak when Alan holds you? Do you get that funny little feeling in the pit of your stomach when you even think about him?"

"I am definitely attracted to him," Lisha said firmly. "And more than that, I trust him. I've had it with hot guys I can't trust."

"So, did you sleep with him?" Karma asked.

"Yeah," Lisha said.

"Yes? *You did?*" Karma cried.

"He was here all night, we slept—"

"That's not exactly what I meant," Karma said. "Did you—"

"I hate him," Chelsea announced, stomping through the front door.

"Who?" Karma asked.

"Nick." Chelsea slammed the door behind her. "I hate him."

"Didn't you just spend the night with him for the very first time?" Karma asked. "Or did I miss something in the continuing saga of you and Nick?"

"I spent the night with him," Chelsea said. "We didn't have sex. We almost did, but then I thought, 'No, the first time I have sex is not going to be like this. It's going to be really, really special. Nick and I will rent the most opulent hotel room in New York, and we'll have champagne, and the bed will be strewn with rose petals. . . .' " Tears filled her eyes. "So, last night, I told him I still wanted to wait. And he was so sweet about it. He said he wanted to make it perfect for me, and he'd wait until I was ready. And now I never want to speak to him again as long as I live!"

"I take it you two had a fight," Lisha stated dryly.

"This morning when we woke up," Chelsea said. "It was so wonderful to wake up with him. And then . . . and then he told me . . . Oh, Lish, you were right. Just because you're attracted to someone doesn't make it love. How could I have believed that I love him?"

"What did he do?" Karma asked.

"I don't know, that's just it," Chelsea said. She sat next to Karma on the couch. "You know how Jazz invited Nick to go to the Rock of Ages Awards with her, and how she's been asking him to come into her office, and flirting with him again and everything? Well, now I know why."

"She wants him?" Lisha guessed.

"Worse," Chelsea said. "I think she already had him. Jazz is pregnant."

Karma and Lisha's mouths hung open in disbelief.

"She's—" Karma began.

Chelsea nodded miserably. "He just told me. It's supposed to be this big secret, but he confided in me. He was afraid I'd be upset, he said. People might jump to conclusions, since everyone knows they were dating, and that's why she told him. That's what he *says*, anyway."

"Oh, my God, this really *is* a soap opera!" Karma cried.

Lisha was incredulous. "You mean to tell me that there's a possibility that Jazz is pregnant with Nick's baby?"

"I don't know," Chelsea said. "But I'm going to find out the truth. If it's the last thing I do."

DIRTY BIG SECRETS

For Sarah, Betsy, Steve, Cara,
and the whole gang at William Morris Agency.
You rule.

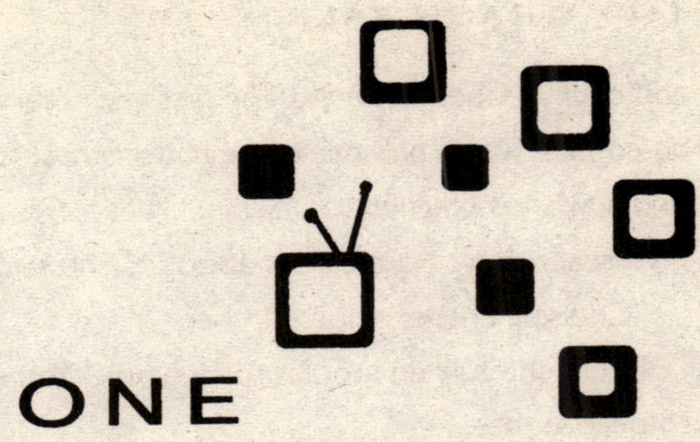

ONE

"Chelsea?"

Chelsea didn't turn around. She recognized Nick's voice. She just continued to pour herself a cup of the sludge that passed for coffee from the Mr. Coffee in the incredibly messy lounge at the *Trash* office.

"You haven't spoken to me for a week," Nick reminded her.

"That's because I don't have anything to say to *you*," she replied. Still she didn't turn around. She just sipped the awful black coffee.

"All I'm guilty of is telling you the truth," Nick said bitterly. "Aren't you glad you heard it from me that Jazz is pregnant, before she announces it on the show?"

Jazz is pregnant. Jazz is pregnant. The painful words echoed over and over in Chelsea's mind. *The first guy I ever really loved, Nick Shaw, dated Jazz, who is only one of the hottest, most famous girls in the world. And now she's pregnant.*

"I really don't want to talk about it," she said, her voice low.

"Chelsea, I never slept with her—"

Finally she turned around to face him. "You don't really expect me to believe that—"

Nick ran his fingers through his dirty-blond hair and shook his head with exasperation. "Believe whatever you want," he told her. "You're going to anyway."

Chelsea gave him a cool look. "Let's just look at the facts, then. You dated Jazz Stewart. Let's see. She's Rod Stewart's alleged love child, host of *Trash,* picked by *People* magazine as one of the hottest new faces of the year. Jazz has the morals of an alley cat in heat. She wanted you. Bad. And you want me to believe you never had sex with her?"

A muscle worked in Nick's chiseled jaw. "Like I said, Chels, believe what you want."

Chelsea could feel her heart melting, and she tried her best to harden it.

He looks way too much like Brad Pitt, she thought. *All I want is to be in his arms. All I want is to pretend he never told me that Jazz is pregnant. If only he'd tell me he loved me and he never loved her. If only . . .*

But wishes were stupid. Facts were facts. And Chelsea wasn't about to get her heart broken by a guy who wasn't even willing to make a real commitment to her.

She took another sip of the terrible coffee. "I guess you think I'm naive enough to believe you—"

"Wrong," Nick said. "I thought you *trusted* me enough to believe me." He gave her a hard look. "But I guess I thought wrong." He turned on his heel and walked away.

Tears came to her eyes. It had been a week since Nick had told her that Jazz was pregnant, and Chelsea hadn't been able to think about anything else.

It was too crazy. She had finally spent the night with Nick. And she had almost been ready to make love with him, but something had stopped her.

And now I'm so glad, she thought. *Because that morning he dropped his bombshell.*

Nick wanted Chelsea to know before Jazz announced it to the press and the world, he'd explained. It's not my baby, he'd explained.

Yeah, right.

Chelsea wandered over to the window and looked down at the street scene of New York. She thought back on how much her life had changed since the first day she'd shown up at the Upper West Side apartment she now shared with her best friends, Alyssa Bishop and Karma Kushner. The three girls, and the three guys who lived in an apartment across the hall, had been chosen from thousands of applicants as summer interns for the most outrageous teen/college daytime talk show in America, *Trash.*

Now the six of us are inseparable, Chelsea thought. *And we're so different from each other, too. Everyone tells me I look like a preppie version of Hilary Duff. Alyssa—or, as everyone calls her, Lisha—looks like a young Angelina Jolie and she dresses like a downtown rocker. And Karma may be tiny and Korean American, but she sounds just like Fran Drescher on* The Nanny, *and her adoptive parents are Jewish hippies from Long Island.*

And yet we're the very best of friends now, she thought. *I can't even imagine my life without them.*

Or the guys.

Nick, Sky, and Alan. They lived right across the hall. Chelsea had lost her heart to Nick Shaw from the very first moment she had set eyes on him. It wasn't just his Brad Pitt good looks, it was the easy, sexy way he had about him. And how she was so sure there was much more to him than met the eye. He was so much more than the Canadian-slacker image he showed most of the world. And then there was Sky, who everyone said looked sort of like Keanu Reeves. He was so steady and dependable, the kind of guy you could trust with your life.

And Alan Van Kleef. A romantic, sensitive guy who dreamed of becoming a great writer, wrapped in a package that looked a lot like Johnny Depp. Once she and Alan had almost—

But no, Chelsea thought. *I love Alan like a brother. Besides, he and Lisha are an item now.*

"Hey, Chelsea," a voice from the door called to her. It was Sumtimes, the only one of the television show's producers that the interns could stand. In spite of her shaved head, Sumtimes was absolutely gorgeous. She had a great figure and her clothes were stunning. Today she wore a white minidress with a halter top and silver patent-leather boots that laced up to her thighs.

Each week or so Sumtimes changed her first name on a whim. This week she was Lourdes Sumtimes, in honor of Madonna's little girl.

Which was why everyone called her by her last name.

"Hi, Sumtimes," Chelsea said. "I was just about to get back to transcribing the calls from the nine-hundred number," she added hastily.

The interns all spent way too much of their time in a room they called Sicko-Central, where they sat in front of computer terminals wearing earphones, transcribing the phone messages that had been left on the 1-900-I'M TRASH line. People actually paid money to leave weird messages and show ideas. It was the interns' job to hone in on any good show ideas from among the thousands and thousands of taped messages they received every week.

"Cool," Sumtimes said, fingering the many earrings in her left ear. "I wanted to let you know that there's a meeting this afternoon at three in the conference room about the 'Teen Kids of Mass Murderers' show. Roxanne wants you there."

Chelsea's heart thudded in her chest. Sweat broke out on her forehead. "Oh, okay," she said, trying to keep her voice steady.

"I think she's finally ready to announce the date for the show," Sumtimes continued. "Man, I haven't seen this much prep for a show in ages. Everyone thinks the ratings are going to be huge. See ya." She wiggled her fingers at Chelsea and walked away.

With a shaking hand, Chelsea poured her coffee into the sink. She had lived with dread ever since she found out that her most despised boss, Roxanne Renault, also known to the interns as "Bigfoot" because of the size of her feet, was planning a show on the teenage offspring of mass murderers.

The cause of Chelsea's dread was that Roxanne didn't know that Chelsea herself was one of them. A kid. Of a mass murderer. A world-famous mass murderer, even.

Sweet, preppie, boring little Chelsea Jennings from Nashville, Tennessee. Class valedictorian. Squeaky-clean virgin. That's how Roxanne thought of her.

Only my birth name is Chelsea Kettering. And my father, Charles Kettering, was one of the most famous mass murderers in recent history, Chelsea thought grimly.

When Chelsea was just a baby, her father, a highly respected lawyer in Johnson City, Tennessee, had gone berserk, and shot all the people in the local Burger Barn restaurant. Then he had headed home to kill his wife and baby.

Only his wife—Chelsea's mom—had stabbed him to death first.

The only people who knew Chelsea's real identity were Lisha and Karma. And she had sworn them to secrecy.

I've never even told Nick, Chelsea realized. *What would he think of me, if he knew? He already thinks I have a terrible temper. Maybe going crazy is in my genes. Maybe one day I'll just get so mad that I'll lose it, and I'll do something horrible, just like Dad, and—*

No. I can never tell him.

And I have to keep my secret from Bigfoot, no matter what. What if she found out?

"Gawd, this room is like, seriously depressing," Karma Kushner said in her trademark nasal whine as she strode into the lounge and opened the small refrigerator. "I am beyond starving. And I left a lemon yogurt in here last week." Her head disappeared into the fridge. "Of course someone ate it. Figures."

"There's a meeting this afternoon about the 'Teen Kids of Mass Murderers' show," Chelsea announced.

Karma closed the fridge. "Really?"

Chelsea nodded. "Sumtimes just told me. Bigfoot and Jazz have set a show date."

Karma thought a moment. "So, you're cool, then. She must have the whole show planned. Which means you dodged a major bullet—with my help, of course—and your secret is safe. The end."

"You think?" Chelsea asked, biting worriedly on her lower lip.

"I know," Karma insisted. "We outsmarted her. Of course, in the case of Bigfoot, that wasn't too difficult to do."

For some time, Roxanne had been determined to find the whereabouts of the daughter of Charles Kettering. She had no idea that, in fact, Charles Kettering's daughter was right under her nose. She even had Karma and Chelsea working on finding this girl. Karma had created an elaborate scheme to convince Roxanne that Kettering's daughter had moved to Australia.

"I'll just feel better when the stupid show is finally over and done with," Chelsea said nervously. "I mean, can you even imagine what Bigfoot would do if she found out the truth about me?" She shuddered at the thought.

"Well, she's not gonna find out, girlfriend," Karma said resolutely. She plopped herself down on the threadbare couch and slipped her feet out of her very high heels. "My dawgs are killing me."

"You are a slave to fashion," Chelsea declared.

Karma looked down at Chelsea's shoes—brown suede loafers. Then she took in her friend's entire outfit—khakis from the Gap worn with a sleeveless white cotton shirt. "Chelsea, I love you like a sister, but your fashion sense is the pits. You look like a poster child for Safe and Boring."

Chelsea laughed. "Can you even imagine me in one of your outfits?"

At the moment Karma had on a tiny, fuzzy sweater in bright orange and plaid hip huggers with flare bottoms. Her gorgeous long hair was up in pigtails, each secured with a scrunchie that featured fuzzy, little yellow dice. Chelsea knew that the sweater was by some expensive downtown designer and had cost a mint. The plaid hip huggers were from a used-clothing store. And the dice hair ornaments were from the kids department at Walgreen's.

Karma was famous for her mix-and-match wardrobe. And she had the money to buy it. She'd earned it herself, through careful investments in the stock market.

"You should have heard the sicko message I just transcribed," Lisha said, walking into the room. "This guy left a message for Jazz saying that he wanted to take photos of her dancing nude with his German shepherd."

"Gag me," Karma muttered.

"What rock do these people live under?" Lisha asked. She lifted the pot from the Mr. Coffee, looked at the coffee, and put it down again. "No one can tell me that what's in there is actually drinkable."

"No one would try," Chelsea agreed.

Lisha sat down next to Karma and cocked her head at Chelsea. "I saw Nick at the elevator."

Chelsea shrugged.

"He looked bummed," Lisha said.

Chelsea shrugged again and leaned against the sink.

"Maybe he's telling you the truth about Jazz," Karma ventured.

"Yeah, right," Lisha snorted derisively. "And maybe I should have married Harley and lived happily ever after."

Chelsea just looked at Lisha. Harley was Lisha's ex, her first love, whom she had fallen for when they both lived in Europe. But Harley had become a crazed drug dealer, had recently come looking for Lisha, and it had all been a terrible, terrible nightmare.

And now Lisha was so bitter about guys.

"Nick isn't anything like Harley," Chelsea said quietly.

"I know," Lisha agreed. "But I'm telling you, you can't trust lust."

"Who said it's lust?" Chelsea protested.

"What, you aren't dying for him?" Lisha asked skeptically.

"It's more than that," Chelsea insisted. "Anyway, it's probably over. I can't compete with Jazz, whether Nick is the father of her baby or not."

"Hold the phone, hold the phone," Karma interrupted. "This is dumb. Nick isn't with Jazz anymore. He wants to be with you, remember?"

"But Jazz is pregnant—" Chelsea began.

"Maybe," Karma said. "And maybe not. Maybe she just told Nick that. She hasn't made any announcement, right?"

"She's going to this afternoon," Chelsea said. "That's what everyone is saying. And why would she tell Nick she was pregnant if it wasn't true?"

"How do I know how Jazz's demented little mind works?" Karma demanded.

"I could see her saying it just to play a mind game with him," Lisha pointed out.

Chelsea felt shivers of excitement race up and down her spine. Could that really be true? Could it just be Jazz playing games with Nick's head?

She sat on the arm of the couch. "Y'all, I would be so happy if it turned out to be just one of her sick jokes." She thought a moment. "Have I been too mean to Nick?"

"Well, if Jazz is playing a mind game with him—and with you—then by dissing Nick you've played right into her hands," Lisha explained.

"I never thought of it that way," Chelsea mused. "Maybe if I—"

"Did someone give the three of you the day off?" a voice barked from the doorway.

The lovely Roxanne Renault, looking every bit as hot as a red-headed Gwyneth Paltrow in her designer suit with a skirt so short it barely covered her crotch, stood glaring at them. The cast on her leg—she had been shot in the foot during a major scandal on live television—had been shortened, and now covered only her foot and her ankle. It was covered in sky-blue material that matched her suit.

"We were just taking a short break," Chelsea explained, getting up from the arm of the couch.

"Interns don't get breaks," Roxanne said icily. "Interns are slaves. Is that clear?"

"Crystal," Lisha said.

"How about you, little Miss Preppie?" Roxanne asked Chelsea. "Is the work here too much for your limited attention span?"

"No," Chelsea said evenly.

"Ducky," Roxanne shot back. "Now get your sorry asses back to work." With that, she hobbled out of the room.

"What a lovely person," Karma said disgustedly.

"I'd like to shoot her in her other foot," Chelsea seethed. "No, in her heart. But that would assume she had one."

"I heard that," Roxanne said, instantly appearing in the doorway again.

The three interns turned red with embarrassment.

"Give me a good reason why I shouldn't fire all your butts this instant," Bigfoot demanded.

"Uh . . . you need slave labor?" Karma queried meekly.

Roxanne managed something that passed as a smile. "I won't fire you because I happen to be in a terrific mood. Ask me why."

"Why?" Chelsea, Lisha, and Karma dutifully asked together.

"Because in addition to firming up plans for the 'Teen Kids of Mass Murderers' show—which I assure you will get unbelievable ratings—Jazz is making a sensational announcement on the show today. This announcement is going to put our ratings through the roof. Ask me what it is."

"What is it?" the interns echoed.

Roxanne snorted derisively. "You're interns. Why would I tell you?" She turned to hobble away.

Chelsea couldn't help herself. "That Jazz is pregnant, maybe?" she called after Roxanne.

"Oh, great," Lisha muttered.

Bigfoot maneuvered herself around. "How did you know?"

"Even slaves have ears," Chelsea replied flippantly.

Roxanne narrowed her eyes. "Don't push me, little girl," she threatened.

Chelsea felt the anger bubbling up in her. She knew that Roxanne hated her, had hated her from the day she had been selected as an intern over Bigfoot's objections.

She also knew she should keep her mouth shut. But—

"I wasn't pushing you," Chelsea said evenly. "And my name is not 'little girl.' "

"She's kidding around," Karma said brightly as she nudged her elbow hard into Chelsea's side. Chelsea knew the nudge meant "shut up."

Roxanne eyed Chelsea thoughtfully. "Oh, I get it now. You're upset because you're hot for Nick. And Nick had a thing with Jazz. And now Jazz is pregnant. So you think—"

"I don't really want to talk about this with you," Chelsea said stiffly. "It doesn't have anything to do with my job here."

Roxanne gave Chelsea a wide-eyed look. "Are you worried that

Nick was the father of Jazz's baby? Is that what has your panties in a wad? Poor little Chelsea! And I was *so* insensitive."

"So . . . Nick isn't the father, huh?" Karma asked Roxanne hopefully.

Roxanne smiled nastily. "Ask him," she said. "Or even better, wait for Jazz to make the announcement." She turned her evil eye on Chelsea again. "You don't really think you can compete with Jazz, do you? Even our Tennessee hayseed couldn't be *that* pathetic. Now get back to work!"

This time when Bigfoot left the room, Karma got up and slammed the door shut to make sure she wouldn't hear them.

"I hate her deeply," Chelsea said.

"My parents would say that her karma is in very bad shape," Karma commented.

"That does not make me feel any better," Chelsea said flatly. "So, it's official. Jazz is announcing her pregnancy today."

"Everyone knew that anyway," Lisha pointed out.

"And that doesn't mean Nick is the father," Karma added.

Chelsea picked up her mini-backpack and swung it over her arm. "It doesn't mean he isn't, either," she said. "I don't know what to believe anymore."

"I think you can trust Nick," Karma insisted.

"Lish?" Chelsea asked.

Lisha shrugged her patented sexy shrug. "Who knows? I'm probably way too cynical. You're right. Nick is nothing like Harley. You should give him the benefit of the doubt."

"Maybe I should," Chelsea agreed.

"Of course you should," Karma said firmly. "The boy is crazed for you. Let's go find him and you can dance naked on his desk. Grab him and push him into the storage room and cover him with kisses. Stuff like that."

Chelsea laughed. "I'll make a date with him, how's that?"

"Okay for a start, I guess," Karma agreed.

"I really do love him," Chelsea confessed. "It's just... it's hard to admit, you know? I mean, we don't have a commitment. And he's so gorgeous. And... well, it's scary."

"If you love him, you have to go for it," Karma advised.

"And if you really love him, you have to trust him," Lisha added reluctantly.

Chelsea smiled at her friends. "Y'all really help me figure things out. I appreciate it."

"We are wonderful, it's true," Lisha said with a grin.

"And you and Nick belong together," Karma added.

They headed for the door. But just before they reached it, the door opened, and Winston, Jazz's gorgeous, dreadlocked Jamaican assistant, stuck his head into the room.

"Did you hear the big news?" he asked in his melodious voice.

"About Jazz?" Lisha asked. "Everyone knows."

"Preggers!" Winston hooted. "Can you believe it? I can't wait to see the show this afternoon."

"We know," Lisha replied. "It's anyone's guess who the father is, huh?"

"Oh, there's no guessing," Winston said. "I know who the father is, for sure. It's Nick Shaw."

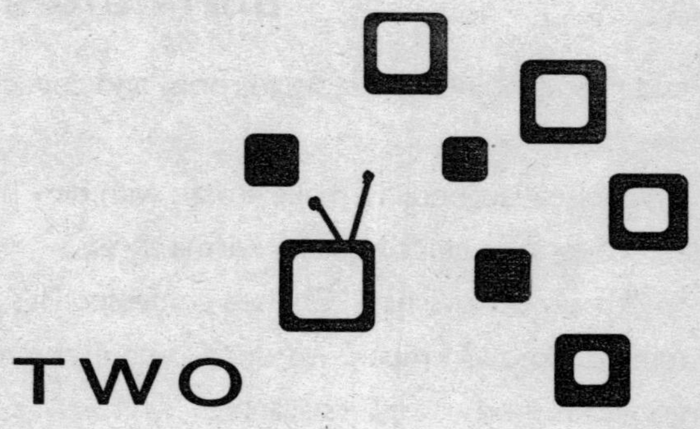

TWO

Nick rubbed the spot on his temples where the earphones pressed into his head and looked sideways over at Chelsea. She seemed completely absorbed in listening to the calls from the 900 tape that she was transcribing and didn't even glance in his direction.

He sighed and pushed the on button on his tape again. "Hey, Jazz, wow, I love your show!" a girl's voice squealed. "Oh, yeah, my name is Burrito Mustings. Guess what my mom was eating when she got pregnant with me! I mean, for real, she says that right at that moment she was actually eating these bean burritos, and—"

Out of the corner of his eye, Nick could see Winston step through the doorway and into Sicko-Central.

My man, my bud, Winston, Nick thought sarcastically. *Yesterday he told Chelsea that I was the father of Jazz's baby. What a pal.*

Jazz had made her big announcement on the air the day before, as predicted. But she hadn't announced who the father was. In fact, she'd been completely coy about it, dropping hints about this person and that. She had been sure that the media would eat up her guessing game, and she was right: the headline of that morning's *New York Post* had been WHO'S POPPA?—with a gigantic close-up of Jazz's abdomen, dominated by her new trademark J-shaped navel ring.

The night before, Nick had once again tried to talk Chelsea out of the notion that he had been the one to get Jazz pregnant, but she still wasn't interested in his disclaimers. Winston had told her the truth, she explained. Winston had no reason to lie.

The whole thing is starting to get really old, Nick thought, looking over at Chelsea again. *Why can't she just trust me? She's willing to believe what anyone else tells her before she believes me.*

"Happy Tuesday, happy Tuesday," Winston called out, his voice a lilting Jamaican singsong. "Good morning to all the slaving interns."

"Hey, Winston," Alan said to him, taking his headset off. "Did you bring us our morning coffee?"

Winston cringed. "You call what you have in this country *coffee,* mon? It's not coffee you drink, it's athletic-sock juice."

"If it's hot and black it's okay for me," Karma quipped, spinning around in her rolling chair.

"You mean hot and *brown,* as in Demetrius, don't you?" Winston asked slyly. Demetrius, who also worked at *Trash,* was Karma's boyfriend. Tall, gorgeous, and golden, with hair halfway down his back, he was half-Greek and half-Hispanic. He was also a truly terrific guy, smart, nice, close to his family. And he was crazy about tiny Karma.

"Works for me," Karma agreed happily.

"As far as coffee goes, try real Jamaican beans, that's the only thing that makes it." Winston smiled. He put his hand on the back of Lisha's chair, but she gave him a cool look and he moved it.

Looks like Winston is still into Lisha, Nick noted as he adjusted his earphones again. And clearly she still isn't interested.

"Anyway, get yourselves quickly back to work. A warning: Roxi's on her way down here to check up on you. 'Nuff respect."

"Thanks for the warning, Winston," Chelsea said. "I know I can count on you to tell me the truth," she added pointedly.

Great, Nick thought. *Just great.*

"Happy to help out," Winston said cheerfully. He headed for the door, then turned around. "Oh, one more thing. Nick?"

"Yeah?"

"Jazz wants to see you in her office."

"When?"

"Now, mon." Winston smiled.

Nick took a quick look over at Chelsea. She was ignoring him. "What does Jazz want?" he asked Winston.

Winston shrugged. "I'm her assistant, not her confessor," he said innocently. "She just sent me to tell you."

"Her Trashiness could have used the intercom," Lisha pointed out.

Winston shrugged again. "Jazz says, I do. I don't question her. I like my job."

Nick took off his headphones and got up. He thought about touching Chelsea on the shoulder as he walked by her, then thought better of it.

She didn't even turn to look at him as he walked by her.

Nick followed Winston out the door, and down the long corridor toward Jazz's office.

"Go right on in," Winston suggested, a knowing smirk on his face. He pointed to the open door of Jazz's office when they reached her suite. "And shut it behind you."

"Listen, Winston—"

"I know nothing, I see nothing, mon," Winston said, holding his palms up to Nick.

"Yeah, right," Nick muttered. He went into Jazz's office. The room was huge, with picture windows offering a view of the Hudson River. The carpeting was thick and white, with a huge, one-of-a-kind black-and-white desk in Jazz's favorite dalmatian print (it matched her two dogs), and a kidney-shaped white velvet couch. Three large-screen televisions dominated one wall. At the moment one was on, and a music video was running, but the sound was turned off.

Jazz was sitting on the white velvet couch by the window, her attention on the TV. Nick had been in her office several times, but had never seen any of the televisions actually in operation.

That's the best TV picture I've ever seen, he thought as Jazz motioned him over to her, indicating with a quick gesture that he should sit down on the other end of the couch from her.

He sat and looked over at the talk-show host, who seemed completely absorbed in watching the TV. She was wearing a tiny, lavender, stretch-velvet T-shirt with an even tinier, lavender, stretch-velvet miniskirt. Her famous abdomen was exposed, as was her new J-shaped navel ring.

Okay, she's hot, Nick admitted to himself. *That's all she is. Hot. No. She's very hot. Very, very hot.*

"Check this out, Nick," Jazz said distractedly, now motioning with her chin toward the television.

It was a music video channel's famous news reporter, Samantha Waring, facing the camera. Samantha, or Sammi, as she was called by her many fans, had long brown hair, a curvy figure, and a ruby-studded nose ring. The gossip rags claimed that Sammi and Jazz were involved in a huge rivalry, but Nick had no idea if this was really true or not. Jazz took the remote in her perfectly lavender-polished fingers—and turned up the sound.

"...and this is what our conversation with Jazz Stewart last night was like," Samantha said, on the TV screen.

The image of Jazz and Samantha together, on two director's chairs facing one another, filled the screen.

"When did you do this interview?" Nick asked Jazz.

"Real late last night, this is the advance tape, now shush!"

"Jazz," Samantha said, looking skeptically at the hostess of *Trash,* "the whole world now knows you're pregnant, since you've announced it on your show. Do you want a boy or a girl?"

"What if it's twins? Twin girls?" Jazz said on TV.

"Have the doctors told you that?" Samantha asked.

"Twin girls, could you imagine?" Jazz continued, not answering Samantha's question. "Could you imagine three of me? I'd name them both Jazz, you know."

"Seriously?" the interviewer asked.

Jazz gave a half smile. "Am I ever serious, Sammi?"

"It's just like you to answer a question with a question," Sammi replied, smiling.

On the TV, Jazz smiled back at her. "Is it?"

"I've heard certain rumors," Samantha said slowly. "That maybe you're not really pregnant at all."

"Oh, well, you know how people love to start rumors," Jazz replied. Nick could hear the steel filtering into her voice.

"Well, can you blame them?" Sammi asked. "I mean, you're the host of *Trash,* you guys scam people all the time, it's practically an art form. So—"

"Excuse me, Sa*man*tha. Are you *doubting* me?" Jazz asked, her smile still in place.

"Just asking," Samantha countered innocently.

Jazz on TV stood up as Jazz on the end of the couch watched, a smile playing at the corners of her lips.

"This part is great," she told Nick, smiling at her image on the TV.

"Where are you going?" Samantha asked.

"I need a little break," Jazz answered.

"But we're in the middle of an inter—"

As Nick watched the television the camera followed Jazz as she went over to her backpack and pulled something out. She held it up dramatically to the camera.

The camera zero'd in on it.

It was a home pregnancy test.

"Where's your bathroom?" Jazz asked. "Although I did hear a rumor that you don't actually have any bodily functions, Sammi, so maybe you don't have one."

Jazz laughed out loud as she watched herself on the television.

Samantha looked uncomfortable. "Uh, there's no bathroom here on the set. Sorry."

Jazz on TV looked triumphant. "Then I'll just mosey over here behind these curtains. Give me thirty seconds. I'll be right back."

"You can't!"

"I'm already there," Jazz said as the camera followed her behind the curtains. It was perfectly obvious what she was planning to do back there, too.

This was fantastic television, and Nick knew it. He looked at Jazz at the end of the couch, and from the smile on her face, he knew that Jazz knew it, too.

Who would have thought that when she picked me up in a club that night last May I'd end up here as an in—

"Nick, pay attention," Jazz ordered. "You're here on my time."

Nick swung his attention back to the television, where the camera came in tight on Samantha, who looked distinctly uncomfortable.

"Score one for me, huh?" Jazz told Nick smugly. She looked at the TV again. "What a hoot! Just look at her! She had absolutely no idea what to do!"

"What if they don't air this?" Nick couldn't help but ask.

"They owe me a half-million bucks, then." Jazz smirked. "Great agents can get you great deals. Keep watching."

Nick did keep watching. Samantha, clearly at a loss for what to do, began to talk about the newest video from Crash Test Dummies. Finally, Jazz reappeared on the screen, holding the pregnancy test in front of her.

It was bright pink and very positive. And there was more color in the test than there was in Samantha Waring's very famous face, when the camera returned to her for a close-up.

"You want to take one now, Samantha?" Jazz cooed on TV.

Jazz in the office snapped off the television monitor and turned to

Nick, laughing. "Now, that was my idea of a good time. Want to know what her next question was?"

"What?" Nick asked warily.

"Watch later," Jazz answered blithely, tossing the remote control across the room, where it clattered once against the far wall before settling into Jazz's very plush office carpeting. "But I doubt if she's going to question if I'm pregnant again. Or if anyone else will, for that matter. Twit."

Nick looked at his watch and stood up. "I'd better be getting back to Sick—to the tape-transcribing room."

"What's your hurry?" Jazz asked him, stretching herself out, catlike, on the couch. One long, tapered finger touched the jewelry in her exposed navel.

"Just trying to do my job," Nick said, trying to sound casual.

"Good," Jazz said, and she stretched out even farther on her couch. She gave him a feline smile. "You're such a good boy."

A muscle twitched in Nick's jaw.

"So, listen," Jazz continued. "I wanted to talk to you about the Rock of Ages Awards. We're still on for that, right?"

"I told you I'd go with you," Nick said.

She put her hands behind her head. Her tiny top rode up higher under her breasts. "You don't have to make it sound like it's work, you know."

"I'm sure it'll be great," Nick agreed. His hair was loose, and he shook it off his face. "So, I'm outta here—"

"Now, now, Nick, someone might think you were in a hurry to get away from me," Jazz purred.

Nick was silent.

"So, listen," she went on. "The press is going to be all over us at the Rock of Ages Awards. So please be sure to look hot."

"Yeah," Nick mumbled.

"Of course, you always seem to look hot, Nick," Jazz added with a seductive smile. "You just can't seem to help it." She stretched her arms farther over her head. Her T-shirt came dangerously close to exposing the bottom of her breasts, which were quite obviously not encased in a bra.

"There's something else I wanted to mention to you," Jazz said. "Did you know that if you're pregnant, you can still make love for several months?"

"I wasn't aware of that."

"But you are now," Jazz said softly. She sat up. And laughed. "Nick, Nick, Nick. If you could just see yourself right now. You look totally freaked out. Are you freaked out, Nick?"

"I'm just listening."

"Uh-huh," Jazz said knowingly. She stood up and pushed a small, discreetly placed button on the table in front of her.

The shades on the picture window fell smoothly and silently to the floor, and suddenly the room was very, very dark.

Jazz pushed another discreetly placed button, and equally discreet lighting filled the room.

She turned to Nick. "It's kind of... hot in here, isn't it?" Her hands reached for the bottom of her velvet T-shirt.

"Listen, Jazz—" Nick began.

"Shhhh," Jazz interrupted. "There's only one word you need to say now. And that word is... yes."

"You mean to tell me that Jazz got you into her office, and then she—whoa!" Alan exclaimed as the taxicab he and Nick were in jolted to a stop at the traffic light at the busy intersection of Ninth Avenue and Thirty-fourth Street. The trains were out of service due to a break in a water main at Fourteenth Street, so they had treated themselves to a taxi ride.

Nick cringed. "What an ugly way to die, almost."

Nick and Alan were on the way downtown after work to Jimi's, the very hip, no-alcohol club in the East Village where Karma had a second job as a bartender. Karma had promised them that she would try to get Lisha and Chelsea to come to the club, too.

The Pakistani cabdriver, who, as he'd been wending his way downtown, had been jabbering away on a CB radio in a language neither Nick nor Alan understood, turned to the two of them, sticking his face into an opening in the bulletproof Plexiglas that separated driver from riders in most New York City taxis.

"Traffic," the cabdriver said and grinned at them. "Rush hour."

"It's nine-thirty," Alan pointed out. "Rush hour ended three hours ago."

"Rush hour," the driver repeated, as if he'd not heard a word that Alan had said.

"Just drive carefully," Alan instructed him. "We'd like to live to see tomorrow."

"Tomorrow, sure. Drive carefully, sure," the driver agreed, and then slammed his foot on the gas pedal the instant the light turned green.

The cab leaped forward.

"Tomorrow, sure." Nick sighed.

"Time be money," the cabdriver responded, hunched over the wheel. "Money be time, time be money."

"Great." Alan sighed. "This guy is here in America maybe a year, and already he's thinking like a New Yorker. Lucky us."

"This great country," the cabdriver said, overhearing them. "You lucky be born here. I love America!"

Alan slid the Plexiglas shut and returned his attention to Nick, who had just finished telling him exactly what had happened to him in Jazz's office that afternoon. "I can't believe Jazz pulled that on you."

"Believe it," Nick said grimly.

Alan shook his head. "It's like something out of some lame fantasy from one of the callers on Sicko-Central."

"Yeah, except it really happened," Nick said. "To me."

"It's sexual harassment," Alan pointed out.

Nick laughed derisively. "Oh, yeah, right. Thousands of guys would pay millions of dollars to have what happened to me today happen to them."

"Hey, man, she had no right to put you in that position. It's not any less sexual harassment if a woman does it to a man than if a man does it to a woman. You could sue her."

"Sue Jazz? Yeah, right. This is Jazz Stewart we're talking about here. I'd sue her for coming on to me? Half of the country wants her to come on to them, and everyone in the Trash bin thinks she's carrying my baby."

"Is she?" Alan asked softly.

Nick shot him a look. "You, too?"

"Well, you two were an item there for a while—"

"Alan, it's not my baby."

The taxi hit a pothole and the Pakistani driver proved he had learned to curse in English.

"I hope you're telling the truth," Alan said. "Because Chelsea . . ."

"What about Chelsea?" Nick asked, his voice hard.

"I just don't want to see her get hurt," Alan finished.

"You think I do?" Nick asked.

"No," Alan replied. "But maybe you're capable of lying to her to save your butt."

"Thanks, man," Nick said sarcastically.

"Look, I'm sorry," Alan said. "Maybe I'm way out of line. But I don't want to see Chelsea—"

"What?" Nick interrupted. "Why are you so concerned about Chelsea? I thought you and Lisha were tight, man."

"Chelsea is my friend," Alan said quietly.

Nick looked at him in the dark taxi. "Maybe more than a friend?"

For a long moment Alan didn't answer. "I just don't want to see her get hurt," he finally said.

"I don't intend to hurt her."

"Yeah?" Alan asked. "What if she finds out about what happened today with Jazz?"

"That was Jazz's doing, not mine!" Nick protested.

"If you want Chelsea to believe that, maybe you really ought to sue Jazz," Alan suggested.

"Forget it," Nick snapped. "Besides, finally, nothing happened. The phone rang right after the blinds dropped, and it was the president of the network. Even Jazz had to snap to for that one."

Alan gazed out the window. "You should probably tell Chelsea before she hears about it from someone else."

"Like I said, nothing happened."

Alan turned to look at him. "Yeah. You got lucky. But what you have to ask yourself is, what would have happened if the phone hadn't rung?"

Nick was silent. *I can't help it if I'm still attracted to Jazz,* he thought. *She really did look so hot. But I don't even like her. I don't care about her. And I would never have played into her little game.*

Would I?

"Sometimes the truth hurts," Alan said.

"I wouldn't have touched her," Nick finally responded.

"You sure?" Alan asked. "I mean, really, truly sure?"

The silence in the cab was deafening.

"Like I said," Alan continued, his voice low, "you'd better take a really good, long look in the mirror. Because I'm not going to stand by and watch you hurt Chelsea. You can bet on that."

THREE

Chelsea looked down at the note that she'd just hastily scrawled on the back of a take-out menu from the local Hunan Cottage Chinese restaurant, and read it quickly to herself.

> Nick—
>
> When you get back from Jimi's tonight, knock on our door (quietly). No matter what time it is. I need to talk to you. No. I *really* need to talk to you. Please.
>
> —Chelsea

She underlined *really* again, then looked up at the clock on the wall. It was already 10:30 P.M., and she was home alone. Lisha had gone downtown to hang out at Jimi's, as had Nick and Alan.

And I would have gone, too, she thought to herself, *if Bigfoot hadn't ordered me to work overtime transcribing the Sicko-Central tapes.*

Ever since Jazz had announced her pregnancy, the phones had been ringing off the hook. And Roxanne had selected Chelsea to be the one to stay late to transcribe them.

Chelsea stretched and rolled her head around on her stiff neck. *At least the mass-murderer-show meeting was put off until tomorrow,* she thought with a sigh. *But everyone says it's official—it airs a week from then. And they're already promoting the hell out of it.*

Chelsea stood up and walked aimlessly around her living room. Her eyes rested on the bizarre painting on the wall—a woman's legs sticking out of a piano—painted by the son of the owners of the apartment. "Which means that in one week and one day all of this will be over," she said out loud. "I won't have to worry every minute that Bigfoot is going to find out my secret."

I hope.

She wandered back over to the coffee table, picked up the note, and padded across the hall to the guys' apartment. She had knocked on their door fifteen minutes earlier, when she'd arrived, so she knew no one was home yet. Quickly she pushed the note underneath their door.

She'd made up her mind. She had to talk to Nick. And she had to talk to him right away.

The note safely deposited, she came back into the apartment, re-locked the triple locks on the door, and went into her bedroom to change into something more comfortable. She threw on her favorite T-shirt and her oldest, most comfortable jean overalls, then looked at herself in the mirror on her dresser. "Oh, sure," she told herself out loud. "*You* can really compete with Jazz Stewart." Then she stuck her tongue out at herself and went back into the living room, plopping down on the couch as she snapped on the remote control on the TV set.

Jazz Stewart was looking at her. And so was the famous reporter from the music-video channel, Samantha Waring. It was the tape of the interview that Nick had watched with Jazz that same morning, in the comfort of Jazz's office.

"Tell me something I don't know, Jazz," Chelsea said out loud to the TV, feeling anger well up inside her. She watched, her face impassive, as Jazz got up to take her impromptu pregnancy test and came back with the positive results.

"Oh, God," Chelsea said, burying her face in her hands. But then she thought of something. *What if it's just another of Jazz's scams?* she wondered again. *What if she had already hid a positive home pregnancy test behind that curtain?*

"You're getting much, much smarter, you Tennessee hayseed, you," Chelsea murmured to herself.

At that moment there was a tiny, almost imperceptible knocking on her door. Chelsea clicked off the TV and sprang to her feet.

Nick.

"I'm an idiot," she said when she saw him.

He grinned. "Hey, I can't have you talking about you that way."

She pulled him into the living room. "I just watched Jazz's interview with Sammi Waring. Have you seen it yet?"

"Uh, yeah," Nick said. "See, this morning I—"

"Don't you think her whole entire pregnancy could be a big scam?" Chelsea interrupted eagerly. "I mean, it just dawned on me!"

"She's capable of just about anything," Nick agreed. He sat down with Chelsea on the couch and held out the Hunan menu. "I got your note."

Chelsea nodded.

"I was surprised. In a good way," he added hastily.

"Listen, Nick, I'm sorry," Chelsea said fervently. "I've been thinking and thinking all day. I am just so sorry. I mean, it finally occurred to me. Jazz might not even be pregnant at all. Why would I believe her before I believe you?"

Nick sat there quietly.

"Well, aren't you going to say anything?" Chelsea asked.

"I have a feeling that you aren't finished," Nick said.

"I'm not. But I wish you would say something. Are you glad?"

"That you believe me?" Nick asked. "Hell, yeah, I'm glad. I'm only sorry that it took you so long."

"It's just . . . try to look at it from my point of view. It's hard to believe that you could have been going out with her and never had sex with her."

Nick was silent.

"You can understand that, can't you?" Chelsea pressed. "And then there's what everyone at work is saying. Winston, and . . . you know. Everyone."

Nick leaned forward and looked directly into her eyes. "Do you really believe that? Do you really believe the gossip that's going around the Trashcan?"

"I don't know," Chelsea said, feeling completely confused. When she'd written that note and then slipped it under the door, she had intended with all her heart to forgive Nick, to make up, to make it the way it used to be with him.

It wasn't perfect before, Chelsea thought quickly. *He always wasn't as serious about us as I am. Still...*

But now, with Nick sitting across from her in the otherwise empty apartment, all the resentments of the previous week were boiling up inside her.

Chelsea couldn't help it. Tears began to roll down her cheeks.

Nick moved closer and put his arms around her. "Shhhhh," he crooned. "It's okay, Chels. I'm sorry this whole thing has you so upset."

"It's not just that." Chelsea wiped her tears on his T-shirt as she spoke. "It's... a lot of stuff."

"Like what?" Nick asked.

Like that my father is the famous mass murderer from Johnson City, Tennessee, she thought. *Like that I'm the teen kid of that mass murderer that Bigfoot is hell-bent on finding.*

"Just... everything," Chelsea improvised. She swallowed one last sob and turned to him. "I'm sorry—"

"You don't need to apologize."

She smiled through her tears. "Hey, I just realized something."

"What's that?"

"You came over without Belch." Belch was Nick's beloved dog, whom he took everywhere. "That means you really, really wanted to make up with me."

"Belch loves you, too," Nick murmured. He leaned over and softly kissed her lips.

"You really, truly never slept with Jazz?" Chelsea whispered.

Nick pulled away. "Chels..."

"Okay, I'm dropping it," she said quickly. She moved closer to him again and kissed him. He put his arms around her and kissed her back. Softly at first, then harder, until she was lost in the heat of his hands, his lips, his body.

"Whoa." She finally shuddered, pulling away from him.

"God, I missed you, Chels," he muttered huskily, nuzzling his face into her neck.

"Hey, I wonder about something," she said. "What did Jazz want with you this morning?"

He sat up. "Jazz?"

"Yeah," Chelsea said. "You know. When she summoned you."

Nick sighed. "Okay, don't go crazy on me because what I'm about to tell you is the total truth. She showed me the uncut video of her interview with Sammi Waring. And then . . . she put the moves on me."

"I knew it." Chelsea's voice was cold.

"Hey, come on," Nick said. "Didn't Barry Bassinger put the major moves on you?"

"Yes," she replied. "But I never dated Barry Bassinger. I'm not remotely attracted to Barry Bassinger."

"Look, nothing happened, Chels. I mean it."

Chelsea tried to smile. "It's just hard, you know? I mean, once that gossip newspaper printed the story of how Jazz picked you up in a club and then offered you a job at *Trash,* well, everyone is so sure that you two are having this big thing."

"Only we aren't," Nick said firmly. "And I can't spend every day of my life explaining that to you. You just have to believe me. Do you?"

Chelsea looked deep into his eyes.

"I believe you," she finally said. And for the moment at least, she did. With all her heart.

"Good." Nick smiled. He pulled her to her feet. "Hey, you up for some green-tea ice cream? I know a great place—"

"I'll stick to chocolate chip." Chelsea put her arms around his neck. "But you can buy me a double-scoop cone."

"Gee, thanks," Nick said. He pulled her close. "I missed you, Chels," he whispered. Gently he pushed some hair off her face. Then his finger traced the line of her jaw, her neck, her collarbone, right down to the lowest part of the V of her T-shirt.

She shivered with happiness. Her eyes closed. "Nick..." she murmured.

He began to kiss her, and the kisses grew hotter, until finally he scooped her up into his arms and carried her back to the couch, all thoughts of ice cream—green tea or otherwise—completely forgotten.

Chelsea's lips lingered against Nick's.

"I missed that," Nick said softly.

"Mmmmm," Chelsea agreed. "I must taste like ice cream." After kissing for more than an hour in her living room, Lisha had come home and interrupted them, and they had finally gone out for ice cream. They had just returned, and now Chelsea was leaning against the door of her apartment, happier than she had been since she heard about Jazz's pregnancy. "Want to come in?"

Nick nodded.

"A lot," he said.

"We have to get up early for work," Chelsea reminded him, her voice low and sexy.

"Ask me if I care," Nick replied, bringing his lips down on hers.

I love how he kisses me, she thought happily. *I love his lips, the way he smells....*

Chelsea opened the door. And the two of them were met by the sound of someone retching their guts out in the bathroom.

"Karma?" Chelsea called. "Lish?"

Alan hurried into the living room. "Thank God," he said, his face worried. "It's you two."

"Who's sick?" Nick asked.

"Lisha," Alan answered.

"But I saw her right before we went out for ice cream," Chelsea protested. "She didn't say anything about feeling sick."

"You know Lish," Alan said. "She started feeling bad down at Jimi's, so we took a cab back. By the time we got here, she said she felt better. I just knocked on the door about ten minutes ago, to make sure she was okay. Well, she's not."

Chelsea quickly went down the hall and knocked on the bathroom door. "Lish?"

"Lisha died," came back Lisha's groaned retort.

"What can I do for you?" Chelsea called in to her friend.

"Tell me not to eat Indian food for dinner again," Lisha moaned. "Oh, God, I feel so sick." There was the sound of retching again.

Alan and Nick came up beside Chelsea. "You think it's food poisoning?" Chelsea asked, concerned.

"You have Pepto anywhere?" Alan asked her. "'Cause we don't. And I didn't want to leave her here alone."

"We don't have any," Chelsea said with a worried frown. "I could go—"

"You stay," Nick said firmly. "I'll run back over to Broadway and find her some."

"You got money?" Alan asked.

"Enough," Nick answered, and then he was out the door as the sound of more retching came from the bathroom.

"Hang in there, Lish!" Chelsea called in to her friend. She turned to Alan. "Did the two of you eat the same thing for dinner?"

Alan shook his head no. "I went vegetarian. She had some kind of lamb thing."

"Wait here," Chelsea told Alan. She went into the kitchen, took out a cold plastic bottle of club soda. She knocked on the bathroom door. "Can I come in?"

Lisha just moaned.

Chelsea tried the door. It was unlocked.

"Go away," Lisha groaned. She was sitting on the bathroom floor, her head leaning over the bowl.

"Hey," Chelsea said gently.

Lisha looked up. "Never buy Indian food from a street vendor."

Chelsea pushed the bottle at her.

"Don't want to drink it," Lisha said, looking away.

"At least rinse your mouth with it," Chelsea suggested.

Lisha took the cold bottle and held it against her forehead. "If you let Alan in here, I'll never speak to you again. That is, if I live."

"I won't come in!" Alan called.

"Oh great, he heard me," Lisha said. "He'll never want to kiss me again."

"Yes, I will!" Alan called in.

Lisha moaned again. "I love you, Chels, but go away. I don't need you to watch."

"You're going to be fine," Chelsea said to her. "Nick's getting you Pepto-Bismol."

"Thank God," Lisha said fervently.

"Want me to get you a cold washcloth or something?"

"No," Lisha said. "Just go away."

Chelsea smoothed back Lisha's hair and went into the living room, where Alan was waiting.

"She'll live," she reported.

"Didn't sound like it." Alan sounded doubtful.

"Well, you know how that feels," Chelsea said. "Stomach stuff is the worst."

"I wish I could help her," Alan said sincerely. "I'd go in there and hold her head, if she'd let me."

Chelsea smiled at him and sat on the couch. "You're the sweetest guy I've ever known in my life, Alan. Did I ever tell you that?"

"Which is why you love me like a brother," he replied.

"That's right," she agreed. "I do. And I just want you to know, I think Lisha is really, really lucky that she got you."

"'Got me'?" Alan raised his eyebrows.

"You know what I mean," Chelsea explained. "I'm happy for the two of you. It's funny, because I always thought it was going to be Lisha and Sky...."

"And I thought it was going to be Chelsea and Alan," he said, his voice low.

"Alan—"

"I'm sorry," he said quickly. "I shouldn't have said that."

"You and I are friends, Alan—"

"I know." He cocked his head to one side as he spoke. "But can I help it if when I look at you I hear... poetry?"

Chelsea got up and hurried to the window. Anything to avoid Alan's eyes. "Don't do this," she whispered.

He came up behind her. She could hear him, feel his breath on her neck.

She turned around. "Alan, I love Nick."

"Do you?"

"I do," she said firmly. "And even if I didn't, you and Lisha are together. She's one of my best friends in the world. And so are you."

He smiled a crooked smile. "Yeah."

"And I love Nick."

"You already told me that," Alan reminded her.

"Right," Chelsea agreed. She felt flustered. Alan was standing so close to her, she could smell the delicious, musky cologne he was wearing. "So . . . there's nothing to talk about."

The door opened. Nick entered brandishing the Pepto. He threw Chelsea's keys on the couch.

"I'll take it to her," Chelsea offered quickly, stepping around Alan.

She knew Nick had seen how close Alan had been standing to her. And she knew that Nick knew that Alan had once wanted her badly.

She looked over her shoulder. Nick and Alan were staring at each other silently. In a rush, she walked down the hallway. But she still heard what Nick said.

"I guess I got back here in the *nick* of time, so to speak," Nick told Alan.

Chelsea's head was spinning. Once, at the beginning of the summer, she and Alan had kind of dated. But that was before Nick. And she was so sure that what she felt for Alan was nothing more than friendship.

No chemistry, was how she had put it.

No chemistry.

So then why did she feel so flustered by what had just happened?

Why?

FOUR

"I can't believe Her Trashiness herself is going to run this meeting," Karma said to Chelsea.

It was the next morning, and the two of them sat next to one another in Studio C in seats that were usually reserved for the studio audience.

"Bigfoot will get her big feet in the door, I'm sure," Lisha added, from where she was sitting in front of Karma and Chelsea.

Chelsea peered at her friend. "Are you sure you're okay?"

"Yeah," Lisha replied. "Why?"

"You know why," Karma answered. "You were still worshiping at the porcelain throne when I got in last night."

"I guess I got it all out of my system," Lisha said. "I can't believe Alan saw me like that."

"Oh, you know how Alan is," Karma said. "He has the soul of a poet. Even when you're barfing, he sees beauty."

"There's a lot to be said for a guy like that," Chelsea said thoughtfully. She looked at her watch. "It's ten-fifteen and Jazz called this meeting for ten. Maybe it's canceled."

"Wishful thinking," Karma said with a snort.

"Hi, how you feeling?" Sky asked, walking over to Lisha.

"Right as rain, big guy," Lisha answered.

"I heard you were really sick last night." His concern was evident in his eyes.

"I'm fine," Lisha assured him.

Sky grinned. "That I already know, Lish." He took a seat near her.

Chelsea looked from Sky to Lisha, then back to Sky again. *He's still crazy about her,* Chelsea realized. *And I always get the feeling that deep down she's crazy about him, too. So what's she doing with Alan?*

"Hi," Demetrius said, sliding his long, muscular body into the seat next to Karma. "Mmmm, you smell good."

"Flattery will get you everywhere," she told him, grinning.

Jazz had summoned every single person in the *Trash* offices to a 10:00 A.M. special all-staff meeting in Studio C. Topic: "Kids Of Mass Murderers." No one was allowed to miss it. In fact, as Chelsea looked around the studio, the only people she didn't see were Sumtimes and Barry Bassinger, the senior show producer. She knew Nick was doing something backstage to prepare for this presentation.

"Too bad we can't have video rolling at this meeting," Alan whispered to Chelsea as he sat down in a nearby seat.

He was talking about the clandestine activity that the friends were involved in, filming an underground video they planned to call *My TRASHY Summer.* It was going to reveal the seamy side of *Trash,* blowing the lid off the country's most celebrated talk show.

"Too bad is right," Lisha said, her voice low. "We leak this to *Hard Copy,* we get paid a million bucks, we all retire."

"That's less than two hundred thousand each," Karma noted. "Not enough for this girl. Where's Nick?"

"Helping to bring out some equipment for our viewing pleasure," Alan said, overhearing. "I think we're going to get the full treatment from the Queen of Trash herself."

Chelsea glanced up at the clock. Ten-twenty. At that moment Jazz and Roxanne emerged onto the set from the left side as Nick, Winston, and Barry Bassinger's nephew, Brian, pushed an enormous video screen and projector on from the right side. Then they went to stand off to one side.

"Hey, gang," Jazz announced. "How's it going?"

Her entire staff murmured back to her that it was going fine.

"Cool," Jazz said. She wore faded hip-hugger jeans and a white suede vest with nothing under it. Shaking her waist-length blond hair off her face, she continued: "So, here's the deal. I do these meetings like twice a year, for the really big shows only. We got one now. Roxi?"

Bigfoot stood front and center. Today she wore a leopard-print miniskirt, with matching leopard-print material covering her cast.

"This is going to be the *Trash* show of all *Trash* shows," Roxanne told the staff. "In fact, Barry is in Virginia right now, signing papers that will get one guest on, and Sumtimes is doing the same in Texas with another."

"Now, if only Barry would stay there," Karma whispered to Chelsea, who nodded in agreement.

"So here's the show," Roxanne continued. "Today's Wednesday. This show will air next Wednesday." She pushed a remote control she was carrying, and the video screen the guys had pushed onto the stage was automatically illuminated.

Chelsea read the breakdown of the show on the screen.

What she read made her heart skip a beat, and by the time she had finished it, she felt as sick to her stomach as Lisha had felt the night before.

Trash #387

KIDS OF MASS MURDERERS

Air date: next Wednesday

Time (EDT):	**Segment**
3:00–3:01 P.M.	Introduction by Jazz
3:01–3:03 P.M.	Video clips from news broadcasts of famous mass murders
3:03–3:05 P.M.	First commercial break
3:05–3:10 P.M.	Peter Elliot, teen son of man who set fire to social club in Dallas (death toll: 35)
3:10–3:12 P.M.	Second commercial break
3:12–3:22 P.M.	Carl McElroy, Stephan Sloan, Janan Winters, Adasha Miller, all teen children of postal workers who have gone berserk (death toll: 16)
3:22–3:26 P.M.	Third commercial break

Time (EDT):	Segment
3:26–3:34 P.M.	Kurt Lamont, teen son of sniper who went on a rampage in Times Square, New York City, on New Year's Eve (death toll: 11)
3:34–3:38 P.M.	Fourth commercial break
3:38–3:40 P.M.	Win-a-dream-date-with-a-kid-of-a-mass-murderer door-prize segment
3:40–3:42 P.M.	Fifth commercial break
3:42–3:52 P.M.	Chelsea Kettering, daughter of Charles Kettering, Burger Barn shooter, all the way from Australia!
3:52–3:54 P.M.	Final commercial break
3:54–4:00 P.M.	Jazz takes us out; panel discussion

Chelsea felt all the color drain from her face. She thought she was going to faint. Cold sweat broke out on her forehead.

I'm Chelsea Kettering! she thought wildly. *The girl in Australia is just a big hoax Karma set up to throw Bigfoot off my trail. Oh, my God!*

"Chelsea?" Karma squeaked, reaching for her friend's hand. "Are you okay?"

"No," Chelsea managed. "I am not okay."

The staff started talking with each other, making sick jokes about serial murderers and what their teen offspring would be like.

"I think I'm going to be ill," Chelsea said, her hands on her stomach.

"Take deep breaths," Karma advised.

"As you can see, this show is going to be the bomb," Roxanne said loudly, taking control of the room again.

"And we owe a real debt of gratitude to a couple of our interns,"

Jazz added. "Chutney Jennings and Karma Kushner. Guys, c'mon up here. Give it up for them, you guys, they deserve it!"

"She's still calling you Chutney!" Alan said with a laugh. "She still doesn't know your name!"

"I can't do this!" Chelsea hissed to Karma as everyone around them applauded.

"Just stand up and smile," Karma told her, helping her friend to stand.

"Oh, God," Chelsea groaned under her breath. She and Karma both stood up. Karma smiled. Chelsea tried and failed.

"Get your butts up here!" Jazz called to them.

The girls made their way out of their aisle and up onto the set.

"Hey, you guys can do better than that!" Jazz called to her staff, and she led them in more applause.

They complied obediently. They only knew that Jazz had said to give Chelsea—she called her Chutney as she had on TV during the show that had turned into an on-air hostage crisis—and Karma a hand. And if Jazz said to clap, everyone on *Trash* knew that they had to slam their hands against each other until they hurt.

Chelsea saw Nick cast her a quizzical look. She tried to smile, and failed once again.

"Gang," Jazz announced, putting her arm around Karma. "These two interns made it possible for Chelsea Kettering to come onto *Trash*. They tracked her down. In Australia."

"It was Karma, really," Bigfoot said. "Chelsea didn't have much to do with it."

"It was both of them, from what you told me." Jazz glared at Bigfoot momentarily. Roxanne immediately backed down.

Jazz turned to face her staff. "This is going to be the highest-rated

Trash of all time which does not involve an actual felony on the air." Her staff laughed dutifully.

There was nothing Karma and Chelsea could do but smile and act as natural as possible.

But there was absolutely nothing natural about how they were feeling.

Jazz thinks we found the actual Chelsea Kettering, and that Chelsea Kettering is going to appear on her show, all the way from Australia, Chelsea thought, feeling nauseous all over again.

But Chelsea Kettering isn't in Australia.

She's right here.

She's me.

"Okay, calm down," Lisha said to Chelsea, who'd been babbling nonstop for the past ten minutes. "I really suggest that you calm down!"

"How can I calm down?" Chelsea nearly shouted. "My life is completely ruined."

"Mine, too," Karma agreed.

"Your lives are not ruined," Lisha told them. "*Yet*. But if you don't calm down, they will be. So chill, okay?"

Chelsea and Karma nodded agreement, but both of them were extremely agitated. They'd been caught totally by surprise when the lineup for the "Kids of Mass Murderers" show had been announced. They'd thought they'd cleverly led Bigfoot on a wild-goose chase, causing her to think that Kettering's daughter and wife were living in Australia and making it impossible for her to bring anyone associated with the Kettering mass murder onto the show.

But now, evidently, Bigfoot had convinced this alleged Chelsea

Kettering, half a world away in Australia, to come to America to appear on the show.

But how can this be? Chelsea kept asking herself, unable to figure it out. *And what's she going to do when she finds out that the whole thing is a scam perpetrated by this girl, as a result of a scam perpetrated by Karma and me? What if the girl reveals on the air that the whole thing is a scam? Jazz will be humiliated. And she thinks that Karma and I led* Trash *to Kettering's daughter.*

She'll fire us. So fast.

My future in television will be over. So fast.

And then she'll probably find out who I really am. I'll have no career in television, and my life will be ruined. So fast.

The three girls were sitting together at a table at a small outdoor café on Broadway, across from Lincoln Center. Jazz had been in an ebullient mood following the morning meeting about the "Kids of Mass Murderers" show, and had given everyone an hour off for lunch—a rarity in the *Trash* offices, where people usually either skipped lunch or ate at their desks.

Chelsea and Karma had grabbed Lisha, and together they had escaped practically on the run to the café. A waiter had quickly brought Chelsea and Karma coffee and Lisha tea, which was all that Lisha could handle after her abdominal episode of the previous night.

"You have to think about this logically," Lisha suggested. They had explained the whole thing to her, and she figured she was the only one of the three who could think objectively.

"I *have* thought about it," Chelsea said. "The whole thing doesn't make any sense."

"Okay, let's go over this again," Lisha said firmly. "You got some friend of a friend in Australia to pretend she was Chelsea Kettering, right? And this girl spoke with Bigfoot on the phone and said she wouldn't do the show, right?"

"Right," Karma confirmed. "So who the hell is Bigfoot planning to bring on the show?"

Chelsea put her head in her hands. "What if it's that girl in Australia?"

"But that doesn't make any sense!" Karma cried. "She's a friend of my stockbroker's! She's an actress!"

"So?" Chelsea said. "What if somehow Bigfoot talked her into coming here? She's an actress who would get a free trip to New York. She'd get on TV. Maybe you've been double-crossed!"

"What, you mean the girl from Australia would actually show up and pretend to actually be Chelsea Kettering?" Karma asked incredulously.

"Maybe," Chelsea said morosely.

"Or maybe Bigfoot hasn't really found Chelsea Kettering yet at all," Lisha mused. "Maybe she's hoping to find her before the show actually airs."

"Of course she hasn't!" Chelsea exploded, practically knocking her coffee off the small metal table. "I'm Chelsea Kettering!"

"Do you girls want to see the menu?" the cute young waiter asked, brushing his blond hair out of his eyes.

"No, thanks." Lisha smiled at him.

"There's a minimum at these tables," he pointed out.

"Okay, bring me a burger," Lisha decided.

"And fries," Karma added. "A double order. And a double espresso."

"You?" the waiter asked Chelsea.

"Nothing, thanks," Chelsea said.

The waiter hurried off.

"How can you eat now?" she groaned.

"I'm hungry," Lisha said with a shrug.

"And I'm always hungry," Karma said. She drummed her fingernails on the table. "Okay, here's the way I see it. Bigfoot would not have put Chelsea Kettering on the show schedule unless she thought she had the right girl—"

"And unless this so-called right girl had already agreed to come on the show," Lisha added. "I mean, Bigfoot announced right there that she was going to Australia this weekend to meet Chelsea Kettering and to bring her back to New York for the show."

"I'm running away," Chelsea moaned. "I'll go to Africa. No, Asia. No, Australia. They'll never find me in Australia. Ha-ha."

"Let's think this through logically," Karma insisted. "What's the worst that could happen if they put the wrong person on the show?"

"Not much," Lisha said. "*Trash* scams people, people scam *Trash*. And it's all meaningless and disposable. That's Jazz's whole philosophy of life."

"Not this time," Chelsea said darkly. "If Bigfoot finds out that Karma and I led her down the garden path, our butts are out of a job. We're blackballed in television. You can bet on it." She thought a moment. "God, my mother will kill me."

"Jazz would probably fire you, too," Karma told Lisha. "Just for being our bud." She groaned. "Gawd, I just thought of something really awful."

"You mean it gets worse?" Chelsea yelped.

"Well, it could," Karma replied. "You know how Winston found out about our secret hidden Trash-cam? Well, once we get bounced from *Trash,* what's to stop him from going to the *Star* or the *National Enquirer* to tell them what we were up to?"

"He could have done that already," Lisha pointed out.

"Not as long as we all work at *Trash,*" Chelsea said. "He wants you, Lish, so he'd never do anything to tick you off. But if we all got fired . . ." Her voice trailed off.

The three friends were silent. The waiter set their food in front of them and walked away. They just stared at it.

"Suddenly I seem to have lost my appetite," Lisha said.

Chelsea buried her head in her hands again. She hadn't considered the Winston angle. "My life was so much simpler back in Nashville."

"And so much more boring," Lisha commented. She thought a moment. "Okay, we're not going to get outscammed by Bigfoot, you guys. I know you said you tried to call this girl in Australia, Karma—"

"Right before we left the office," Karma said. "Her answering machine said she's on a scuba-diving vacation off the Great Barrier Reef."

"Well, you'll just have to keep trying her," Lisha informed her. "We can't give up."

"I feel sicker than you felt last night," Chelsea told Lisha. "I hate lying and sneaking around. I hate it!"

"So why don't you just skip into Bigfoot's office and tell her the truth, then?" Lisha demanded sarcastically. "Oh, by the way, Bigfoot?" she continued, imitating Chelsea. "I meant to mention that I'm really Chelsea Kettering. Isn't that a hoot?"

Karma gave Lisha a look. "Not funny."

Chelsea thought for a long moment. No, it wasn't funny.

But maybe it wasn't all that crazy, either.

"Y'all," she began slowly, "what if . . . what if I really *did* tell her the truth?"

Her two friends just stared at her.

"Come again?" Lisha finally said.

Chelsea cleared her throat. "I said, I could tell Bigfoot the truth."

"You're kidding," Karma said flatly.

"No, I'm serious," Chelsea insisted, her Tennessee accent getting thicker, as it often did when she was tired or upset. "It would be horrible, the whole world would find out my secret, my mother would kill me, it would ruin my life, but at least it wouldn't ruin y'all's lives. And I wouldn't have to live a big lie anymore."

"You can't do it," Karma protested.

"Don't do it," Lisha said firmly. "The media will eat you alive."

"I guess it *is* a crazy idea," Chelsea admitted. "I mean, I haven't even had the nerve to tell Nick. Maybe I ought to try it out on him before I throw myself at Bigfoot's big feet and plead for mercy."

"And you know she wouldn't show you any," Lisha added.

"I know." Chelsea nodded. "But... I don't know if I can go on like this. And I'd rather tell her the truth in person and right away than have her find out when she goes to pick up this girl in Australia this weekend."

Karma reached for Chelsea's hand. "You realize it would change your life. I mean, like, forever."

"Forever," Lisha echoed.

"I know," Chelsea acknowledged. "But maybe I should do it anyway."

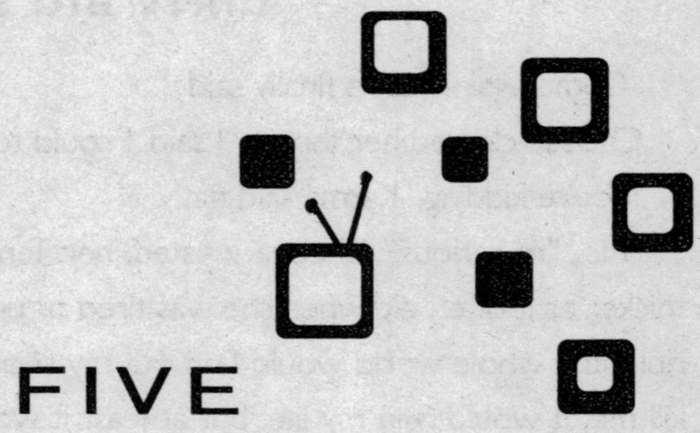

FIVE

Demetrius's warm voice poured out of the studio speakers and, through the wonder of broadcast television, into family rooms, summer-session college dorm rooms, manicure and beauty shops, restaurants, and countless other locales all over North America and the world.

"Let's give a warm welcome to our six summer interns! *Trash* interns, c'mon out here and meet today's studio audience!"

The *Trash* studio audience went berserk as Karma, Lisha, Chelsea, Alan, Sky, and Nick walked out from the wings onto the *Trash* set. Jazz stood to greet them, and motioned them over to the long couch that was usually reserved for her special guests. She lifted one of the inflatable-doll people who lounged on the couch and threw it toward a stagehand. Then she motioned for the interns to sit down next to her.

I can't believe Jazz asked all of us to be on the show, Chelsea thought as she nervously adjusted the neckline of her T-shirt. Over it she wore a short denim jumper. Lisha wore black flared pants and a black poorboy-style sleeveless sweater. And Karma, always the style queen, had on pink polyester hot pants from a thrift store, high-heeled thigh-high boots, and an orange, yellow, green, and pink Stella McCartney top.

As Chelsea took a seat on the couch she glanced over at Nick, who had just sat down in one of the canvas director's chairs. Nick grinned at her, then he gave the audience a quick thumbs-up, to which they responded with cheers. Some girls in the audience stood up and yelled out his name.

They know who he is because of that article in Star *magazine,* Chelsea realized. JAZZ'S HOT DATE GETS HOT SUMMER JOB AT *TRASH,* the headline had read. The tabloid had come out two weeks earlier, but the innuendos about Nick and Jazz would not quit.

It was the next day, Thursday, and with no warning, all six interns had been summoned down to the studio in order to be a part of the show.

"But why?" Chelsea had blurted out, scared to death that it all had something to do with the Chelsea Kettering fiasco. "What did we do wrong?"

Sumtimes, who had informed them of the summcns, had given her a weird look. "Uh, Chelsea, it's not exactly a punishment to be on national TV."

"Right," Karma had said quickly. "Chelsea knows that. She was... joking. Yeah, that's it. What a jokester!"

Shrugging, Sumtimes had then proceeded to usher all the interns down to the studio, explaining along the way just what would happen.

"Here's the deal," Sumtimes said as they hurried down the hall. "Jazz is going to pick one person out of this studio audience to be 'Intern for a Day.' This lucky person will come to *Trash* tomorrow and have their day captured on videotape. And then, this person will be featured on the show, and Jazz will show the tape. Pretty cool, huh?"

"So, does this lucky person get to clean up after Jazz's dogs like we do?" Alan asked archly.

Sumtimes had the good grace to laugh. "I doubt it."

And now here we are, Chelsea thought, trying not to squint under the bright lights. *Live. On* Trash. *Whoopee.*

"So, these are my interns," Jazz now said, when all six of them were seated on the set. She turned to her audience. "You have to admit, I picked some hot-looking interns." She flashed a smile, then turned back to the group of six. "So," she said to Karma, "how does it feel to be an intern?"

"It feels a lot better than working in my parents' health-food store," Karma said, her voice its characteristic Long Island nasal whine, "which is what I did last summer. All I can say is, tofu sucks."

The audience cheered.

"How about you, Chutney?" Jazz asked as a boom mike swung across the set toward Chelsea. "You've had quite the summer here at *Trash.*"

Quite the summer is right, Chelsea thought fearfully. *A summer that could be over in about a week.*

"Gang, how many of you watched the show where Chutney here was a hero?"

The audience went crazy. They'd all seen it. In fact, most of the world had seen it, either live or on videotape. The snap ratings for that particular day's *Trash* had beaten the O. J. Simpson verdict.

"That's our Chutney," Jazz said proudly. "So, Chutney, how would you describe your summer here so far?"

Chelsea smiled as courageously as she could. "It's been . . . fun," she began. "And a lot of work."

"A lot of work," Jazz repeated thoughtfully. "You know, you might think we were making you guys just slave away here."

"Oh, no," Karma said brightly. "It's great!"

"We're learning a lot," Alan answered.

"Really?" Jazz asked, wide-eyed. "Like, what have you learned?"

"About how TV really works," Sky said. "It's a complicated business."

"Yeah, it is," Jazz agreed. She looked at Chelsea. "And I guess you learned how great it is to work with someone as brilliant as Roxanne Renault, huh?" She turned to the studio audience. "Roxanne is my ace producer. She and Chutney have gotten really close." She turned back to Chelsea. "Roxi tells me she's become kind of a special mentor to you, right?"

She hates my guts, Chelsea thought. *And you know it.*

"I work with her a lot," Chelsea managed.

"Cool," Jazz said. She looked over at Nick. "So, Nick," she purred. "You and I have . . . a special relationship. Wouldn't you say?"

"I do what all the other interns do," Nick said, his voice flat.

"Oh, right," Jazz said, a laugh in her voice, "and much, much more!"

The audience hooted their approval.

"So, you guys, how would you describe your jobs—no-brainers, or pretty demanding?"

"Pretty demanding," all the interns answered at once.

"A breeze, or a challenge?"

"A challenge."

"A lot of work, or a picnic?"

"A lot of work," they all said.

"Part-time hours or long hours?"

What is she getting at? Chelsea thought. *I honestly don't know.*

"Long hours."

"Long lunch breaks, yes or no? Be honest!"

"No," they all said.

Jazz turned to the studio audience. "Okay, gang," she said, "you see what our interns go through. They say this is a tough job. That it's a job that makes them think, which is no picnic at all. Maybe it is that way. And maybe it's not. Who of you want to do it with them?"

Every single person in the audience jumped to their feet, waving their arms wildly.

They'd been cued to do this, Chelsea thought as she sat under the uncomfortable glare of the bright studio lights. *But I bet it looks great on TV.*

"Demetrius," Jazz instructed, "pick me six. Three girls, three guys."

Demetrius waded into the audience and quickly chose six people, all of them good-looking and photogenic. He sent each of them up to the stage, where they formed a line by Jazz.

"Okay, you potential Interns for a Day, are you ready to go through the rigorous *Trash* screening process?"

The six people selected all nodded.

"I *guarantee,*" Jazz said, "that this is *exactly* the same way we picked the six hardworking young men and women whom you see before you."

The six potential interns for a day looked eager and hopeful, as if they couldn't believe their good fortune to be on stage with Jazz Stewart, possibly about to be chosen as Intern for a Day on live TV.

"You guys ready?"

They all nodded enthusiastically.

Demetrius rolled something onto the set. It was a larger-than-life-size cardboard cutout of Jazz herself.

Nude. From the back.

"Poetry in cardboard, huh, gang?" Jazz commented.

The audience cheered and whooped again. Some guy yelled out, "I love you, Jazz!"

"I love you, too," Jazz replied. "I want to have your baby."

This sent the audience—who all knew that Jazz was pregnant—into gales of laughter.

Demetrius handed Jazz a paper bag. She reached into it and took out a small paper bikini bottom that would fit perfectly over the cardboard likeness of her bottom. Then Demetrius handed her a blindfold.

"Okay," Jazz said, "Time for you trashy potential interns to go through the same rigorous selection process as our real interns. Let's play pin the tail on me. The one who comes closest to getting these bottoms in the right place is our pick for Intern for a Day!"

"On you or on the cardboard you?" one guy asked. "Because I'd rather pin it on the real you!"

The audience exploded, screaming and yelling their approval.

"Hmmmmm," Jazz mused. "You might just be *Trash* material! We're going for the cardboard me today."

All six of the lucky audience members were blindfolded, spun around until they were dizzy, and then each had the chance to pin the bikini bottom on Jazz's cardboard form.

Five minutes later they had a winner. Her name was Brianna Burnett, though she told Jazz to call her Breezy. She was eighteen, tall, redheaded, and from Minnesota, and she was visiting her cousin in New York for the week.

"So, Breezy, you psyched?" Jazz asked, putting the microphone in the girl's face.

"I can't even believe it!" the girl yelled. "It's the greatest thing that ever happened to me!"

"Yeah, lucky you," Jazz said laconically. "I'm sure the other interns will be really nice to you tomorrow." She gave Nick a smoldering look. "Especially Nick. And I know how really, really *nice* he can be."

"Nick, mon, Jazz wants to see you," Winston said, sticking his head into Nick's cubicle.

Nick looked up from the 1960s back issues of the *National Enquirer* he'd been assigned to peruse in search of story ideas for the show.

"Doesn't she ever use the intercom?" he asked.

"Not with you, mon, evidently," Winston said. "I'm heading to the travel agent to get Roxi's tickets for the weekend. I think she wants you to chaperon Breezy tomorrow. Breezy. Can you imagine? Naming yourself after a weather report?"

Nick looked at his watch. It was almost 6:00 P.M.

Long day, long day, he thought. *Now she wants me to escort this girl around here all day tomorrow. Chelsea's going to love that idea, I'm sure.*

"Hey, Nick, let me ask you a question." Winston leaned against the door to Nick's cubicle.

"Shoot."

"What's it take to get next to Luscious Lisha? I've used all me tricks and I'm getting nowhere fast."

"Got me, man." Nick shrugged. "I think she's got a thing going on with Alan."

"Just my luck." Winston sighed.

"Hang in there," Nick suggested. "You never know when the girl will change her mind." He got up and walked down to the end of the corridor, to Jazz's office.

He walked right in.

This time, Jazz wasn't on the couch waiting for him.

She was wearing a silver leotard with the middle cut out, and she was lying on the floor, doing leg lifts.

"Oh, don't mind me," she said to him as he came in. "I'm just doing some stretching. The doctor says it's good for me to be limber. Sit down," she instructed him, motioning to the floor next to her.

"I'll use the couch," Nick said, sitting down.

"You don't seem able to follow instructions very well," Jazz observed, not missing a count on her leg lifts.

"Look, is there a reason that I'm here?" Nick finally said.

"Aren't we touchy," Jazz replied. She sat up and stretched, catlike, then gracefully rose to her feet and went to the couch, where she sat down next to him.

"So, you guys ready for Breezy and Intern for a Day tomorrow?" Jazz asked.

"Sure. It should be . . . fun," Nick said noncommittally.

"Could be," Jazz agreed. She smiled at him. "Do you think I have that special glow that pregnant women are supposed to get, Nick?"

"You look great," he admitted. "How do you feel?"

"Morning sickness, that kind of thing, you mean?" Jazz asked.

"That's what I mean," Nick answered.

"The funny thing is," she confided, "it changes every day. Some days, I feel like I'm pregnant. Others, I feel like I'm not pregnant at all."

"Well, maybe that's because you aren't," he said carefully.

"Aren't?"

"Aren't really pregnant," Nick said.

Jazz gave him a wide-eyed look. "Now, would I pull a scam like that?"

"In a word, yes."

She laughed. "Oh, you know me so well."

"So, is it a scam?" he asked.

"I never said that." She cocked her head at him. "I have a feeling you don't really think I'm pregnant, do you?"

"You just said yourself that—"

"I'm asking what you think." Her voice was low and serious. "I happen to care what you think."

Games, Nick thought. *Jazz plays all these games. There is no right answer here.*

He got up. "Look, Jazz, if that's what you called me in here for, then I'd better get back to work."

"Sit down, Nick."

"No, thanks," Nick said. "Look, fire me if you want to, but you can't keep summoning me in here and playing these little mind games with me, Jazz. The gig doesn't mean enough for me to put up with it!"

She walked over to him and looked up into his eyes. "I'm sorry."

He looked down at her. "You actually sound sincere."

"I am. Please. Sit down. I really do want to talk to you. No games."

Nick sat. So did Jazz.

"You think I've made the whole thing up, that it would be just like me to make the whole thing up, and I'm having a great time making the whole thing up," she said. "Well, it isn't like that."

"No?"

Jazz went to her desk, reached into a drawer and pulled something out. It was a half-eaten box of Saltines. Then she pulled out a catalog for Babies "R" Us.

"This is real," she said, her voice low.

"Those could be props," Nick pointed out.

"But they're not. I get really queasy in the mornings. My breasts hurt all the time. I crave ice cream. Nick, I'm pregnant."

God, she really seems sincere, Nick thought. *So maybe it's true. I can't imagine her as a mother. But then I couldn't imagine Madonna as a mother, either.*

"Well, if it's what you want, then I'm happy for you," he finally said.

"Thank you," Jazz replied. "And about the morning-sickness thing. Please don't tell the staff. They think I'm impervious."

"Okay," he said.

Jazz came over to sit next to him again. "I suppose like everyone else in the world you'd like to know who the father is."

"I admit I'm curious."

"You know the rumor in the office is that you're the dad," Jazz said.

"Dumb rumor." Nick's tone was dismissive. "You and I know that isn't true."

"Well, I'm a celebrity," Jazz went on, "and we were a hot little item there for a while, weren't we?"

"We dated," Nick allowed.

"Dated . . ." Jazz mused. "What a quaint way to put it. Dated." She moved close to him. "Remember that time in the back of my limo?"

I couldn't stop kissing her, Nick remembered. *She was so wild. But we stopped before we even got our clothes off, and went into some trendy downtown club. And then not long after that, I really fell for Chelsea. Chelsea is twice the woman that Jazz will ever be....*

"Nothing happened," he said, his voice flat.

"Is that how you remember it?" Jazz asked. "That's not how I remember it."

"Come on, Jazz," Nick said. "We messed around, went to a club, we never—"

"I didn't realize I was that forgettable," she interrupted.

"What are you talking about?"

"That night," Jazz said. "We were so hot in the limo. We went to the club and danced for hours. You had a bad cold, remember?"

"Yeah," Nick recalled.

"And you were taking some kind of flu medicine that made you really groggy. You had a few beers. I don't think the two mixed very well."

"I woke up the next morning on your couch," Nick remembered.

"Right," Jazz agreed. "But what do you think happened between the beers and the time you passed out?"

Nick's heart hammered in his chest. "Nothing happened. If I was so wasted from the cold medicine and the beers that I passed out, nothing *could* have happened—"

"That's not the way I remember it," Jazz told him. "You know, if a guy is turned on enough, then he can... well, all I can say is, I had a wonderful time that night."

All the color drained from Nick's face. "Are you trying to tell me that we had sex and I just don't remember?"

"It's okay," Jazz said soothingly. "I remember well enough for both of us. And it was great, Nick. Really great."

The silence in Jazz's office was deafening.

"This is just another one of your scams," he finally said.

"Wrong," she replied serenely. "I'm only sorry you don't remember what a fantastic evening it was." She patted her still-flat stomach. "I only have one question."

Nick gulped hard. "What's that?"

"If it's a boy, do you think we should name the baby Nick Junior?"

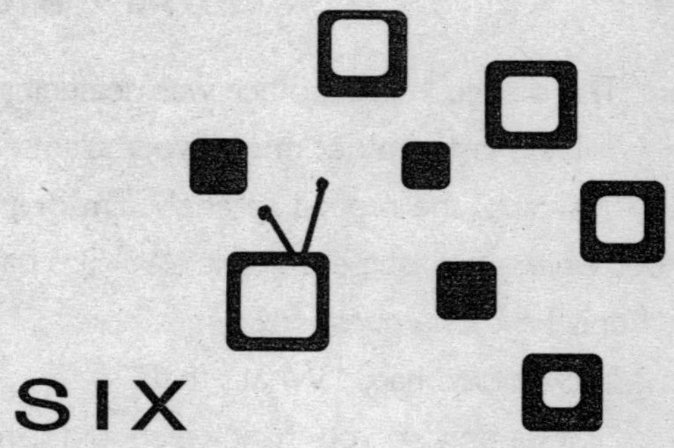

SIX

"I just can't believe this is really happening to me!" Breezy cried as Chelsea escorted her toward the *Trash* lounge the next morning. "I keep thinking I'll wake up and this will all have been a dream!"

"It's really happening," Chelsea assured her. "You got lucky."

"I'll say," Breezy agreed. "So, when do the cameras start to follow us?"

"Sumtimes told me they'd be in the lounge when we get there," Chelsea explained as they rounded the corner.

"Do I look okay?" Breezy asked nervously.

"Darling," Chelsea said honestly.

Jazz's personal makeup artist had done Breezy's makeup, and a wardrobe consultant had picked out a really cute hot-pink minidress for her to wear. Her hair had been styled by a top stylist, and all in all, she looked fabulous.

"You don't know how lucky you are to really work here," Breezy said fervently.

You don't know the half of it, Chelsea thought, but she kept her mouth shut.

"So listen," she began, "our lounge is always a little grungy. A lot grungy, actually. So don't be surprised that it isn't some grand—"

Chelsea's jaw hung open. They had just entered the lounge. At least it was *supposed* to be the lounge. But it bore no resemblance to the filthy, tacky room with the burned sludge that passed for coffee where Chelsea and her buds usually hung out.

In the middle of the room was a long table, which was covered with a breakfast buffet spread of muffins, bagels, various cheeses, smoked salmon, and four different kinds of exotic fruit juice. Three different coffeemakers were labeled regular, decaf, and espresso.

And the room was spotlessly clean.

"Wow, this is great!" Breezy exclaimed.

"Breezy, hi!" Sumtimes said, hurrying into the room. A young woman wielding an expensive video camera came in after her.

"Just act naturally," Sumtimes instructed Breezy. "We want to get your really natural reactions all day. Please, help yourself to breakfast."

"Thanks," Breezy said.

"Oh, you, too, Chelsea," Sumtimes added.

The room filled up with the other interns, and various other staff people, who filled their plates with food.

"Do you believe this?" Sky whispered to Chelsea.

"No," she replied. "I can't even believe this is the same hideous lounge."

Chelsea took a seat next to Nick. Breezy was on his other side, eating a bagel and chatting with Karma.

"I called you last night," she told him. "You weren't home."

"Yeah," Nick said, sipping his coffee. "I was . . . out."

"Oh," Chelsea said. She took a bite of a chocolate-chip muffin. "So, you want to do something tonight?"

"I'm busy," Nick said.

He sounds like he's mad at me, Chelsea thought. *But why would that be?*

"Listen, are you okay?" she finally asked him.

"Yeah, fine." He sipped his coffee.

"You say it but you don't mean it," Chelsea accused.

"It's nothing," Nick said. "I've just got something on my mind."

"Maybe I can help," she offered.

"Forget it," he snapped. He turned to Breezy. "So, Breezy, as you can see, we interns get treated to a delicious and lavish breakfast every morning."

"It's so cool!" the Intern for a Day exclaimed.

Chelsea took a sip of juice and tried to hide her hurt. *Why is he treating me like I did something terrible?* she wondered. And then a horrible thought occurred to her. *Oh, God, what if he found out the truth about me? What if he found out I lied to him. He'll never, ever trust me again.*

That has to be it.

She put her hand on his shoulder. "Nick, listen, I—"

"Time to go to work!" Sumtimes called from the doorway. "Interns, you'll all be in Studio C, practicing your onstage mike technique."

"Our *what?*" Lisha asked incredulously.

"Onstage technique with a microphone," Sumtimes explained.

"You know. How we're training you so that someday you can all have your own shows. And then we'll work on your on-camera technique."

Karma stifled a laugh. "Oh, yeah, Sumtimes. I *love* it when we do that!"

"I'm ready!" Breezy said eagerly, getting up from the table.

Nick got up, too.

"Nick," Chelsea said. "I'd really like to talk to you about—"

"I can't talk now," he said quickly. "I promised Jazz I'd show Breezy around today."

"When can we talk, then?" Chelsea pressed.

"Soon," he said vaguely, then hurried after Breezy, who was already at the door.

Chelsea just stood there, rooted to the spot. "He knows," she told Karma.

"Who knows what?" Karma stuffed the last bite of a bagel with cream cheese and smoked salmon into her mouth.

"Nick knows the truth about me," Chelsea explained. "I can tell."

"Get outta here," Karma scoffed, taking a long sip of her espresso. "No way does he know."

"He knows," Chelsea insisted.

"Girlfriend, you are being mighty paranoid," Karma said. "Come on. Let's go have a typical day in the life of a *Trash* intern. It should be amusing."

"... so then I had to go to the prom with the other guy," Breezy was saying. "You know, because I had already promised him before the guy I really liked got around to asking me. Isn't that wild?"

"Wild," Lisha agreed.

The three female interns were sitting outdoors with Breezy at a hip restaurant on Broadway called Max. They had been given an hour and a half for lunch. And *Trash* was footing the bill.

"This is just so incredible," Breezy marveled as she bit into her Swiss cheeseburger. "I can't believe you guys get to live like this every day."

"Neither can we," Lisha muttered.

Breezy sipped her third Coke. "So, what's up for this afternoon?"

"We're doing an interview with Tabitha Shaynheart," Karma reported.

Breezy's jaw hung open. "Tabitha Shaynheart? The girl who got the lead in the new movie with Josh Hartnett? The one who's dating Tobey Maguire?"

"That's her," Lisha said.

"Unreal." Breezy shook her head. "Being a *Trash* intern is, like, the greatest job in America! And Jazz and Roxi and everyone there is just so nice, don't you think?"

"Super nice," Karma agreed.

"I need to run to the ladies'," Breezy said. "Excuse me. Oh, can we order dessert?"

"Sure," Chelsea told her. "It's on *Trash*."

"Cool!" Breezy disappeared into the restaurant.

"What a joke." Lisha frowned in disgust. "Like we've ever had a day like this before at the Trash-can."

"No scooping up Jazz's monster dogs' poop," Karma said, ticking it off on her fingers. "No picking up Jazz's laundry, or Barry's special coffee beans, or listening to the calls from Sicko-Central—"

"No rubber bands being snapped at us," Chelsea added, recalling the time that Bigfoot had actually shot a rubberband at her.

"Have you tried calling Australia again?" Lisha asked Karma.

"Only every half hour," Karma replied. "I just get the same recording."

"Bigfoot is supposed to fly to Australia early Saturday morning," Lisha said, shaking her head. "I wish I knew what was really going on."

"Well, I know this much," Chelsea said. "I can't go on like this. I still think I should just tell Bigfoot and Jazz the truth."

"I'm telling you, Chels, it's not a good idea," Lisha insisted.

Chelsea fiddled with the paper from her straw. "But don't you see, Lish? All my life I've had to live this lie! It's like... like some huge weight on my back, all the time. Always worrying, always wondering if someone is going to find out the truth. I'm just... I'm so sick of it!"

"I understand," Lisha said sympathetically.

"You don't—"

"I do," Lisha insisted. "It's not like I didn't have plenty of secrets of my own, remember? About Harley? And what happened in Europe?"

"So, don't you feel better now that we know the truth?" Chelsea pointed out.

"Yeah, I do," Lisha admitted.

"But, Chelsea, there would be a lot more fallout if you tell the truth," Karma told her. "You'd be even more of a celebrity than you already are. If you want to live some kind of normal life, telling the truth isn't going to get you what you want."

"Telling the truth about what?" Breezy asked, coming over to the table.

"About her recent sex-change operation," Lisha deadpanned. "You really can't tell that she was recently a guy, can you?"

Breezy laughed. "Hey, you guys work for *Trash*! Anything is possible! Now, who's going to have dessert with me?"

Chelsea knocked on the door of Nick's apartment. She looked at her watch. It was after ten o'clock. She had been knocking every fifteen minutes for the past two hours. No answer. She knocked again, louder, and waited, hoping that he was home. She couldn't stop thinking about how weird he had been acting all day, and she felt that she just had to talk with him.

Alan opened the door. "Nice surprise," he said with a smile. "Come on in. I just got home. I went to the Truffaut retrospective at the Angelika film center. Lisha said she was too tired to go. It was great."

"I was looking for Nick, actually," Chelsea admitted, walking into the living room.

"He went to the Usher concert with Breezy," Alan explained.

When the interns had returned from lunch, they all found tickets to the concert in their inboxes. It turned out that only two of the tickets were real—the others were dummy tickets. Sumtimes took them aside and told them later. "Sorry, you guys, but two front-row seats were all I could scrounge up last minute. And Jazz didn't want Breezy to think that we'd give you guys crap seats."

"So, what you're telling me is that Jazz forced Nick to take Breezy to the concert?" Chelsea asked Alan.

"Something like that," Alan acknowledged. "Only I guess 'forced' is too strong of a word. You want some coffee? A Coke?"

"A Coke, I guess," Chelsea said, sitting on the couch. "Listen, did Nick say anything about me today?"

"No, why?" Alan asked, getting her a Coke from the fridge.

"Nothing." She stared out the window.

Alan handed her the Coke and sat down. "So, how about that Intern for a Day scam, huh?"

"Amazing," Chelsea agreed. "Breezy was nice, though."

Alan stared at her. "What's wrong, Chels?"

"Nothing."

"Hey, this is Alan you're talking to. I know you too well to fall for that."

"Nothing is wrong," Chelsea insisted, but she wouldn't meet his gaze.

Gently, Alan took her chin and turned her face to him. "What?"

"It's... I can't tell you," she blurted out.

"How come?"

"Because... because you'd hate me!"

Alan's eyes searched hers. "Don't you know how I feel about you by now, Chels? I could never hate you."

I want to tell him so badly, Chelsea thought. *It would be easier than telling Nick. Less risky. Alan would understand.*

"Alan, I... there's something you don't know about me," she began slowly.

"I'm listening." He smiled encouragingly.

"Something bad," Chelsea went on. She gulped hard. "It's... it's about my family. About my father, really. I... God, this is so hard."

"Chels, whatever it is, you can tell me," Alan said. "Believe me, I know all about messed-up families. My macho dad thinks I'm a sissy because I like poetry instead of football, remember? Besides, nothing you could tell me would make me think less of you. I promise." He reached for her hand.

"Well, you know how Bigfoot is planning that big show on teen kids of mass murderers?" Chelsea began.

Alan nodded.

"I . . . I kind of have a connection to that show. In fact, I—"

At that moment the door opened, and Sky came barreling into the apartment. A cute girl with long brown hair was with him. "So, this is the humble abode," Sky announced. "Guys, this is my friend Claire. Claire, that's Alan and Chelsea. She lives across the hall."

"I was just leaving," Chelsea said, getting up quickly.

"You don't have to go," Sky protested. "We can put on some tunes, pop some popcorn. Claire's a PA on that new Josh Hartnett movie, and she was just telling me this amazing story about Tabitha Shaynheart."

"I really do have to go," Chelsea insisted.

"I'll come with you," Alan offered.

"No, no, that's okay, I'm kind of tired," Chelsea said. "Nice to meet you, Claire."

She fled from the apartment and hurried into her own, closing and triple-locking the door behind her.

I can't believe I almost told Alan the truth, she thought, her back pressed against the door.

"Chels? What's up?" Lisha was standing there in a T-shirt and panties, carrying a box of cookies.

"I can't believe it," Chelsea told her. "I almost just blurted out the truth to Alan."

"Alan is a really understanding guy," Lisha responded.

"But I haven't even told Nick!" Chelsea cried. "Why would I tell Alan before I tell Nick?"

"Maybe you're closer to Alan than you think," Lisha said.

"I love him like a brother, Lish," Chelsea said. "You know that."

"Do I?"

"Of course you do," Chelsea declared.

"And I suppose he loves you like a brother, too."

"Lish, come on. You and Alan are a couple. I would never—"

"I know you wouldn't," Lisha said. "Forget I even said anything." She held out the bag of cookies. "Cookie?"

Chelsea took one and bit into it. "Tomorrow is my last chance to tell Bigfoot the truth before she leaves for Australia."

"Well, maybe Karma reached that girl in Australia from Jimi's tonight. Don't give up hope."

"Karma would have called us by now," Chelsea said. Suddenly the cookie tasted like sawdust. "I have to tell her, Lish."

"You sure?"

"No," Chelsea replied. "I'm not sure about anything."

"Well, see how you feel in the morning, then, okay?"

"Okay," Chelsea agreed. "But I have a feeling I'm not going to sleep at all tonight."

"Might as well sleep," Lisha said, reaching for another cookie. "It might be your very last night of privacy before your face is plastered on the cover of every sleazy tabloid in America. Not to mention every trash TV talk show that isn't *Trash.* Not to mention being the focus of the Howard Stern radio show for about three weeks. Is that what you want?"

"Of course it isn't," Chelsea said miserably. "What I want to do is to run away."

"Well, don't." Lisha gave her a quick hug. "Whatever you decide, you know Karma and I are with you, right?"

"Right," Chelsea agreed.

But as she padded down the hall to her room, she realized that she had never felt quite so alone in her entire life.

SEVEN

Chelsea gave a quick wave to Antoine the doorman as she walked by his post in the lobby of her building, took another quick look outside to verify that the day's predicted rain showers had not yet materialized, and then walked through her building's revolving door onto West End Avenue.

It was early Friday morning, and the rush-hour traffic on West End Avenue was intense, as was the pedestrian traffic on the sidewalk. Everyone seemed to be rushing somewhere—to buy The New York Times, *to find a taxicab, to catch the subway, to get to work.*

Chelsea turned left out of her building—Karma and Lisha had already left for work, which was why she was alone—and started to walk the few short blocks to the Trash offices, just as a few raindrops began to fall from the sky.

She reached into her backpack and took out one of the cheap black umbrellas that street vendors sold on the street corners, and struggled to get it open. At that moment a teen guy she didn't know came abreast of her.

"Chelsea?" he asked.

Chelsea got the umbrella open, smiled politely, and walked away. She felt rude not speaking—her mother had raised her to be polite at all times. But ever since she'd been involved in the Sela Flynn affair, strangers sometimes recognized her on the street, and she really hated it.

I never even dreamed about being an on-air personality, she thought. I've always been a more behind-the-scenes kind of girl. I hate being recognized on the street.

"Chelsea!" the guy called out. "Hey, Chelsea!"

He's following me, she realized. She walked a little faster.

"Hey, I don't mean to bother you!" he called. "I'm from Tennessee, too! Can I just have your autograph?"

If I sign an autograph for him, he'll go away. Besides, it will only take a second. And he's from Tennessee, Chelsea thought, her native Southern politeness piercing her tough-girl adopted-New-Yorker exterior for just a moment.

She turned and smiled at the guy, who was dressed nondescriptly in jeans and a T-shirt, and who wore a lightweight army-fatigue jacket over the shirt.

"Thanks for stopping," the guy said earnestly. "Say, you're even prettier than your pictures!" He handed her a notebook to sign.

"Thanks." Chelsea pulled a pen from her purse. "What do you want me to say and who do you want me to sign it to?"

The guy smiled at her. "Just sign it 'in memory of your father,' " the guy said.

"That's a strange thing to want," Chelsea commented as she began to write.

"No, it isn't," the guy said as Chelsea wrote what he had instructed and then signed her name. She handed the notebook back to him.

He stared at her with admiration. "You're really something, you know that?"

"Thanks," Chelsea said. "Well, it was nice—"

"I mean, you didn't have to stop and talk to me, but you did. You're not stuck-up at all. No, sir." His Tennessee twang was thick and melodious.

"Well, have a nice day." Chelsea began to put her pen back in her purse.

"Dang," the young man said, looking down at Chelsea's signature, "my daddy would be right proud."

"How did you lose your dad?" Chelsea asked, her voice sympathetic. "Has it been a long time?"

The teen guy smiled at Chelsea. "Oh, it's been about sixteen or seventeen years now."

Like my dad, Chelsea thought.

"I'm sorry," she said.

"Not as sorry as I am," the guy replied. "You see, Charles Kettering—your father—killed my father, when I was just a little, bitty kid. And now it's payback time!"

The guy pulled a revolver out from his fatigue jacket, pointed it at Chelsea, and squeezed the trigger.

Chelsea screamed.

The sound of her own scream woke Chelsea up.

She was bathed in sweat, trembling with fear and horror.

"Chels?" Karma was standing in her doorway. "I heard you scream or something."

"I had a nightmare," Chelsea confessed.

"You want hot chocolate?" Karma offered sleepily.

In spite of the fact that she was still shaking, Chelsea managed to smile. "You are going to make a terrific mother one day."

"Gawd forbid." Karma grimaced. "Well, at least not for a really, really long time. Can you sleep now?"

"I don't know."

"You want to talk about your dream?"

"No," Chelsea said. "I'm okay. Go back to sleep."

"Night." Karma yawned. "Try counting designer sweaters on sale. It always helps me fall right to sleep."

Chelsea lay back down. But she knew that counting designer sweaters wasn't going to help her.

She was afraid to close her eyes.

Chelsea knocked on the door of the guys' apartment, still groggy and shaky from both lack of sleep and the dream she'd had the night before.

It seemed so real, she thought. *What's going to happen when the kids of all those people my father killed find out who I am? What if they really do blame me?*

They can't blame you if they never find out who you are, a voice in her head told her. *Why rock the boat?*

"Because I can't go on living a lie," she said out loud, and knocked on the door again.

I'm going to tell Roxanne the truth, she resolved. *I have to. And I have to tell Nick before I go and tell Roxanne. For all I know, someone already told him. I have to find out if he knows. And if he doesn't know, I have to tell him before he hears about it from someone else.*

Chelsea knocked on the guys' door again.

Alan answered.

He was clad only in a short towel wrapped around his waist, and the lower half of his face was covered with shaving cream.

"Hi," he said with a grin. "You've caught me at my very best."

"Hey," Chelsea answered. "Can I come in for a minute? I need to talk to Nick."

An odd look clouded Alan's face, or as much of it as Chelsea could see. "What's wrong?" she asked.

"Uh . . . he's not exactly . . . here," Alan said.

"Not here?" Chelsea echoed. "You mean he went to *Trash* early? Karma and Lisha got called in to do some file-footage stuff for a show and—"

"I mean not here as in never came home last night," Alan explained reluctantly.

Chelsea was stunned. "You're kidding."

"I could be wrong."

"You're just saying that to make me feel better, aren't you?" Chelsea guessed.

"Yeah," Alan admitted. "Listen, come in, drink some coffee, let me finish shaving and get dressed, and we can walk to *Trash* together."

Chelsea nodded dumbly.

Where could he be?

Did he spend the night with Jazz?

Twenty minutes later Alan and Chelsea were on their way to Trash. Just as it had been in Chelsea's dream, it was a gray and rainy day. Alan held an umbrella over them as they stepped around puddles.

"I had a terrible nightmare last night," Chelsea said, sidestepping another puddle, "but now I feel like I'm living one."

"Maybe there's some kind of logical explanation for why he didn't come home," Alan suggested.

"And he didn't even call?" Chelsea asked for maybe the tenth time in the last twenty minutes. "You checked your answering machine?"

"Twice." Alan nodded as they hurriedly crossed a street against the light, as most New Yorkers do when they see an opening in the traffic. "You know, Chelsea, that's just the way Nick is. I mean, he's a good guy, he's my bud, but he's not the most responsible guy in the world."

"Once a slacker, always a slacker, you mean," Chelsea said with a sigh.

Alan didn't respond.

"But he's changed lately," Chelsea added, as if Alan had argued with her. "Don't you think he's changed?"

"Maybe." Alan sounded guarded.

"And maybe not?" Chelsea asked.

"Well, let's just say that before you moved in across the hall, Nick pulled this stunt, like, three times. He wouldn't call, he'd just stay out all night. Clubbing, usually. And if I tried to tell him that I was concerned, he just blew me off."

"He met Jazz clubbing," Chelsea recalled bitterly.

"That's right," Alan said. "He's got that all-night thang down to an art form." He looked sideways at her. "That doesn't mean he doesn't care about you, Chels, because he does."

"But maybe he doesn't care enough," she said softly.

Again, Alan didn't answer.

They walked into the lobby of the *Trash* building, and Alan closed his umbrella. "Look, you'll see him here at work today. Y'all will make up."

She smiled at her friend. "You think?"

"Yeah," Alan replied. "He's not dumb enough to let you get away."

"You're really a great friend, Alan."

"Thanks," Alan said. "I think." He hesitated a moment. "Just... here's some unsolicited advice...."

"What?"

"I suggest you tell Nick what's on your mind," he advised. "And what a jerk you think he is."

"Maybe he was out someplace and wasn't feeling well," Chelsea suggested, grasping at straws. "That stomach-virus thingie."

"Chelsea, he could have picked up the phone."

"Maybe he was too sick for the phone."

He just stared at her.

"I get your point," she said. "I get your point."

She glanced toward the elevator, where various members of the *Trash* staff were waiting, sipping their cups of morning coffee. "I am so not into being here today."

"What was it you wanted to talk to Nick about so badly, anyway?" Alan asked, buying a copy of the morning *Times* from the news vendor in the lobby.

"I can't tell you," Chelsea said.

"I didn't mean to pry—"

"You weren't," she said quickly. "Not at all. It's just..." Her words trailed off.

"You have to tell Nick first," Alan guessed.

"Something like that."

Chelsea smiled a little and looked up at her Texan friend.

Alan would never stay out all night on Lisha without calling.

Alan wouldn't be somewhere else when I had something I had to tell him.

"Lisha is the luckiest girl I know," Chelsea said.

A smile flickered across Alan's sweet face. "The funny thing is, Chelsea, it could have been you. It absolutely, totally, could have been you."

"Chelsea?"

She looked up from the papers she was filing for Sumtimes. It was Galaxy, the new receptionist. Galaxy had short, jet-black hair and very white skin. She always seemed to dress all in black. She had a tattoo of stars circling one slender wrist.

"You are Chelsea, right?"

"Right," Chelsea replied.

"Nick called and left this message for you." Galaxy thrust a piece of paper at her. "He said to make sure you got it."

"Thanks," Chelsea said automatically.

"So, how do you like working at *Trash*?" Galaxy asked.

I am not in the mood to make chitchat with you, Chelsea wanted to say. But as usual, her good manners wouldn't allow her to be rude. "It's fine," she answered.

"Yeah, it's the bomb, ya know?" Galaxy said. "Can you believe I interviewed for, like, about a hundred jobs before I got this one?"

Of course I can, Chelsea thought. *You look like a space cadet.*

"Really," she murmured politely.

"But you know, here they appreciated that I have, like, my own look," Galaxy went on. "Well, that and the fact that I graduated from Mount Holyoke with honors. See ya."

Chelsea had to laugh. *It figures,* she thought. *Everyone wants to work at* Trash. *Trust them to find the only girl who looks like she just stepped out of a horror movie and who also graduated from Mount Holyoke with honors.*

She looked down at the note from Nick.

Chelsea—

Nick called and said he was sick and he wasn't coming in today. He said to tell you.

Galaxy

Right, Chelsea thought. *Calling in sick from someone else's apartment. With no phone number where I can reach him. How convenient.*

How stupid does he think I am?

She put her head in her hands. *What difference does any of it make, anyway?* she thought. *Lies. Deceit. Maybe Jazz is right. Maybe everything I think is valuable in my life is really just all trash.*

Only I don't want to live my life as a liar. Not anymore.

Chelsea crumpled up the note and threw it viciously in the garbage. Then she picked up the phone and punched in an extension number.

"Roxanne Renault," Bigfoot barked into the phone.

"Roxanne?" Chelsea said, her heart hammering in her chest. "It's Chelsea Jennings. I have to talk to you."

"So, make an appointment with my secretary," Bigfoot answered, and hung up the phone.

Chelsea angrily punched in the digits of Roxanne's extension again. She was filled with cold fury at Roxanne, at Nick, at the whole two-faced, hypocritical world.

"Roxanne Renault."

"I'm coming to talk with you now," Chelsea said, her voice steely.

"Just who do you think you're—"

"If you want to fire me when I get there, fire me. Or you can listen to me. Your choice." She slammed the phone down.

Roxanne's newly hired secretary was absent from her desk. Chelsea marched right into Bigfoot's office.

"You pull a stunt like this ever again and I *will* fire you," Roxanne threatened from behind her desk, the red color in her cheeks matching the bright red of her minidress, and the red of her new cast cover. "Now, what the hell is your problem?"

Chelsea sat across from Roxanne. Now that she was actually here, in Bigfoot's office, she could barely open her mouth.

"What?" Roxanne exploded. "I'm waiting."

"I have something to tell you," Chelsea finally said.

"I gathered that," Bigfoot said dryly. "So say it and stop wasting my time."

"It's not easy to say."

"You're quitting," Bigfoot guessed gleefully. "Good. Now no one can blame it on me. We here at *Trash* will miss you very much and wish you all the best in your future endeavors," she added, her voice deadpan.

"I'm not quitting," Chelsea said.

"Pity." Roxanne made a tsking sound. "Then what?"

Chelsea had thought about this moment many, many times. Other than sharing her secret with Lisha and Karma, she'd never told anyone. Oh, she'd often thought about it—thought she'd be telling Nick. Or a psychologist. Or a minister.

But I never imagined I'd be sitting here, about to tell the truth to the person I hate most in the whole world, she thought.

"Look, *Chutney*." Bigfoot sneered derisively. "Don't yank my chain. Say what you have to say and then get the hell out of my office."

Chelsea gulped hard. "I . . . I lied about something."

"Goody. Go tell a priest."

"I mean I lied to you," Chelsea said evenly. "About Chelsea Kettering. Chelsea Kettering isn't in Australia. You see . . . *I'm* Chelsea Kettering."

Roxanne stared at her for a moment, and then leaned back in her chair. And then she laughed. And laughed and laughed and laughed.

"I didn't expect you to find it so funny," Chelsea said stiffly.

Finally, Roxanne got a hold of herself. "That's really a good one."

"You mean you don't—"

"You are truly pathetic," Bigfoot marveled. "No, pitiful. No, pitiful *and* pathetic. You must really be desperate for attention, that's all I can say."

"But it's true!" Chelsea exclaimed. "I really am Chelsea Kettering!"

"Right," Roxanne snorted. "And I'm her mother. Now get out."

Chelsea jumped up. "But I'm telling you the truth! My mother changed our last name to Jennings, she changed the way she looks, she moved us to Nashville when I was just a little kid—"

"You are too sad for words," Roxanne scoffed.

"My father had no brothers or sisters, and his parents were dead. He's buried in a cemetery in Johnson City behind the Johnson City Baptist Church. He married my mom on August fifth! Now, how would I know all of that?"

"Nice research, Chelsea," Roxanne said. "How would you know? Because it's been your job to research the chick, that's how you'd know! Duh!"

"But there's more!" Chelsea cried, leaning over Bigfoot's desk. She tried to get out every single fact that she could recall about her father so Roxanne would believe her.

But Roxanne didn't believe her. In fact, she just started laughing again.

"Stop, stop, my stomach hurts from laughing," Bigfoot said, waving her hand at Chelsea. "You know, the truly pitiful thing is that you're so desperate for attention that you would come in here and give me a story like this."

Suddenly a thought seemed to flit across Bigfoot's face. "Wait, I get it! It's because your little Nicky-poo knocked up Jazz! That's it, isn't it! You actually think your stupid little story is going to help you compete with Jazz! This is the biggest laugh I've had in weeks!"

And then Bigfoot laughed some more.

"Get out of here," she finally said. "Go back to your cubicle. And get to work on the murderers show."

Feeling numb, Chelsea headed for the door.

"Oh, one last thing," Bigfoot called.

Chelsea turned around.

"Get some psychological counseling, honey. Because you are really a head case. Have a nice day."

EIGHT

That evening, Chelsea lay on the couch in her living room, staring up at the ceiling. Karma sat across from her, her legs thrown over the arms of the overstuffed easy chair.

"I can't believe I actually told Bigfoot the truth," Chelsea said, "and she didn't believe me."

"Well, maybe that's a good thing," Karma said. "I mean, she can never accuse you of lying about it again."

"It sure doesn't feel like a good thing," Chelsea replied. "It was so humiliating. It makes my stomach hurt."

Karma looked at her watch. "I have to get ready to go to Jimi's. You want me to fix you some dinner?"

"Not hungry," Chelsea mumbled.

"Chicken soup?" Karma wheedled. "You know chicken soup cures everything."

"Not this." Chelsea shook her head.

Karma walked over to her. "It's not just this thing with Bigfoot that has you bummed out, is it?"

"Right on the first guess." Chelsea looked at Karma. "Where was Nick last night? And why did he call in sick to work today?"

"I wish I knew, Chels," Karma replied sympathetically. "You want me to beat him up for you?"

"I want to beat him up myself." Chelsea looked over at Karma. "How could he do this to me?"

"'Cuz he's a guy," Lisha answered, padding through the living room in her bare feet. She opened the freezer and took out the ice cream. "Anyone else want some?"

"I thought you had a date with Alan," Chelsea said.

"He canceled," Lisha said. "He thinks he might be getting the stomach thing I had."

"I thought that was food poisoning," Karma piped in.

"I thought so, too." Lisha shrugged. "Maybe Alan just wanted to cancel our date." She scooped three huge balls of butter-pecan ice cream into a soup bowl.

"I gotta get ready for work," Karma announced. She cocked her head at Chelsea. "Hey, cheer our roomie up, okay?"

Lisha brought her ice cream into the living room. "There could be a perfectly innocent reason Nick didn't come home last night, you know."

"Such as?"

"Such as... he crashed at a friend's house," Lisha suggested, spooning some ice cream into her mouth.

"She must be some friend," Chelsea said darkly.

"Look, I'm not exactly a cheerleader when it comes to guys," Lisha said. "But I really don't think Nick is cheating on you."

"He wouldn't even look at it as 'cheating,' " Chelsea responded. "I mean, we don't have any kind of a commitment. We're free to see other people."

"Only you don't want to see other people," Lisha pointed out.

"And I guess he does," Chelsea said. "I really would like to kill him right about now." She sat up. "So, what are you doing tonight?"

"Eating junk food." Lisha emphasized her words by swallowing more ice cream. She looked into the almost empty bowl. "I am such a pig."

"You are not—"

"Yes, I am. I can't believe how much I've been eating lately."

"It's okay, Lish—"

"What if I gain back all the weight I lost?" She shuddered at the thought.

"I'll go running with you this weekend," Chelsea offered.

Lisha wrinkled her nose. "I hate running." She scraped the last of the ice cream from her bowl. "And I'm still hungry."

"Eat something healthy, then," Chelsea suggested.

"What I need to do is to get out of the house so I won't eat at all," Lisha said.

Just then the phone rang.

"I'll get it!" Karma yelled from her bedroom.

"It's probably Demetrius," Lisha said, "calling to tell her how fantastic she is."

"Aren't you happy for her that she has such a great boyfriend?" Chelsea asked.

"Yeah," Lisha admitted reluctantly.

"You have a great boyfriend, too," Chelsea reminded her.

"Yeah," she said again. "It's just that sometimes . . . I know this is sick, Chels, but sometimes Alan is just too *nice* for me."

"Don't hurt him, Lish," Chelsea said, her voice low.

Lisha jumped up. "I clearly have to get out of here. If I don't, I'm going to eat my way through the kitchen. You want to go see a movie or something?"

"I couldn't concentrate," Chelsea said. "I keep thinking that Nick will call."

"All the more reason for you to get out of here," Lisha told her. "You absolutely should not be waiting by the phone."

"I'm not."

"Hey, you guys." Karma stuck her head into the living room. "Winston is on the phone. He called to invite all of us to a party at his friend's loft in SoHo. He says some really hot reggae band is playing. I told him I have to work. You guys in?"

"I'm not in a party mood," Chelsea said.

"Oh, come on," Lisha wheedled. "Go with me. It's just what we need." She lifted her roommate off the couch. "Tell him we're there," she called to Karma. "Get the address."

"Lish, I really don't want to—"

"Too bad," Lisha said. "We're young, free, single, and living in the greatest city in the world. Now let's go party!"

"No need to knock, I see," Lisha observed as they headed out of the freight elevator on the third floor of the downtown loft building where the party was being held.

Loud reggae music competed with the voices of the party goers, wafting all the way into the hall that led to the loft and the party in progress. The industrial-gray door was propped open. Lisha and Chelsea walked in, working their way through the crush of people.

"Quite the bash!" Lisha yelled to Chelsea over the noise.

"No kidding." Chelsea felt a little awkward since she didn't recognize anyone she knew.

"Maybe we can find a drink," Lisha yelled.

"Share mine, pretty girl," a handsome guy with spiky black hair and a nose ring offered.

"No thanks," Lisha said. "Where's the kitchen?"

"Thataway," the guy said, cocking his head to the side. "Hope to see you again!"

Lisha and Chelsea dodged bodies and found the kitchen. There was a half-empty liter of Coke on the counter. All the ice in nearby buckets had melted.

"Warm Coke," Chelsea said. "Yuck."

Lisha opened the refrigerator and peered inside.

"You shouldn't do that!" Chelsea admonished her. "We don't even know whose loft this is!"

"Orange juice or cold Diet Pepsi?" Lisha asked, ignoring Chelsea's comment.

"Lish—"

"Oh, come on, Chelsea. It's a loft party. Everything is fair game."

"I've never been to a loft party before," Chelsea admitted.

Lisha took out the orange juice and found them both paper cups. "Well, here's to your first," she toasted. "It should be wild."

"Luscious Lisha!" Winston cried, coming into the kitchen. "You honor me with your beauty, girl."

Lisha laughed. "You're a big suck-up, Winston."

He laughed and held out his hand. "Come and dance with me."

Lisha put her juice down. "Why not?" She reached for his hand, then turned back to Chelsea. "You okay?"

"Oh, sure," Chelsea assured her, even though she felt kind of self-conscious and awkward. "Go have fun."

Winston led Lisha into the main room where the reggae band was playing.

Chelsea sipped at her orange juice and leaned against the counter. She just wasn't in the mood to join the party.

I guess you really can feel totally alone even when you're with lots of people, she thought sadly. *Where are you, Nick? Why didn't you come home last night? Why weren't you at work today? Why don't you call me?*

"Chels?"

She looked up.

And there, as if she had willed it, stood Nick.

"What are you doing here?" she blurted out, her voice accusing.

"The same thing you're doing here, I imagine," he said.

"Where have you been?" she demanded.

Nick sighed. "Don't do this, Chels—"

"Don't do what?"

"Talk to me like you're my mother. I have a mother. And you ain't her."

Tears sprang into her eyes. She turned and started out of the kitchen.

"Chelsea, wait—" Nick called to her.

"Go to hell!" she yelled, throwing herself into the crowded party.

"Wait, please!" Nick called.

But Chelsea kept going. Her eyes were blinded by tears. She forced her way through the crowd, as far away from Nick as she could get.

Finally she found herself in the hallway that led to the elevator. Up ahead she saw a door. She opened it. Narrow stairs led to the roof of the loft building. She climbed up and stepped out on the roof.

And there, alone at last, she let herself cry. She sobbed great, heaving sobs. For her father. And her mother. And the little girl who had grown up to become her, who had to hide the truth about who she really was.

"Chelsea?"

It was Nick. He had found her.

"Go away."

"Chelsea, please." He walked over to her. "I'm an idiot."

"I know." She sniffed.

"I shouldn't have yelled at you like that. It's just . . . seeing you took me by surprise," Nick explained.

"Why, got a hot date?" she asked bitterly.

Nick sighed. "I came alone. I don't even know *why* I came."

"I don't know why I came, either," she confessed. She wiped the tears from her cheek with the back of her hand. "Look, I know you don't have to explain yourself to me, okay? And I know we aren't some big, exclusive couple—"

"Chels—"

"But I was worried about you," she said. "Alan told me you didn't come home last night. I wasn't checking up on you. I really needed to talk to you. It was important. But you've been avoiding me, and I don't know why."

In the moonlight Nick's face looked anxious and haggard. "You're right," he finally said. "I have been avoiding you."

Chelsea's heart clutched with fear. She gulped hard. "Well, if you want to break up with me, just do it."

"That's the last thing I want." He came closer to her.

"It's about me, isn't it?" Chelsea said. "Someone told you the truth about me—"

"What are you talking about?" Nick looked baffled. "What truth about you?"

Chelsea was surprised. "You mean you really don't know?"

"Know what?"

"Know what I told Bigfoot today," she said slowly. "I thought you already knew, and were avoiding me because someone told you—"

"Told me *what?*" Nick was getting more confused by the second. "I have no idea what you're talking about."

As her eyes searched his she realized he was telling the truth. *He really doesn't know. So this is my chance to tell him.*

Taking a deep breath, she opened her mouth to begin. *Now,* she thought. *I'll tell him right now.*

No sound came out.

Instead Nick said, his voice low, "Chelsea, I . . . I have a problem."

"So do I," she confessed. "There's something you need to know about me." She took another deep breath. "God, Nick, this is really hard."

"I have to tell you something first," he insisted. "After you hear what I have to say, you might not want to speak to me at all."

Chelsea felt as if she couldn't breathe.

"It's about Jazz, isn't it?" she guessed, her voice low.

Nick nodded miserably. "I've been doing a lot of thinking. Last night I walked all over the city, just thinking. Finally I crashed at a friend's place in Brooklyn. A guy friend. And then today . . . I called in sick because I still needed more time to think."

"Think about what?" she asked, even though she knew she didn't want to hear what he was about to say.

"Jazz. I think she really is pregnant," he said sadly.

"By you?" Chelsea whispered, the words torn from her throat.

"It's not how it looks—"

"No?" Chelsea asked, her voice rising hysterically. "How is it, then?"

"It's complicated—"

"No," Chelsea snapped. "It isn't. It's really very simple. All you have to do is to answer this question. Is it possible that Jazz is pregnant with your baby?"

Nick didn't answer. A pigeon took off from the roof. The stars twinkled above them. It was a beautiful night.

And Chelsea felt as if her whole world was crashing down on her head.

"Oh, Nick," she whispered, the words catching in her throat. "How could you? How *could* you?"

"It's not what you think—"

Chelsea could feel the rage building, swelling inside of her like some force of nature.

"It's not what I *think*?" she yelled. "How stupid do you think I am?"

He reached out for her. "If you'd just listen to me—"

"I'm through with listening to you, Nick," Chelsea cried, jumping away from him. "I never want to listen to anything you have to say, ever again. You disgust me, understand? You disgust me!"

She ran past him, savagely pulling the door open. Then she ran down all six flights to the street and hailed the first taxi she saw.

She huddled in a corner of the back of the cab, crying her eyes out.

How could he lie to me that way? she thought, sobbing even harder. *He really did sleep with Jazz. How can I ever trust him again? How?*

It wasn't until the cab had stopped in front of her apartment building that she realized she had no money.

The Asian cabbie turned around and stared at her. "Miss?"

She choked back her tears. "I . . . have a little problem."

"You owe seven dollar," the cabbie said.

"I . . . uh . . . don't seem to have any money," she said, her voice small.

"You owe seven dollar," he said again, more firmly.

"I don't have it," she repeated, "but I'll get it for you. Can you wait?"

"I wait one minute," the cabbie said. "You leave purse. You get money or I get cop!"

Chelsea hurried into her building, hoping that Antoine the doorman would loan her seven dollars.

A swarthy, heavyset man Chelsea recognized as one of Antoine's cousins was at the front desk, reading the *Daily News*.

"Where's Antoine?"

"Yonkers, playing the trotters, little lady," the guy said, winking at her. "He got a hot tip."

"I don't suppose you could loan me seven dollars, could you?" she asked meekly.

"I'm busted," the guy said with a shrug.

Lisha's at the party. Karma's at work. Sky went out of town for the weekend. Nick is . . . I can't think about Nick now. My only hope is that Alan really did stay home with the stomach flu. She asked the guy at the desk to buzz Alan's apartment.

"Yeah?" Alan's voice came through the tinny sound system.

"It's Chelsea," she told him. "I hate to bother you, but I took a taxi home and I owe the driver seven dollars."

"I'll be right down," Alan said.

Meanwhile the taxi driver had entered the lobby. "Meter still running!" he yelled at her. "Now you owe eight dollar!"

"My friend is on his way downstairs with the money," Chelsea assured him.

It seemed to take forever, but finally there was Alan. He hugged Chelsea and handed her a ten-dollar bill, which she handed to the cabbie.

"You no want change?" he asked, pocketing the ten.

"Keep it," Chelsea told him.

"Nutcase," the cabbie said under his breath, handing her the purse she'd left with him. Then he hurried back to his taxi.

"Thanks," Chelsea said as she and Alan rode up the elevator together. "I'll pay you back tomorrow."

"You look like you lost your best friend," Alan said.

"I lost Nick," she said, tears seeping from her eyes again.

"You want to come in and talk about it?" Alan offered.

"You have the stomach flu—"

"False alarm," Alan said. "I was actually staring at my computer trying to work on my novel."

"I don't want to interrupt your writing—"

"If I were actually writing, you might be interrupting," Alan said dryly. "Come on in."

Chelsea entered the guys' apartment. Belch immediately jumped up on her, happy to see her.

"Down, Belch," Alan ordered. "Go play with your ball."

Chelsea sat on the couch. Alan sat next to her. He handed her a Kleenex and she blew her nose and wiped her eyes.

"I was at a party downtown," she said, shredding the Kleenex between her fingers. "Nick showed up. And he . . . he admitted that he could be the father of Jazz's baby."

"Wow," Alan said, at a loss for words.

Tears filled Chelsea's eyes again. "He lied to me, Alan. It's all over."

"He really told you that he slept with Jazz?"

"He didn't need to," she said. "He told me that there was a chance that the baby could be his. What more do I need to know?"

"I guess he lied to me, too, then." Alan reached out and gently touched Chelsea's hair. "I'm really sorry, Chels. I can't stand to see you hurting like this."

"I never should have believed him," she said bitterly. "I never should have trusted him." She looked into Alan's eyes. "He's not like you."

And then, the next thing she knew she was in his arms.

His lips were on hers.

"Chelsea," he moaned, holding her close.

For just a moment she closed her eyes and gave herself up to the sizzling kiss. It felt so wonderful to be loved by someone who would never break her heart. So wonderful, so safe, so . . .

"Oh, my God, what are we doing?" Chelsea cried, pulling away from Alan.

"Chelsea, I—"

She jumped up. "I'm sorry," she babbled. "This is my fault—"

"No—"

Chelsea headed for the door. "You and Lisha are . . . and she's my . . . oh, God, I'm so sorry. Please, forget this ever happened. Please."

She ran across the hall to her own apartment, pushed open the door, and slammed it behind her.

Dear God, Chelsea thought, *what have I done?*

NINE

"You guys ready to order?" the waitress asked, fiddling with the small ring that pierced her right eyebrow.

It was Saturday afternoon, and Karma had coaxed Chelsea and Lisha out to brunch with her. They had gone downtown to a new place called Madness, which was co-owned by a famous psychiatrist who had her own show on cable and three of the Hollywood stars she had treated. Large photos of famous people throughout history who'd had serious mental problems decorated the walls—from Van Gogh and Napoléon to Kurt Cobain and Patty Duke. According to the gossip columns, famous movie and rock stars hung out at the café all the time.

"I'll have a bagel with everything—no, make that two bagels with everything, and a double espresso," Karma ordered.

"Do you have fat-free muffins?" Lisha asked.

"Nope," the waitress replied.

"Fat-free anything?" Lisha tried.

"Fat-free air," the waitress answered, rolling her eyes.

"I'll have a veggie omelette made with egg whites, then," Lisha said. "And please tell the chef not to use any butter or oil."

"Yeah, right," the waitress said, dutifully writing it down. "You?" she asked Chelsea, not bothering to look up from her pad.

"Just coffee. No, make that tea."

I'm so upset about Nick and guilty about what happened last night with Alan that I feel as if I'll never want to eat again, Chelsea thought.

The waitress looked up for the first time, and her eyes lit up when she noticed Chelsea. "Hey, aren't you—?"

Oh no, Chelsea thought. *She recognizes me from all the publicity I got with Sela Flynn.*

"No," she said quickly. "Everyone just tells me I look like her."

"No kidding," the waitress agreed. "Anyway, I heard that Hilary is in Chicago shooting some movie, and I guess she couldn't be two places at once, huh?"

When the waitress left the table, Lisha and Karma cracked up.

"Too funny!" Karma hooted. "She thought you were Hilary Duff!"

"It's a good thing Bigfoot didn't believe you yesterday," Lisha said, liberally buttering a roll from the basket on the table. "You'd be a lot more famous than Hilary."

Chelsea slunk down in the booth. "What are we going to do?"

"We're going to pray that when Bigfoot comes back from Australia, she comes back alone," Karma said.

Lisha took a sip of her water. "You really think this friend of your stockbroker's would pretend she was Chelsea Kettering and agree to appear on *Trash*?"

"No." Karma was emphatic. "No way."

"Maybe you're wrong," Chelsea said glumly. "Maybe Jazz is right, and everyone really does have a price. And Jazz paid more than you paid."

"And maybe the girl is outscamming Jazz," Lisha mused. "Like, she'll travel all the way to America on Jazz's dime, and then on national television she'll confess that she really isn't Chelsea Kettering after all."

"And we'll get fired for pretending that we found Chelsea Kettering," Chelsea said. "By six o'clock Wednesday night, our jobs will be history. Our futures will be nonexistent."

The three girls looked at each other.

"Try calling Australia again," Lisha urged Karma.

"I've tried over and over and over." Karma drummed her fingers on the table. "Look, I still say there's something weird going on here. I just don't believe Bigfoot is really on her way to Australia."

"So what's her scam, then?" Lisha wanted to know.

"I don't know," Karma confessed. "Something."

"We're fired," Chelsea predicted. "We are so unemployed."

"Eat something," Karma urged Chelsea, pushing the basket of rolls toward her friend.

"Eat?" Chelsea was incredulous. "Eat? I'm about to lose my job, get blackballed from the field of television forever, and my boyfriend lied to me and got Jazz Stewart pregnant. I may never eat again."

That morning, she had told Lisha and Karma about her encounter with Nick at the loft party. She had apologized to Lisha for leaving the party without telling her, but Lisha had said under the circumstances, that she understood.

"You know, I don't want to be right when I say that guys are scum," Lisha said, finishing her roll and reaching for another. "It's not like it's satisfying."

"This thing with Nick makes about as little sense as this thing with Bigfoot going to Australia to get Chelsea Kettering," Karma said. "Are you telling me that Nick admitted to you that he had sex with Jazz and he didn't use a condom?"

"Not in so many words," Chelsea stated.

"He's not that crazy," Karma said. "And neither is Jazz. She's brilliant. She would not risk it. That means that she and whoever is the dad of the baby deliberately didn't use a condom. And that doesn't sound like Nick."

Lisha agreed. "And I can't believe he'd be that stupid. He might be a slacker, but he's a smart slacker."

"I can," Chelsea insisted. "His problem was, he didn't know if he could get away with it. I mean, once the baby is born they can do a blood test to determine if he's the father. And if it's a match, well... then he's the daddy."

"So, then, how did he think he could get away with the lie?" Karma asked. "That's the part that isn't logical."

"Guys aren't logical," Lisha said, reaching for a third roll. "Take Alan, for example. He's supposed to be crazed for me, right? Well, lately he's been breaking dates with me, acting kind of cool. If I didn't know better, I'd say there was another girl."

Hearing these words, Chelsea felt like throwing up. She couldn't look at Lisha.

"But Alan is probably the only guy on the planet with too much integrity to two-time a girl," Lisha continued, biting into her roll. "My theory is that I was much more attractive to him when I was hard to get. Typical guy behavior."

Lisha reached for another roll. The basket was empty. "Please tell me I didn't eat every roll in that basket."

"With butter," Karma informed her.

Lisha put her hands on her stomach. "I hate myself."

"Don't beat yourself up over food, Lish," Chelsea said, relieved to change the subject. "It isn't worth it."

"That's easy for you to say," Lisha moaned. She shook her shaggy bangs out of her eyes. "Do I look like I've gained weight?"

"No," Karma replied. "Have you weighed yourself?"

"Do we own a scale?" Lisha's question was clearly rhetorical.

"Guess not," Karma said. "Anyway, you look great."

"Yuh, but for how long?" Lisha asked anxiously.

"Hey, I know a feature they should add to this café," Karma said. "Booth-side shrinks! Like, a shrink could come sit with you while you eat brunch and you could tell her your problems!"

"Ha-ha," Lisha said.

"Actually, I think it's a great moneymaking concept," Karma mused, "with very low overhead."

"I don't need a shrink," Lisha insisted. "I need to stop shoveling food into my mouth."

"Veggie omelette, two bagels, double espresso, coffee, and tea," the waitress said, setting their food and beverages on the table.

"I should just skip the omelette." Lisha eyed her food as she spoke.

"Please, don't tell me you're gonna get all obsessive about your weight," Karma said. "I mean, you live with me, the junk-food queen."

"You wear a size two." Lisha rolled her eyes. "You can afford to eat junk food."

Karma took a sip of her double espresso. "This is about Harley, isn't it?" she guessed.

Lisha denied this quickly.

"Yeah, it is," Karma said. "You feel guilty that he . . . did what he did. Like you're responsible. So now you're taking it out on yourself by stuffing your face."

"Thank you, Dr. Kushner." Lisha sounded unimpressed.

"You're welcome," Karma replied. "See, I told you booth-side shrinks would work. Pass the salt."

Chelsea sipped her tea, then put down the cup. "I really don't feel well," she told her friends. "I should just go back to the apartment—"

"We're not going to let you go home and mope," Karma said. She thrust half a bagel at Chelsea. "Pretend you're Jewish. We always eat in times of crisis."

"In that case, I must be Jewish, too." With a sigh, Lisha cut into her omelette.

"Lisha, dearest," Karma crooned, "kindly get over yourself. Chelsea has a reason to be bummed. You don't."

"You're right," Lisha said. "Totally right."

"Of course I'm right." Karma smiled. "I'm also feeling rich today. One of my stocks split. And I got my paycheck from Jimi's. So . . . after brunch, we are going out to buy Chelsea a present."

"Oh, Karma, you don't have to—" Chelsea began.

"I know," Karma said. "But I want to. I am going to buy you the hottest outfit you have ever owned. Something guaranteed to make guys everywhere fall at your feet—"

"But I never—"

"Wear stuff like that," Karma finished for her. "I know. That's the whole point." She bit into her bagel. "It's time to create a whole, new Chelsea."

"You're kidding," Chelsea said, staring at her reflection in the full-length mirror.

"Why would I be kidding?" Karma whined. "It's fabulous!"

"You do look hot," Lisha agreed.

"What I look is naked," Chelsea said. They were in an East Village clothing store called Racey Lacey, owned by a punk rocker and clothing designer named Lacey Corkrin, who was actually a friend of Jazz's. Her designs were the hottest thing happening with the hip, young, downtown urban set. The salesgirl, who looked a lot like Kate Moss, had diffidently offered to help them, but Karma had assured her that they didn't need any help.

After that, Karma had selected three different outfits for Chelsea to try on. The first consisted of plaid bell-bottoms with a lacy bra top—Chelsea instantly vetoed that. Next came a long, knit tube dress in red and orange, which Chelsea thought looked like an oversized potholder. And then, finally, came the outfit Karma had forced her to actually try on.

Chelsea was wearing a tiny, short-sleeve, lime-green, fuzzy sweater that bared her midriff, and an even tinier black-green-and-yellow-plaid miniskirt.

"Karma, I could never, ever wear this," Chelsea said.

Karma ignored her. "The problem is the shoes," she decided. "Of course you couldn't wear it with those weenie loafers you've got on. What size shoe do you wear?"

"Seven and a half," Chelsea said. "But—"

"Oh, these are to die for," Karma decreed, reaching for a pair of bright orange patent-leather, knee-high, clunky-heeled boots set in a display against the wall. "Try them on."

"Karma—"

"Oh, go ahead," Lisha urged. "You know she'll be relentless unless you give in."

Chelsea slipped out of her loafers and pulled on the boots. She stood up awkwardly. "Great, I'm six feet tall."

"Oh, I'm good," Karma concluded with satisfaction, looking Chelsea over.

"I look like some kind of freak," Chelsea stated.

"Actually, you look very hot," Lisha said, leaning against the wall.

Chelsea took a couple of steps. "How do girls actually walk in these boots?"

"A girl has to suffer for beauty," Karma intoned seriously.

"Not this girl." Chelsea sat down to pull off the boots.

"Okay, okay, forget the boots," Karma said quickly. Her eyes scanned the shoe display again. She picked up a pair of neon-yellow velvet slippers with magenta piping and looked inside at the size. "Ah, you're in luck, they're your size. Put these on."

Chelsea complied dutifully. "At least I can walk in them," she commented after standing up.

"You know, Chels, you have a great figure," Lisha said. "I never actually realized it before. I mean, the clothes you wear are so . . . so . . ."

"Bor-ing," Karma put in. "I'm buying you this outfit," she told her friend. "Now, the finishing touch would be a small tattoo right on your—"

"Forget it!" Chelsea said, laughing.

Karma grinned back. "That's better."

"Karma, I love you, but I can't let you buy me this stuff. It must cost a fortune. And besides, I'd never have the nerve to wear it!"

"Don't you know how rude it is to turn down a gift?" Karma told her. "Okay, here's my compromise. Let me buy you the sweater. You can wear it with jeans. How's that?"

Chelsea hesitated. "I don't know."

"Put your jeans back on and see how it looks," Lisha suggested.

Chelsea went into the dressing room and slipped her jeans back on, then she returned to the others.

"Now, that is really hot," Lisha said. "Hotter than with the skirt."

"That settles it, you own it," Karma decided. "In fact, keep it on and wear it now." She pulled a credit card out of her purse. "I'm about to go use plastic the way God intended it to be used."

Ten minutes later the three girls walked out into the bright afternoon sunshine. Chelsea was still clad in the tiny, fuzzy, lime-green sweater.

"Hi!" a guy said, grinning at her appreciatively as he walked by with his friend. "Nice sweater!"

"Nice what's *in* the sweater!" the other guy said, walking backward so he could keep looking at Chelsea.

"Oh, great," Chelsea groaned. "This is just the kind of attention I want."

"Male attention can cure what ails you," Karma declared. "Now I have to take you guys to this thrift shop you won't believe."

Suddenly a lump formed in Chelsea's throat. *I don't need male attention,* she thought. *I need Nick. Oh, Nick, how could you do this to us? I thought you really cared. But you didn't.*

"Chels?"

"Huh, what?" Chelsea asked, startled.

"I asked if you wanted to get an Italian ice from that vendor on the corner," Lisha said.

Chelsea turned to her friends. "Listen, Karma, I love the sweater. I really do. And I appreciate that the two of you are trying to cheer me up. But... I think I need to just go home and be alone for a little while, okay?"

"Are you sure?" Lisha asked.

"I'm sure," Chelsea said. "Y'all go have fun. I'll just get a taxi and—"

She stopped mid-sentence. Because at that moment a very familiar-looking limousine was pulling up in front of Racey Lacey's. A limousine with one-of-a-kind dalmatian-print doors.

Jazz's limousine.

Chelsea felt rooted to the spot. She watched as Jazz got out and spoke to her driver, watched as Jazz turned to walk into the store, watched as Jazz spotted her three interns standing on the sidewalk.

"Well, well," she said, sauntering over to them. She took in Chelsea's lime-green sweater. "That's a Lacey original, isn't it? You've got good taste."

"We were just leaving," Karma told Jazz brightly, pulling on Chelsea's arm. "Ducky running into you, Jazz."

"I guess I won't be able to wear Lacey's stuff for much longer," Jazz commented, staring coolly at Chelsea. "I mean, she doesn't exactly design clothes for pregnant women."

"Just think, Jazz," Lisha said maliciously, "soon you'll be really, really fat."

"You mean like you used to be?" Jazz quickly returned.

Lisha gasped, and the color drained from her face.

Without pausing to savor her triumph, Jazz looked at Chelsea again. "The sweater looks great on you. You ought to show off your body more often."

Chelsea couldn't speak.

"Nick likes clothes like that, you know," Jazz continued, her tone conversational. "He likes girls who are confident enough to strut their stuff. And you're a confident girl. Aren't you, Chutney?"

Chelsea opened her mouth. No sound came out.

Jazz smiled a dazzling smile. "Hope you guys have a great day," she finished, turning to head into the store.

"How did she know I used to be fat?" Lisha gasped.

"It's probably in her files on us or something," Karma said, staring after Jazz. "Something isn't right here."

"But it's so creepy," Lisha said. "We secretly video her to get the dirt on her, and all the time she already has all the dirt on us!" She grabbed Karma's arm. "Do you think she knows about Harley, too?"

"Oh, my gawd, I am beyond brilliant." Karma hit herself in the forehead.

"Y'all, I truly feel sick," Chelsea said. "I have to go home—"

"Wait," Karma said. "Listen to me. We need to hide the Trash-cam in Jazz's office. Like right away."

"I thought we all agreed we were going to lay low with all of that for a while," Lisha reminded her friend. "Remember how we almost got caught?"

"That was then, this is now," Karma said impatiently. "Don't you realize what just happened?"

"Jazz got to make us all feel about two inches tall?" Chelsea asked.

"No, Jazz just gave herself away," Karma said. "If she was really so sure that Nick was the father of her kid, she would not need to psych out you, her lowly intern, about him on the street, Chelsea! Don't you see that?"

"No," Chelsea said bluntly.

"I know I'm right," Karma told her. "Either she isn't pregnant at all, or she knows it isn't Nick's."

"Karma, you have sunstroke," Chelsea observed.

"I'm telling you, I'm right," Karma insisted. "If we get the Trash-cam going in her office, sooner or later she's going to give herself away!"

"Karma, that is all wishful thinking," Chelsea said, her heart breaking. "I've got to go." She stepped into the street and raised her hand to hail a cab.

"Chels, come on—" Lisha began.

"Have fun," Chelsea called to her friends as she got into a cab that had just pulled over.

"Where to?" the driver asked.

Chelsea gave her address. *At least I stopped at an ATM this morning and I know I have money to pay him,* she thought, letting her head loll back. She closed her eyes. *How did everything get to be such a mess? How?*

The traffic was light for once, and in only minutes the taxi pulled up in front of the girls' apartment building. Chelsea paid the driver, waved to Antoine—who was actually on duty—and took the elevator up to her floor.

All I want to do is sleep, she thought as she stepped out of the elevator. *I want to pretend that Bigfoot isn't on her way to Australia to pick up some girl who claims to be me, that everything is great with Nick, and that Alan and I never—*

"Chelsea?"

It was Alan, just locking the door to his apartment.

"Hi," she said softly.

"Chelsea, we have to talk."

"No—"

"Yes," Alan said firmly. "It's time for us to tell Nick and Lisha about how we really feel about each other."

TEN

Nick rapped on the girls' apartment door.

No answer.

Dejectedly, he walked back across the hall, opened the door to his own apartment, and went back inside. He'd been making this same trip across the apartment hallway every half hour since noontime, and it was now nine-thirty at night. Each time, there was no answer. Clearly neither Chelsea, Karma, nor Lisha were home.

Or maybe they are home, Nick thought, *and they're just not answering. I'm sure Chelsea told Lish and Karma about our conversation at the party last night. Now all three of them think I'm this lying, low-life scum. Chelsea never even gave me a chance to explain.*

Typical hotheaded Chelsea.

Nick sighed and clicked on the TV. Some stupid sitcom. He clicked it back off again. Belch jumped up on the couch, his ball in his mouth, eager to play.

"Not now, big guy," Nick told him, ruffling his fur. Belch slunk off to play by himself.

Nick picked up the Arts and Leisure section of the Sunday *New York Times* and scanned it idly. In the "television" heading of that section was a feature story about the upcoming "Kids of Mass Murderers" *Trash* episode set to be aired on Wednesday. Nick turned to it.

IS JAZZ MASS-MURDERING *TRASH?* CRITICS PROTEST, BUT RATINGS SAY: "WE WANT MORE!"

"Sorry, Jazz," Nick said out loud, "I'll be taking a big fat pass on you today."

He angrily tossed that section of the newspaper back on the sprawling pile of papers on the coffee table. Then he reached for the cordless phone half-buried under the sports section and punched in the girls' number.

"Yeah, it's Nick," he said, when the answering machine picked up. "Chelsea, please gimme a call, I have to talk to you. And if I'm not home, I've got a new beeper number. It's 917-555-NICK. Just call. I mean it. We need to talk." He hesitated a moment. "Please," he added. "See you."

Just as he was hanging up, Sky let himself into the apartment.

"Hey man," Nick said to his roommate. "'Sup? How was your weekend? You get to see the kid?"

Nick knew that Sky had spent both Saturday and Sunday with his family in Brooklyn, helping his dad do some renovations on the basement of their house. He also knew that Sky was a "big brother" to a boy in the Big Brother/Big Sister program, and that he was hoping to spend part of his Sunday with his "little brother," a nine-year-old named Ricky.

"It was cool," Sky said, dropping his overnight case on the floor. "I took Ricky to the Coney Island Aquarium."

"Sounds like fun," Nick remarked.

Sky looked down at his left hand. "More fun than pounding nails was," he said. "I smashed the hell out of my thumb yesterday." He held it up. "You think I can get Lisha to kiss it and make it all better?" He grinned and began to pull off his T-shirt as he headed into the shower.

"Not if you hang with me, you can't," Nick called to him. But Sky didn't hear him.

The next thing Nick heard was the shower being turned on. He gave in and played with Belch for a while, throwing the dog his ball, which he eagerly retrieved and returned, his tail wagging furiously. "I'm never in the doghouse with you, huh, Belch?"

"Ah, I feel much better," Sky announced, padding back into the living room in a pair of gym shorts, towel-drying his hair. "So, what did you say before, something about hanging out with you?"

"I said none of the Three Musketeers across the hall are speaking to me," Nick said, putting his hands behind his head.

"How come?" Sky asked, sitting in the leather chair. "You break Chelsea's heart again or something?"

"Not on purpose," Nick mumbled.

Sky stopped drying his hair. "I was joking, but I have a feeling you're serious."

"Forget it," Nick said tersely. "It's a misunderstanding. That's all."

"Okay," Sky said easily. "No biggie." He got up and went to the fridge, and pulled out a Coke. "Where's Alan?"

"Out," Nick said.

"Yeah, I gathered that," Sky said, amusement coloring his voice. "I mean, I figured it out when I saw he, like, wasn't here."

"How should I know?" Nick asked. "He hasn't been here all day."

"Touchy," Sky commented. He took a slug of the Coke and reached for the sports section of the *Times*. "You okay, big guy?"

Nick had no intention of spilling his guts to Sky—they were roommates and friends, yes, but Nick wasn't a guy who was into that male-bonding thing.

I've always kept my problems to myself, Nick realized. *Ever since I was a kid. My dad used to say that whining about your problems never did anyone any good.*

Of course, my dad was wrong about almost everything.

Nick hesitated a moment. He looked over at Sky, who had his face buried in the sports section. "Uh, actually," he began self-consciously, "I'm not so okay."

Sky put the paper down and waited.

"You don't wanna hear this," Nick said.

"I do if you wanna tell me," Sky said simply.

Nick gave a short, sharp laugh. "It's complicated. It could take a year to explain."

"My time is your time," Sky said easily.

Nick started at the beginning, and told Sky the whole story about Jazz, Jazz's pregnancy, and Chelsea.

"...so you see," he concluded several minutes later, "Jazz says I'm the dad. Knowing her, she's going to tell the world that I'm the dad. And like I said, I never even got a chance to explain to Chelsea because she got all bent out of shape before I could explain. So now she just thinks I lied to her." He ran his fingers through his hair anxiously.

"But, man, I don't see how I could have had sex with Jazz and not even remember."

"Yowza." Sky shook his head. "I've got to hand it to you, man, that's the best story I've heard in a long time."

"I didn't tell you to entertain you."

"I know," Sky said. "But . . . well, I'm human. Jazz a is walking work of art. An homage to the female form. And she clearly wants you bad, buddy-boy."

"Well, I don't want her," Nick replied.

"Yeah?"

"Yeah," Nick said firmly. "There was a time when I did, I admit it." He got up and paced across the room. "I mean, it was really flattering, how strong she came on to me. And she is hot—"

"You can say that again," Sky agreed.

"But so what?" Nick asked, turning back to Sky. "I don't care about her. I never did."

"You care about Chelsea," Sky said.

Nick threw himself back on the couch. "Yeah. Even if she drives me crazy. So now what the hell do I do?"

"It just so happens you confided in the right guy," Sky said, stretching his legs out.

"Don't tell me this happened to you, too—"

"No chance." Sky reached for the phone.

"If you're calling Chelsea, I've already left six messages for her," Nick said.

"I'm not calling Chelsea. I'm calling my uncle Harvey."

"Who?" Nick asked.

"Harvey," Sky said, punching some numbers into the phone. "Harvey Glickstein, the doctor who runs the Upstate Sex Therapy and

Dysfunction Center in Albany. He married my mom's sister. He's a little bit famous. *Cosmo* interviewed him."

"Hey, man, I don't need a—"

Sky shushed Nick. "Too late."

"But—"

Sky silenced Nick with a wave of his hand and waited for his uncle to answer the phone. "Hey! Uncle Harvey!" he said into the phone. "It's Sky! . . . Yeah, I'm great, how's everyone? . . . Great! . . . Listen, I have a question for you, it's about sex . . . no, Uncle Harvey, I am not too young to be asking!"

He put his hand over the receiver of the phone and turned to Nick. "He's a big jokester, my uncle."

"Yeah, I'm laughing over here," Nick said flatly. "Don't use my name."

"Listen, Uncle Harvey, is it okay if I put us on the speaker so my friend . . . Belch can hear? It's Belch that has a problem."

"Your friend Belch?" Nick mouthed.

Sky grinned and punched on the speakerphone.

"Uncle Harvey, are you there?" Sky asked.

"Right here," said a voice as professional sounding and sonorous as a TV commercial voice-over. "Dr. Harvey at your service. And how are you today, Belch?"

"Just fine, sir," Nick said, giving Sky a murderous look.

"So, Belch, I hope you didn't get that nickname because you drink too much beer. Beer can play havoc with sexual function, did you know that?"

"Uh—" Nick began.

"So, Belch, what can I help you with?" Harvey asked. "Just ask away. I'm not Dr. Ruth, but I'm a little bit taller!" He laughed at his own joke.

Nick winced. Then he took a deep breath and quickly outlined his problem.

"So is there any chance I could have gotten her pregnant, if I was too out of it to even remember?" he concluded.

"Doubtful," Harvey replied.

"What does *doubtful* mean?" Nick asked.

"Doubtful means doubtful," Sky's uncle said. "You were passed out on her couch from beer and cold medicine. If you're passed out, it's doubtful that you'd have sexual function. If it's doubtful you'd have sexual function, it's extremely doubtful you'd get her pregnant."

"What would you say the odds were?" Nick pressed.

"You want odds, go to Vegas," Harvey told him. "Okay, I'll give you odds. Strictly nonscientific, so we'll call them Harvey's guess odds. I would say . . . one in a thousand."

"No kidding?" Nick asked eagerly.

"Could be even longer odds than that," Harvey said.

"One in a thousand," Nick echoed happily.

"But like I said, this is not an exact science," Harvey warned. "And don't hold it against me if I'm wrong. Maybe you're a one-in-a-thousand kind of guy, Belch!" He laughed at another of his own lame jokes.

"Thanks, Uncle Harvey," Sky said.

"Anytime," Harvey said. "And Belch?"

"Yeah?" Nick said.

"Next time, when you find yourself in that situation, Belch," Harvey advised, "do yourself a favor. Stay away from the alcohol. I promise, you'll sleep much better the day afterward."

"Jazz," Nick said into the phone, "I have to talk to you."

"I was sleeping," Jazz said groggily. "What time is it?"

"Eleven or something," Nick said.

"Where are you?" she asked.

"At a pay phone on Greene and Spring," Nick said. "And I'm coming over."

"Oh, unexpected male company." Her voice was low and throaty. "How nice. You know how I hate to sleep alone, Nick."

"I'll be over in five," Nick said, and hung up the phone.

It was scarcely a half hour after his conversation with Sky's uncle. A few seconds after he'd hung up, he had grabbed his wallet and headed out the door.

"Where are you going?" Sky had asked him.

"Jazz," was Nick's reply. He'd practically run over to the downtown number "1" subway at Seventy-second and Broadway and had been lucky that the train was just pulling into the station.

Now he was going to confront his boss with the truth.

And then he was going to talk to Chelsea.

I'll make her listen, he told himself. *I'll find a way.*

When Nick got to Jazz's building, the security man downstairs let him in immediately. There were only four floors in the building—Jazz occupied the huge, three-thousand-square-foot loft on the fourth floor that used to be a warehouse space. He took Jazz's private elevator up, which opened directly into her apartment. Formerly a freight elevator, it was huge. Jazz had put in plush carpeting and designer wallpaper.

"Well, well, well," she said, greeting Nick in a short white silk robe. "Come on in."

"I don't want to come in," Nick said, still standing in the large former freight elevator.

"Okay." Jazz shrugged. "I'm up for anything." She stepped into the elevator with Nick. Then she leaned against the wall and slid down it, until she was sitting on the lush, white carpet. She reached up for Nick. "Join me?"

Nick just stood there.

"Is there a problem?" Jazz asked.

"Yeah, there's a problem," Nick said.

"You know, you're the one with the problem, Nick. You take life way too seriously. You need to get out and have some fun."

"Jazz," Nick said, "I'm serious."

"So am I," Jazz replied. She smiled at him. "We used to have a lot of fun together, didn't we?"

"I can't be the father of your baby," Nick said tersely. "That is, if you really are going to have a baby."

"You are and I am," Jazz answered blithely.

Nick crouched down so he could look into her eyes. "Look, you might really be pregnant or you might not. I honestly don't know. But I talked with this doctor, who told me that it basically would have been impossible for me to make love with you that night. He said there was a thousand-to-one chance against it."

Jazz patted her tummy. "What's this ignorant doctor's name? Maybe we should name our baby after him."

"Harvey Glickstein."

"Harvey Glick . . . ?" Jazz began. Then she threw her head back and laughed. "Harvey Glickstein? You talked to *the* Harvey Glickstein?"

"So?"

"I had him on one of my first shows, back when we used to have so-called experts on," Jazz explained, still laughing. "He's the sex therapist that makes all those lame jokes!"

"Well, Harvey says it couldn't have happened," Nick maintained.

Jazz smiled at him. "No, that's not what he said. He said that there was a one-in-a-thousand *chance* of it happening."

Jazz got to her feet and moved very close to Nick. "Don't you think I'm one-in-a-thousand, Nick?"

"Gee, Harvey made the same lame joke," Nick replied coldly.

Jazz moved even closer. She stared at his mouth.

"Don't even think about it," he told her, his voice low.

"Think about what?" Jazz asked.

"Whatever it is you're thinking," Nick said.

"I was thinking about Chelsea," Jazz said, leaning against the wall of the elevator. "Are you madly in love with our little intern, Nick? Is that what this is all about?"

"This doesn't have anything to do with Chelsea."

"I doubt that." Jazz stepped out of the elevator, then turned back to him. "No one in the entire world would believe that you'd choose her over me, you know."

Nick was silent.

"Well, anyway, we'll do a blood test when the baby comes to prove your paternity," Jazz said. "I'm sure you'll be eager to give a blood sample. Maybe we'll even do it on the air."

It's a bluff, Nick thought, staring her dead in the eye. *It's got to be a bluff.*

"Thanks for stopping over, Nick," Jazz continued. She yawned and ostentatiously stretched her arms over her head. "Mmmmm, I'm sleepy. I guess I'll go back to bed. Care to join me?"

"No, thanks."

"Why? Do you have plans with Chutney?" Jazz mocked, deliberately using the wrong name. There was an edge to her voice.

"You're jealous!" Nick realized.

"Oh right," Jazz said, laughing. "America will really believe that one."

"America doesn't have to believe that one," Nick responded. It was like a lightbulb going off in his head. "It's finally all making sense to me. Even though you dumped me, you can't stand the idea that I'd fall for an intern instead of pining away for you!"

Jazz shook her head. "You're delusional, Nick. Really. Nice try, though." She pressed the down button for the elevator and the door closed between them.

"Have a nice trip!" she called after him. Then she added an afterthought: "Daddy!"

I'm right, Nick thought as the elevator took him down to the street level. *I know I'm right.*

Now all I have to do is to convince Chelsea.

ELEVEN

"May we who are about to die salute you," Chelsea told her own reflection in her living-room window. She lifted her glass of milk and toasted her reflection, then took a sip.

It was Tuesday night. The feeling of dread in her stomach over the arrival of Chelsea Kettering—the impostor Chelsea Kettering—had been keeping her up nights. In fact, she had barely slept in days.

And nursing a broken heart doesn't help either, she thought. *Nick keeps calling and leaving messages, and trying to corner me at work. Well, why should I listen to him? I listened before, and look what happened. I must be the biggest sucker of all time.*

And then there's Alan. I refused to talk to him the other night. What am I supposed to say? Nick lied to me but I love him, anyway? I kissed you because I felt scared and lonely and flattered that you care about me so much? In other words, I used you?

I can't believe I let him kiss me.

And I kissed him back.

If Lisha knew, she'd hate me forever. Some kind of best friend I am.

Chelsea took another sip of her milk. A little of the milk spilled onto her T-shirt, but she didn't much care. The T-shirt was hardly clean. Neither were the jeans she was wearing. They kept falling down onto her hipbones because she hadn't really been eating, either. Her hair was a greasy mess, up on top of her head in a sloppy ponytail. A pimple had erupted on her chin. She didn't care. She was too depressed for grooming.

"We're going out for burgers," Lisha said, entering the living room with Karma. "You want to come?"

"No," Chelsea replied. "In fact, I've decided never to leave this apartment again."

"Karma is convinced—well, half-convinced, anyway—that somehow everything is going to work out tomorrow," Lisha said.

"Well, just call me a pessimist, then," Chelsea said, sipping her milk. "By tomorrow at this time I will be unemployed. Maybe you'll dodge a bullet, Karma. Bigfoot likes you. She'd just love an excuse to fire me." She sat on the couch. "And then maybe Nick and Jazz will get married and live happily ever after. That would be a lovely ending to this whole saga, don't you think?"

"I think lack of nutrition is getting to your brain," Karma declared. "That milk is the first thing I've seen you consume in days."

"I'm not going to work tomorrow," Chelsea announced. "Why show up for my own execution?"

"But, Chels, remember that you told Bigfoot the truth and she didn't believe you," Karma reminded her.

"Right, after we scammed her for weeks," Chelsea pointed out.

"True," Karma agreed. "I guess I should be freaked out, here, but somehow I'm not. Not too much, anyway."

"Because love has short-circuited your brain," Lisha said.

"Partly," Karma admitted. "But I also don't think that—"

A knock on their door interrupted her.

"If it's Nick, I left town. Permanently," Chelsea added.

"It's Demetrius," Karma said, opening the door. "He was over at the guys' apartment."

"Ready?" Demetrius asked Karma.

"Sure." Karma reached up and wrapped her arms around his neck. He lifted her off the ground and kissed her.

"Such a happy couple," Lisha said, laughing.

"Sure, rub salt in my wounds," Chelsea said darkly.

"Aw, come on, Chels," Lisha wheedled. "I'll loan Alan to you, if it will cheer you up."

Chelsea felt her face grow warm. "No, thanks," she managed.

Karma gave her a quick hug. "Want us to bring you back—"

"Nothing," Chelsea said. "Thanks, anyway."

"I'll find a way to get some food into you," Karma threatened, waving good-bye.

Chelsea wandered over to the couch and lay down, staring up at the ceiling. She went over and over the current facts of her life yet again, and yet again she could find no way out.

I'm about to get fired.

The guy I love lied to me and slept with someone else.

My life sucks.

And with that cheery thought, she fell asleep.

Bzzzzz!

What was that?

Bzzzzz!

Chelsea had been in the middle of a terrible dream, something about her mother forcing her to have plastic surgery so that no one would know she was really Chelsea Kettering, when an insistent buzzing woke her up.

Bzzzzz!

There is was again.

Chelsea opened her eyes. Someone was insistently buzzing the downstairs buzzer.

She rolled off the couch and stumbled to the intercom box near the front door.

"Who is it?" she croaked.

"Pizza delivery," came Antoine's voice.

"I didn't order a pizza."

"This guy insists it's for your apartment," Antoine said.

Karma, Chelsea realized. *She must have ordered a pizza and sent it to me in the hopes that I'd eat something.*

She could feel her stomach growling with hunger. "Okay, send him up," she said through the intercom. She stumbled sleepily around the living room, trying to locate her purse, which she finally found under the cushion of the chair. Just as she got out her wallet there was a knock on the door.

"Coming," Chelsea called. She counted her money. Seven dollars. "I only hope she didn't order a large or I can't pay for it," she mumbled as she went to the door and opened it.

And there stood Nick.

Chelsea started to shut the door.

He put his foot in the way. "I'm not letting you run away from me this time," he said.

"Get your foot out of my door," Chelsea said coldly. "How did you get Antoine to lie for you and say you were a pizza delivery, anyway?"

"He can be bought," Nick said.

Chelsea tried to close the door again. Nick's foot stopped it.

"Give it up, I'm coming in and we're going to talk." He pushed the door open.

"Fine," Chelsea said curtly. "Great." She went over to the chair and sat down, folding her arms. "Well?"

Nick sat on the couch. "You look terrible."

"Thanks, you're lovely, too," she snapped back.

"No, I mean you look skinny. I noticed that at work today, too. Are you eating?"

"Did Karma get you to ask me that?"

"I'm asking because I care," Nick said softly.

"Oh yuh, right."

Nick stood up. "Okay, that's it. Get up."

"Don't tell me what to—"

"Get up, go take a shower, and get dressed. I'm taking you somewhere."

"I don't have to listen to you!" Chelsea bellowed.

"No," Nick said with a sigh, "you don't." He went over to her and knelt down on one knee and gazed up into her eyes. "Please. Please come out with me so we can talk. Just hear me out. And after that, if you hate my guts and you never want to speak to me again, I promise I'll leave you alone forever. Okay?"

Chelsea looked into his beautiful blue eyes and gulped hard. She didn't want to care about him still, but she did.

"All right," she finally said. "Where are we going?"

"It's a surprise," Nick said.

A half hour later Chelsea had showered and changed into a lemon-yellow sundress that she knew Nick liked, and they took the elevator downstairs together. They didn't stand close to each other in the elevator. And they didn't look at each other, either.

"You two kiss and make up?" Antoine asked as they walked by.

"No," Chelsea said.

They walked out of the building.

And there, on the street, was a red carriage driven by two white horses. As soon as the driver saw Chelsea and Nick, he jumped out and held the door open for them.

Chelsea turned to Nick. "What is this?"

"It's called transportation," Nick said. "Just get in."

Chelsea allowed the uniformed driver to help her into the carriage. The horses took off at a slow trot.

"Once you told me you always wanted to take a ride with me in one of these," Nick said.

"That was before," Chelsea said, her voice sad.

"Before what?"

"Before you lied to me and slept with Jazz."

"Chelsea, I'm going to explain it all to you, and you're not going to be able to run away this time," Nick said firmly.

"So that's why you got the carriage," Chelsea realized.

"Just listen," Nick said.

As the horse-drawn carriage made its way downtown through the sultry, summer night, Nick told her the entire story.

"So, that's it," he concluded. "I don't believe I ever did have sex with Jazz. If I did, I don't know about it. And like I said, the expert said there is next to no chance that I did."

Chelsea struggled with her feelings. "Am I really supposed to believe you?"

"Yeah, you are," Nick said. "Because it's the truth."

"So there's . . . there's some tiny, little chance it really could be your baby," Chelsea said slowly. "But that would mean that Jazz took advantage of you."

"It isn't only guys who take advantage of girls, you know," Nick said mildly.

Chelsea sighed. "You know that no one in America would believe this story. Especially not after the tabloids printed all that stuff about how Jazz picked you up in a bar."

"I don't give a red-hot damn about those trash rags," Nick said impatiently. "I don't care what any of them think. They wouldn't know integrity if it jumped up and bit them. Neither would Jazz."

"But you would," Chelsea observed, her voice dubious.

"I'm not telling you I wasn't attracted to Jazz. Or flattered that she came on to me like she did," Nick said. "I am telling you that I never knowingly or willingly had sex with her. And I sure as hell never made love with her." His eyes bore into hers.

"I want to believe you." She gulped hard.

"I never made love to her, Chels, because I didn't love her. I don't love her. I love you."

"You—?"

"I love you, Chelsea," Nick whispered, and in the glow of the streetlights she could see tears in his eyes.

"I love you, too," she confessed.

And then she was in his arms, laughing and crying, and he was kissing the tears off her cheeks. Then he was just kissing her, over and over, until the stars in the sky were spinning, and she felt giddy with happiness, hope, love.

"Uh, excuse me," the driver called back to them.

Chelsea and Nick broke apart.

"We're here," the driver said with a grin.

They were in front of a small restaurant on the corner of Eighth Avenue and Twenty-sixth Street. The tasteful sign in front said DANIELLA'S.

Nick hopped out and helped Chelsea descend, and paid the driver.

"What is this place?" Chelsea asked as Nick held the door open for her.

"My favorite restaurant in New York," Nick told her.

They went inside. There were perhaps twenty tables, covered in crisp, white tablecloths, being served by handsome men in tuxedos.

"Nick!" a short, handsome man in his fifties bellowed when they entered. "So, this is the girl, huh?"

"Hey, Tony," Nick said, embracing the man. "Yeah, this is her." Nick turned to Chelsea. "Tony is a friend of my favorite cousin back in Windsor," Nick explained. "When I first got to New York, he used to feed me for free. And he makes the best Italian food in town."

"Pleased to meet you," Chelsea said.

Tony embraced her in a bear hug. "Nick told me he was bringing in the girl he loved," Tony said. "You got yourself a great guy, Chelsea!"

Tony seated them at a front table.

"You are full of surprises," Chelsea told him. "How did you know that everything was going to work out, anyway? What if I didn't let you in with your pizza delivery? Or what if I refused to make up with you?"

"I'm a hopeful guy," Nick said. He smiled at her. A candle danced on the table in front of them. He reached out and took her hand. "You look really beautiful, Chelsea."

Her eyes searched his. "We won't let Jazz come between us," she whispered. "Will we?"

"No," Nick said firmly. "No chance."

"Grilled Portobello-mushroom appetizers," Tony said, putting steaming, fragrant plates of food in front of them.

Nick looked up. "We didn't order yet."

"You trust me, right, Nicky? I have prepared a feast for you and your lady love that can't be beat." He leaned in close to them. "I served it to my wife the first time she came in here. That was before she was my wife. Food can be very seductive."

Nick laughed. "In that case, Tony, we put ourselves in your hands."

Tony nodded his approval and took off for the kitchen.

"I missed you so much," Chelsea whispered.

"Never again," Nick promised. "We'll never be apart again."

TWELVE

"At least when I get fired today I'll still have a love life," Chelsea announced. It was the next morning. She was in the again-decrepit lounge at *Trash* with Karma and Lisha. She had gotten in the night before really late, but both her roommates were still up. She filled them in on what had happened with Nick, and they were both really happy for her.

But that didn't change the fact that she, and probably Karma, too, were both about to lose their jobs.

"Oh, God. Fired." Chelsea buried her head in her hands.

"Something about all of this stinks, I'm telling you," Karma insisted. She unwrapped her third candy bar of the still-young day and took a bite.

"How can you eat that now?" Chelsea moaned.

"Nerves make me eat," Karma said with a shrug. "Let's review, shall we? I got a friend of my stockbroker's who lives in Australia to pretend she's Chelsea Kettering. Of course, she isn't really Chelsea Kettering. You're Chelsea Kettering. And this friend of my stockbroker's already told Bigfoot that she wouldn't come on *Trash* for any amount of money. So I ask you, what the hell is going on here?"

"We are so screwed," Chelsea moaned.

Lisha, who was leaning against the wall over by the coffeemaker, gave one of her patented shrugs. "Whatever happens, happens," she said.

"Easy for you to say," Chelsea said. "You aren't going to get the big ax."

"Maybe there will be no Kettering," Karma suggested, polishing off the candy bar. "Maybe there'll be a last-minute glitch or something."

"Right," Lisha sounded dubious. "Maybe."

"Well," Karma said, "we're all meeting in the fifth-floor ladies' room later, at a quarter to three, right? We can talk about the end of the world then."

"I liked it better when you were convinced that everything was going to work out okay," Chelsea said gloomily.

"Me, too," Karma confessed.

All of *Trash* was high-energy that morning because of the big show. It had been hyped endlessly in the press and on the tube. Political pundits had debated the ethics of the topic on CNN's *Crossfire*. Everyone seemed to be talking about it.

A nervous Sumtimes had come by their cubicles first thing that morning to assign them their duties for the show.

Lisha is chaperoning two of the kids of postal workers, Chelsea remembered, *and she's also in charge of dealing with print media—newspapers and magazines.*

Karma has two of the other postal-worker kids. And she and Demetrius are to meet and greet any television reporters who want to monitor the show. But there's going to be no other cameras in the room besides Trash *cameras.*

And me, I get all the on-line-services news reporters. And foreign reporters. But no kid of a mass murderer.

Lucky me.

Sumtimes stuck her head in the employee lounge.

"Chelsea?" she asked.

Chelsea looked up at her. A feeling of dread filled her stomach. "Did some reporters arrive?"

"Break's over, you guys," Sumtimes called. "This is a big day. Let's get cracking!"

Lisha threw her foam coffee cup into the trash.

"Chelsea, come with me," Sumtimes ordered, disappearing down the hall.

"Good luck," Chelsea told her friends, hurrying after Sumtimes.

"Pretty low-energy in there," Sumtimes remarked as Chelsea caught up with her. "Everything cool?"

No, everything is not cool, Chelsea wanted to say. *In six hours, Karma and I are going to be out of a job, and we're never going to work in television again. Because we scammed* Trash. *And we got caught.*

But she didn't say any of that. "Just tired," she said.

"Well, you'll be whipped by tonight," Sumtimes said as she led Chelsea down the hallway toward the green rooms. "This is gonna be one red-letter day here at *Trash.*"

You can say that again, Chelsea thought anxiously.

"So, am I meeting some of the foreign press now?" she asked.

"Not exactly," Sumtimes said. "Okay, we're here."

It was Sumtimes's own office. She pushed her office door open and stepped inside.

Chelsea followed.

Sitting on the small love seat against the wall was a girl of about Chelsea's age.

She looked like a stereotypical girl next door—pretty but not too pretty, long brown hair tied back with a blue scrunchie, brown eyes, a slender nose, and thin lips. She was dressed in a light blue miniskirt, not too short, and a short-sleeve light blue cotton sweater. She had a notebook on her lap.

A reporter for a foreign teen magazine? Chelsea guessed.

She saw Sumtimes standing expectantly, waiting for her to do something.

I'd better introduce myself, Chelsea thought quickly, *instead of standing here like a total idiot. She might write for a really important online service or something.*

She smiled brightly and walked over to the girl. She stuck out her hand.

"I'm Chelsea Jennings," she said brightly, mustering her best Southern manners and best Southern-girl smile. "I'm an intern here."

The girl rose to her feet. "Nice to meet you, Chelsea," she said. "Hey, we have the same first name!"

A feeling of terrible dread filled Chelsea's stomach. She felt dizzy, faint.

She knew what was coming next.

"My name," the other girl said, "is Chelsea Kettering."

"Excuse me a minute," Chelsea Jennings said to the girl who was pretending to be Chelsea Kettering, "I have to go use the bathroom."

"Sure," Chelsea Kettering said. "I'm not going anywhere. Thanks for talking to me about all this. I'm really nervous."

"No problem," Chelsea Jennings said, trying to smile through stiff lips. "You'll be great. I'll be right back."

"I'll be here."

Chelsea left Sumtimes's office and closed the door behind her, checking her watch as she did so. It was 2:45 P.M., exactly the time that she, Karma, and Lisha had agreed to meet. She turned left, practically trotted down the hall to the fire exit, opened the door, and scooted up the stairway. The bathroom was just at the top of the stairs, on the other side of the fifth-floor fire door.

She opened the bathroom door, and exactly as they'd planned, Karma and Lisha were standing there waiting for her.

"Oh my God, you aren't going to believe it," Chelsea said breathlessly.

"Sort of like being on death row, isn't it?" Karma commented. "Let's talk fast, I've only got like eight minutes."

"I've got five," Lisha said.

Chelsea grabbed her friends' hands. "I have spent the last two hours in Sumtimes's office. With Chelsea Kettering."

"No way," Karma said.

"It's true," Chelsea said. And she recounted for her friends the events of the past couple of hours—how Sumtimes had introduced her to the Kettering impostor, how she and this girl had been talking for nearly two hours, and how the Kettering impostor seemed to know every single detail there was to know about Chelsea's mother and father and their life up to and including the deadly day, but had concocted a completely false history of what her life had been like since then.

"Did she say anything about Australia?" Karma asked her.

"All she said was that Roxanne came to meet her there," Chelsea said.

"Does she have an Australian accent?" Lisha asked.

Chelsea shook her head no. "She had all the facts down—how she's lived in America until recently, how she's going to school in Australia. I'm telling you, this is crazy!"

"Look, call me nuts, but I don't believe my stockbroker's friend turned on us," Karma whined.

"Maybe they paid her a fortune," Lisha suggested.

"I'm telling you," Karma insisted, "something is bizarre about all this."

"I'll say," Chelsea said fervently. "You should hear the lies she made up about my mother!"

"Like what?" Lisha asked.

"Like that my mother's a stripper in Reno, Nevada. And my mother had this massive breakdown and got addicted to Valium! God, my mother will absolutely die if she hears this girl! My mother is the most clean-living, conservative Southern lady you could ever meet!"

"That's a good one," Lisha snorted. "Your mom, the church-choir director, a drug-addicted stripper!"

"Who, according to this girl, has been married four times," Chelsea went on.

Lisha started to laugh.

"What's so funny?" Chelsea asked her.

Lisha laughed some more. And then some more. Her laughter echoed in the tiled bathroom.

"I can't believe you're laughing!" Chelsea screeched.

"It's just so perfect!" Lisha cried. "I'm laughing because I just figured this whole scam out! And it's just so brilliantly trashy."

"What?" Chelsea demanded.

"Tell us quick," Karma demanded.

"Well," Lisha said, "this Chelsea Kettering isn't Chelsea Kettering at all."

"Of course she isn't!" Chelsea exclaimed, her voice rising hysterically. "*I'm* Chelsea Kettering!"

"No," Lisha said, "I mean she isn't the girl from Australia who you guys got to pretend to be Chelsea Kettering."

"Who is she, then?" Chelsea asked.

"Chels, *Trash hired* her," Lisha said. "They hired her, and trained her, and coached her to be Chelsea Kettering. She's *their* plant."

There was silence for a few moments. The only sound was a slightly dripping faucet.

"Omigawd, it's so perfect," Karma said softly.

"But—" Chelsea was still trying to figure it out.

"I get it," Karma said. "*Trash* hired her to pretend to be Chelsea Kettering."

"So either the whole world believes her," Lisha continued, "in which case, Jazz wins, she has scammed the world, or the real Chelsea Kettering gets upset over this girl who's pretending to be her, and the real Chelsea Kettering comes forward."

"In which case, Jazz would also win," Karma concluded.

Chelsea let all of this settle in her mind. "You know, y'all might actually be right," she finally said.

"And the truly great part, the truly hilarious part," Lisha said gleefully, "is that even though Jazz is going to get away with her little scam, she has no idea that the real Chelsea Kettering will never come forward, because she's right under her very nose."

"That's not the great part," Chelsea said. "The great part is that if you're right, Karma and I still have our jobs."

Chelsea Jennings stood in the wings of the Studio C set, with the Chelsea Kettering impostor not more than three feet from her. They'd been there since 4:00 P.M., watching the show together.

And the show was going great.

They'd gone through the children of postal workers who had gone berserk, and through some of the other guests. They'd had the segment where a few lucky studio-audience members who wanted to go out on dates with the guests were matched with guests who were willing to go out with them.

And now they were in the middle of a four-minute commercial break. It was the break right before the Chelsea Kettering segment of the show.

Jazz walked over to the two Chelseas.

"You doing okay, Chelsea?" she asked.

"Fine," they both answered at the same time.

"I meant our guest," Jazz said pointedly.

"Oh, of course," Chelsea Jennings said, flustered. "Sorry."

"I'm a little nervous," the Chelsea Kettering impostor said.

"You'll be great," Jazz said, giving her hand a reassuring squeeze. She turned a cool eye on the other Chelsea. "Talked to Nick lately?"

"I—" Chelsea began.

"He was over at my place the other night," Jazz said smoothly. "It was great."

"One minute, Jazz," the assistant director called.

"So remember, Chelsea," Jazz said to Chelsea Jennings. "You escort our special guest out, with you upstage of her, your right hand on her left arm."

"Got it," Chelsea said nervously.

"See you out there," Jazz said, giving the Chelsea Kettering impostor's arm one last squeeze.

Chelsea Jennings's heart was hammering in her chest. She looked over at the impostor.

What if I just told her the truth? she thought wildly. *I know you aren't who you're pretending to be. Don't go on national television and say those awful things about my mother. How can you—*

"Chelsea?"

It was Bigfoot.

"Yes?"

"I want to thank you for doing such a great job on this story. You and Karma worked really hard. And we really appreciate it." She walked away.

But before Chelsea could stop and think about the fact that Bigfoot had just been nice to her, the stage manager was indicating that it was time.

"Five, four..."

Three seconds later Jazz was again on camera.

"We're got one more guest for you, gang," she announced, facing camera one. "Ask your parents about the Burger Barn shooter.

Because today, here on *Trash,* after years in hiding, we've got the Burger Barn shooter's only daughter, ready to tell her story. Gang, let's give our trashiest welcome to Chelsea Kettering!"

Deafening applause and cheering from the audience.

"Let's go," Chelsea Jennings said, taking the impostor's arm as Jazz had instructed.

Together, the two girls walked across the set, to Jazz's desk. On the edge of the desk, instead of on the couch, was one of the famous inflatable people. This one had handcuffs on.

"Welcome, welcome!" Jazz said as the two Chelseas approached her. She reached her hand out to Chelsea Kettering.

"Thanks for coming on, Chelsea Kettering," Jazz said to the girl.

The impostor smiled. "Great to be here, Jazz. I really love your show."

"Thanks," Jazz said.

Chelsea Jennings tried to smile. She felt like an idiot, just standing there.

I guess I must be out of camera range, she thought, taking a small, self-conscious step backward.

"So, this is really a big moment," Jazz told the impostor Chelsea Kettering. "Chelsea Kettering comes out of hiding."

"Well, there's just one thing, Jazz," the girl said.

"What's that?"

"I'm not really Chelsea Kettering."

The audience gasped.

Jazz looked quizzical. "Really? Then who is?"

The impostor stepped forward, turned, and then pointed at Chelsea Jennings.

"Jazz, here she is."

One of the rolling cameras closed in on Chelsea, until it was right in her face.

Chelsea felt frozen to the spot. She couldn't move.

All she could do was look into the camera, and know that her face was being broadcast all over America and the world.

But this time she was no hero.

"Here's the girl you're looking for, Jazz," the impostor said. "This is Charles Kettering's daughter."

"This is the real Chelsea Kettering."

It's the hottest summer job ever...

HOT TRASH

Cherie Bennett & Jeff Gottesfeld

Six girls and boys are about to have one hot summer. They've been chosen to move to New York City to be interns on the new reality talk show *Trash*.

But what goes on while the cameras are rolling is nothing compared to the happenings behind the lights.

Includes the first two books in the popular series: *Trash* and *Love, Lies, and Video*

0-425-20120-1
www.penguin.com